The Watchers of the Plains: A Tale of the Western Prairies

Ridgwell Cullum

Illustrated by J. C. Leyendecker

HIS EYES WERE INTENT UPON THE DARK HORIZON

The Watchers of
The Plains

A Tale of the Western Prairies

By RIDGEWELL CULLUM

WITH FRONTISPIECE
BY J. C. LEYENDECKER

1909

To

B. W. M.
my good friend and counselor
I affectionately dedicate
this book

CONTENTS

CHAPTER I

A LETTER

A solitary hut, dismal, rectangular, stands on the north bank of the White River. Decay has long been at work upon it, yet it is still weather-proof. It was built long before planks were used in the Bad Lands of Dakota. It was built by hands that aimed only at strength and durability, caring nothing for appearances. Thus it has survived where a lighter construction must long since have been demolished.

And it still affords habitation for man. The windows have no glass; the door is a crazy affair; there is an unevenness in the setting of the lateral logs which compose its walls; the reed thatching has been patched where the weather has rotted it; and here and there small spreads of tarpaulin lend their aid in keeping out the snows of winter and the storms of summer. It occupies its place, a queer, squat sentry, standing midway between the cattle ford and the newer log wagon-bridge lower down the river toward its mouth, where it joins the giant Missouri some two hundred miles distant. It backs into the brush fringing the wood-lined river bank, and is dangerously sheltered from the two great Indian Reservations on the other side of the river. Dangerously, because it is at all times dangerous to live adjacent to woods when so near such a restless race as the Indians on the Rosebud and the Pine Ridge Reservations. Still, it has stood there so long, and yet bears no sign of hostile action directed against it by the warlike Sioux, that it seems safe to reckon it will continue to stand there in peace until decay finishes it off. And the fact is significant.

Those who lived in that hut must have had reason to know that they dwelt there in safety.

The present tenant of the hut is a white man. He is seated on the tread of his crazy doorway, holding an open letter in one hand, while he stares in an unpleasantly reflective manner out across the prairie in front of him.

And the letter, which is slowly crumpling under the clutch of his nervous fingers, is worthy of attention, for it is written on crested

1

paper which is blue. And the ink is blue, too, and might reasonably indicate the tone of the blood of the sender, though hardly of the recipient.

Still appearances are deceptive on the prairie with regard to human beings, even more so perhaps than elsewhere. This man has a something about him which speaks of a different life—a life where people live in greater ease and more refined surroundings. But even so, his face is very mean and narrow; an appearance in nowise improved by its weather-stained, unwashed condition.

Nevil Steyne—for that is the man's name—has read the letter, and now he is thinking about it. And as he thinks, and mentally digests that which a right-minded man would accept as its overwhelmingly kindly tone, his anger rises slowly at first, but ever higher and higher, till it culminates in a bitter, muttered exclamation.

"The crawler!" he said under his breath.

Suddenly he looked down at the paper, and proceeded to straighten it out. And his pale blue eyes were glittering as he read the letter again from beginning to end. The very crest at the top was an aggravation to him. And he conjured meaning between the lines as he went, where meaning lay only in what was written.

The heading bore a date at New York. It had been written on the second of June—ten days earlier. And it was a letter that should have put joy into his heart, rather than have raised his anger and hatred.

"MY DEAR BROTHER (it ran)—

"It is possible that a letter from me may not be as welcome as I try to hope. I can only trust that your resentment against me has abated in these long twelve years since you cut yourself out of my life. I know you blamed me for what happened at our father's death. You said nothing, would not see me, or the whole thing could have been adjusted then. You went off believing what was not true. Whether father treated you justly or unjustly you are the best judge. From my point of view it was the latter. It was always a mystery to me that he cut you out of his will. I was as disappointed as you, and it is for that reason that, for twelve years, I have been seeking you, to restore to you your share of the property. My dear boy, I'm sure you cannot imagine what joy it is to me that at last I am able to write this, that at last I shall be able to say it to you. We both know what a martinet father was, and what a disappointment it was to him when you refused to adopt the army and join me in following in the old boy's footsteps, but, unless there was something else between you, that was insufficient reason for the injustice of his will.

"Well, all that is past now. What I have set aside as your share is untouched, and has been accumulating all these years. It is waiting for you. If you refuse it, I shall never touch it. In that case it remains tied up for my little daughter, at such time as she shall marry. But of course I have done this only as an emergency. You will not, I know, refuse it.

"Thank God, I have found you at last, dear old boy! Now, listen! I have set my plans with great care, and hope you will appreciate them. I do not want to subject you to any curiosity among our friends—you know how inquisitive people are—so I have come out here ostensibly on a big game shoot in the Rockies. Alice, my wife— you remember Alice Travers—and little Marjorie, our daughter, are with me. They know nothing of my secret. We shall break our journey at Sioux City, and then come across to you by road. And, lo! when we arrive my little surprise for them—Marjorie finds an uncle, Alice a brother.

"In conclusion, I hope to be with you on the 16th at latest; we shall come by way of the south bank of the Missouri River, then across the Pine Ridge Reservation, and so on to Beacon Crossing. I hope to find you as young in spirit as ever. I have many gray hairs, but no matter, so long as I find you well I shall be more than satisfied. *Au revoir.*

"Your affectionate
"LANDOR."

"*Au revoir,*" muttered the man, as he viciously tore the letter into the minutest fragments, and ground them into the hard earth with a ruthless heel. "*Au revoir,*" he said again, and louder. Then he laughed. "But we haven't met yet. Why should I take a share when you and your wife, and your brat are the only people who stand between me and the lot?"

And after that he relapsed into silence, and his thoughts flew on apace. The unwashed face grew meaner and more brooding, the fair brows drew closer over the large blue eyes, the jaws were shut as tight as they well could be, for he was painfully overshot, and his chin was almost hidden, so far receding was it under the long, drooping, tobacco-stained moustache.

That letter, it would seem, required no depth of thought, unless it were the happy thought that he possessed such a brother. It seemed to be a moment for nothing but happiness. And in such a man one might reasonably have expected to see him mount the horse tethered a few yards away in front of the hut, and ride into Beacon Crossing, where he could tell his associates of his good fortune, and celebrate it in the usual manner.

But there was nothing of happiness in the face that stared so steadily out at the hazy sky-line in the direction of the Cheyenne Reservation away to the north. There was a hard look, such as is to be seen only in pale blue eyes;—a look of unyielding hatred and obstinacy; a look which, combined with the evident weakness of character displayed in his features, suggested rather the subtle treachery of a coward than the fierce resentment of a brave man.

Never was a character more fully laid bare than was his at that moment. He was conscious of his isolation. There was no one to see. He hated his brother as a weak nature hates a strong. He hated him because years ago he, Nevil, had refused to go into the army for the reason of an obstinate cowardice, while his younger brother gladly embraced the profession of which their father, the stern old general, had been such an honored member. And so he had eschewed his mother country, leaving England, when he had been disinherited, for the wilderness of South Dakota, and had become one of those stormy petrels which, in those days, were ever to be found hovering about the territory set apart for the restless Indians. Yes, and with his destruction of that kindly, simple letter his resolve had been taken. He would have nothing at the hands of the man who had ousted him.

It was not thoughts of his resolve that gave his face its look of treacherous cunning now, but something else. Something which kept him sitting on his door-step thinking, thinking, until the sun had set and the twilight darkened into night. Something which, during that time, brought cruel smiles to his lips, and made him glance round on either side at the brush that marked the boundary of the Sioux camping ground.

Something which at last made him rise from his hard seat and fetch out his saddle from within the hut. Then he brought his horse in from its tethering ground, and saddled it, and rode off down to the ford, and on to the tepee of old Big Wolf, the great chief, the master mind that planned and carried out all the bloody atrocities of the Pine Ridge Indian risings.

"*Au revoir*, eh?" this tall renegade muttered, as he dismounted before the smoke-begrimed dwelling. "There's only we two, Landor; and your precious wife and child, and they are—no, we haven't met yet." And he became silent as he raised the hide door of the tepee, and, without announcing himself, stepped within.

The dark, evil-smelling interior was lit only by the smouldering embers of a small wood-fire in the centre of the great circle. Though it was summer these red heritors of the land could not do without their fire at night-time, any more than they could do without their skins and frowsy blankets. Nevil Steyne glanced swiftly over the dimly outlined faces he saw looming in the shadows. The scene was a familiar one to him, and each face he beheld was familiar. The puffy, broad face of the great chief, the fierce, aquiline features of the stripling who was sitting beside him, and who was Big Wolf's fifteen-year-old son, and the dusky, delicate, high-caste features of the old man's lovely daughter, Wanaha.

He saw all these and entered in silence, leaving his well-trained horse to its own devices outside. He closed up the doorway behind him, and squatted upon his haunches in their midst.

Big Wolf removed the long-stemmed, red-clay pipe from his lips and held it out to the newcomer. The newcomer took it while the other said "How." And all those about him followed suit and welcomed the white man in chorus with this customary greeting.

Then a conversation started which lasted far into the night. It entailed much subtle argument on the part of the visitor, and the introduction of many dusky warriors into the tepee, who also smoked the pipe in council, with many deliberate grunts of approval at the words of wisdom the white adviser spoke.

And all this was the result of that crested letter.

CHAPTER II

ON THE PLAINS

There is no place in the world which affords more cheerful solitude than the prairie. One may be miles and miles away from human habitation and yet there is an exhilaration in the very sunlight, in the long nodding grass, in the dusty eddies of the breeze which is never actually still on the plains. It is the suggestion of freedom in a great boundless space. It grips the heart, and one thanks God for life. This effect is not only with the prairie novice. It lasts for all time with those who once sniff the scent of its delicious breath.

Dakota and the more southern Nebraska are not the finest examples of the American plains, but they will do. What is better they will make one ask for more, and that is an excellent sign.

It is curious to gaze out over this wonderful virgin grass-land and seek for signs of other human beings. Not a speck in view, except perchance a grazing steer or horse. Not a movement but the eddying whirls of dust, and the nodding of the bowing grass heads as they bend to the gentle pressure of the lightest of zephyrs. And yet no doubt there are human beings about; aye, even within half a mile. For flat as those plains may seem they are really great billows rolling away on every hand into the dim distance, hiding men and cattle and houses in their vast, open troughs.

A little party of six had just appeared over the brow of a rising, which was the last great wave toppling monstrously down toward that great expanse of the shallow valley, in the midst of which flows the Missouri. This tiny party, so meagre and insufficient-looking as they faced the sun-bound plains, had just left the river route to strike in a more westerly direction. As they topped the rise a great, wholesome love for the wide world about them welled up in the heart of the woman who was riding in the wagon, and found vent in a low, thrilling exclamation.

"Wonderful!" Then louder and with eyes sparkling: "Beautiful!"

A child of about eleven summers, with fair curling ringlets flowing loosely beneath a wide, flat sun-hat, whose wide-open violet eyes stared a little awe-struck at the vast world which greeted them, nestled closer to the woman's side on the seat of the jolting wagon without comment, but with a sharp little intake of breath. She had no words to add to her mother's.

At that moment one of three men riding ahead detached himself from the others and dropped back to the wagon, to speak to the woman and child. It was easy to understand the relationship between them by the affectionate smile that greeted him He was a tall man and much tanned by a life spent largely in military camps in hot countries. He had the well-set-up figure of a fighting soldier.

"Well, dearie," he said cheerfully to his wife, "how do you like the prairie?"

The woman nodded.

"I'm so glad we came on by road, Landor. The hotel people were quite bothersome about the restlessness of the Indians. I suppose that is a bogey they thrust before all strangers. I am glad you did not change your mind."

The man understood his wife's strong character, and her reply made him feel as though his responsibilities had been suddenly increased. He looked at his companions riding in scout fashion in front. They were pointing at something on the horizon, and he followed the direction indicated.

At last he looked round and encountered the gaze of his wife's gray eyes.

"I thought you would be, Al," he said quietly. "You see the Indians are always restless. Besides, if I——"

"Yes."

The man laughed happily.

"No not yet, dear. My secret must remain a little longer. You are a wonder, Al. You have known that I have a secret for nearly two months, and still you refrain from questioning me."

Alice shook her head, and stooped to readjust their daughter's hat. Her action hid the smile at her husband's simplicity. A good wife learns many things without questioning.

"You see I know I shall be told when it becomes expedient. How would you like to make hay in these lovely open fields, Marjorie?" she asked the violet-eyed child, gazing so steadfastly at this new world about her.

But Marjorie shook her head. She was a little overpowered.

"It's so big, mamma," she murmured, doubtfully.

At that moment one of the two horsemen ahead beckoned to the man a little peremptorily, and he rode off. Then the child turned to her mother.

"What did you mean about the Indians, mamma?"

But the mother did not answer; she was watching her husband, who had just joined the others, and she saw that all three were watching something that looked like smoke on the northwestern horizon.

"Don't Indians eat people, mamma?" asked the child presently.

Her mother laughed shortly, and answered, "No." The answer came a little more sharply than she usually spoke. Suddenly she leant forward and touched the driver on the shoulder. He turned round instantly.

"What is that smoke on the horizon, Jim?" she asked.

The man looked into her steady gray eyes. Then he glanced down at the beautiful child at her side, and, in a moment, his gaze came back to the handsome dark face of the mother; but instantly he turned back to the horses.

"Don't know," he threw back brusquely over his shoulder.

And the woman who learned so much without asking questions knew that he lied.

The vehicle creaked on. The steady jog of the horses kept the neck-yoke rattling in the harness with a sound that was almost musical. The sun was very hot, and the sweat was caked in white streaks all over the hard-working animals' flanks. Mother and child sat on in silence. Those two pairs of lovely eyes were looking out ahead. The child interested, and the mother thinking hard and swiftly. Curiously that smoke on the horizon had set her thinking of her husband and child, but mostly of the child. The driver chirruped at his horses as he had done from the start. He munched his tobacco, and seemed quite at his ease. Only every now and then his keen eyes lifted to the smoke. He was an old prairie hand.

The horsemen on ahead had halted where a higher billow of grass-land than usual had left a sharp, deep hollow. A hundred yards to the right of the trail there was a small clump of undergrowth. The men had dismounted. When the wagon came up the husband stepped to its side.

"We are going to camp here, Alice," he said quietly. "There is good water close by. We can spare the time; we have come along well."

Alice glanced at the faces of the others while he was speaking. One of the men was a long-haired prairie scout; his keen black eyes were intent upon her face. The other was a military "batman," a blue-eyed Yorkshireman. His eyes were very bright—unusually bright. The teamster was placidly looking round his horses.

"Very well," she answered, and passed little Marjorie out into her father's arms. Then she sprang lightly to the ground.

Then the teamster drove the horses away into the brush, and the wagon was hidden from view. The scout and the batman pitched two "A" tents, and the mother noticed that they were so placed as to be utterly hidden in the thick foliage. The horses were off-saddled, and, contrary to custom, were tethered further still from the road, down by the water.

Little Marjorie went off with the men who were securing the horses, and Alice stood watching her husband's movements. She was a beautiful woman of that strong, dark Celtic type, so common in Ireland. Her strong supple figure was displayed to perfection in a simple tweed suit with a jacket of the Norfolk pattern. She stood for some moments watching with deep contemplative eyes. Then she abruptly turned away.

"I will gather some fire-wood," she said deliberately to her husband.

He looked up from his work and their eyes met.

"Don't bother," he said; "we will use the oil stove."

And without further explanation the camp was arranged. There was no bustle or excitement. Yet each member of that little party, with the exception of the child, knew that the camp had been made in emergency — grave emergency.

A hearty meal was partaken of. Then the man and the scout disappeared. The others occupied themselves around the camp. The afternoon wore on. At tea the scout and his companion reappeared. The wife still asked no verbal questions. Her eyes told her all she wished to know.

During the evening meal little Marjorie made a discovery.

"Mamma," she exclaimed, "you've got a belt on like daddy's. What are these?" And she fingered a revolver holster, of which her mother's belt supported two.

It was the rough, long-haired scout who saved the woman a deliberate falsehood.

"Guess them's playthings," he said, with a sombre laugh. "B't don't figger they're fer kiddies to monkey with."

After supper the man and the scout again disappeared. Three hours later the moon was high in the starlit sky. It was a glorious summer moon, and the whole country was bright with its silvery light.

Two men were lying upon their stomachs conning the northwestern sky-line.

The scout at last spoke in his slow drawling way.

"Guess it's played out, Colonel," he said. "We're up agin it."

It didn't seem clear to what he referred, but the other understood him.

"Yes, they're working this way," he replied. "See, something has been fired away to the right front. They may be working round that way and will miss us here. What are our chances?"

"Nix," responded the scout decidedly. "Them critturs hev got to git around this way. They're on a line that'll strike Fort Randall, wi' a heap more military 'n they'll notion. They'll strike south an' sweep round sheer through to Wyoming. We're dead in their line."

"Then we'd best get back and prepare. Mrs. Raynor and Marjorie will have turned in; we can do it quietly."

"Yup."

They rose and returned to camp.

Colonel Raynor had intended to avoid his wife's tent. But Alice was waiting for him on the outskirts of the camp. The scout saw her and discreetly passed on, and husband and wife were left together.

"Well?"

The woman's tone was quite steady. She was used to a soldier's life. Besides, she understood the man's responsibility and wished to help him. And Landor Raynor, looking into the gray eyes that were to him the gates of the heart of purest womanhood, could not resort to subterfuge.

"They will be on us before morning, dearest," he said, and it was only by the greatest effort he could check a tide of self-accusation. But the woman understood and quickly interposed.

"I feared so, Landor. Are you ready? I mean for the fight?"

"We are preparing. I thought of sending you and little Marjorie south with Jim, on saddle horses, but — —"

"No. I would not go. I am what you men call 'useful with a gun.'" She laughed shortly.

There was a silence between them for some moments. And in that silence a faint and distant sound came to them. It was like the sound of droning machinery, only very faint.

The wife broke the silence. "Landor, we are old campaigners, you and I."

"Yes, Al."

The woman sighed ever so lightly.

"The excitement of the foreknowledge of victory is not in me to-night. Everything seems—so ordinary."

"Yes."

"When the moment comes, Landor, I should not like to be taken prisoner."

"Nor shall you be, Al. There are four good fighting men with you. All old campaigners like—you."

"Yes. I wasn't thinking of that." The gray eyes looked away. The man shifted uneasily.

There was a prolonged silence. Each was thinking over old scenes in old campaigns.

"I don't think I am afraid of much," the woman said slowly, at last. "Certainly not of death."

"Don't talk like that, Al." The man's arm linked itself through his wife's. The woman smiled wistfully up into the strong face bending over her.

"I was thinking, dearest, if death faced us, little Marjorie and me, in any form, we should not like it at the hands of an Indian. We should both prefer it from some one we know and—love."

Another silence followed, and the sound of machinery was nearer and louder. The man stooped down and kissed the upturned face, and looked long into the beautiful gray depths he loved so well.

"It shall be as you wish, Al—as a last resource. I will go and kiss Marjorie. It is time we were doing."

He had spoken so quietly, so calmly. But in his soldier's heart he knew that his promise would be carried out to the letter—as a last resource. He left the woman, the old campaigner, examining the revolvers which looked like cannons in her small white hands.

One brief hour has passed. The peace of that lonely little trail-side camp has gone. War, a thousand times more fierce than the war of civilized nations, is raging round it in the light of the summer moon. The dead bodies of three white men are lying within a few yards of the tent which belongs to the ill-fated colonel and his wife. A horde of shouting, shrieking savages encircle that little white canopy and its two remaining defenders. Every bush is alive with hideous painted faces waiting for the last order to rush the camp. Their task has been less easy than they supposed. For the defenders were all "old hands." And every shot from the repeating rifles has told. But now it is different. There are only two defenders left. A man of invincible courage—and a woman; and behind them, a little, awe-struck child in the doorway of the tent.

The echoing war-whoop sounds the final advance, and the revolvers of those two desperate defenders crack and crack again. The woman's ammunition is done. The man's is nearly so. He turns, and she turns to meet him. There is one swift embrace.

"Now!" she says in a low, soft voice.

There is an ominous crack of a revolver, but it is not fired in the direction of the Indians whom the man sees are within a few yards of him. He sees the woman fall, and turns swiftly to the tent door. The child instinctively turns and runs inside. The man's gun is raised with inexorable purpose. His shot rings out. The child screams; and the man crashes to the earth with his head cleft by a hatchet from behind.

CHAPTER III

AN ALARM IN BEACON CROSSING

A horseman riding from White River Homestead to Beacon Crossing will find himself confronted with just eighty-two miles of dreary, flat trail; in summer time, just eighty-two miles of blistering sun, dust and mosquitoes. The trail runs parallel to, and about three miles north of the cool, shady White River, which is a tantalizing invention of those who designed the trail.

In the whole eighty-two miles there is but one wayside house; it is called the "half-way." No one lives there. It, like the log hut of Nevil Steyne on the bank of the White River, stands alone, a relic of the dim past. But it serves a good purpose, for one can break the journey there, and sleep the night in its cheerless shelter. Furthermore, within the ruins of its old-time stockade is a well, a deep, wide-mouthed well full of cool spring water, which is the very thing needed.

It is sunrise and a horseman has just ridden away from this shelter. He is a man of considerable height, to judge by the length of his stirrups, and he has that knack of a horseman in the saddle which comes only to those who have learned to ride as soon as they have learned to run.

He wears fringed chapps over his moleskin trousers, which give him an appearance of greater size than he possesses, for, though stout of frame, he is lean and wiry. His face is wonderfully grave for a young man, which may be accounted for by the fact that he has lived through several Indian risings. And it is a strong face, too, with a decided look of what people term self-reliance in it, also, probably, a product of those dreaded Indian wars. He, like many men who live through strenuous times, is given much to quick thought and slow speech, which, though excellent features in character, do not help toward companionship in wild townships like Beacon Crossing.

Seth is well thought of in that city—whither he is riding now—but he is more respected than loved. The truth is he has a way of liking slowly, and disliking thoroughly, and this is a disposition the reckless townsmen of Beacon Crossing fail to understand, and, failing to understand, like most people, fail to appreciate.

Just now he is more particularly grave than usual. He has ridden from White River Farm to execute certain business in town for his foster-parents, Rube Sampson and his wife; a trifling matter, and certainly nothing to bring that look of doubt in his eyes, and the thoughtful pucker between his clean-cut brows. His whole attention is given up to a contemplation of the land beyond the White River, and the distance away behind him to the left, which is the direction of the Rosebud Indian Reservation.

Yesterday his attention had been called in these directions, and on reaching the "half-way" he had serious thoughts of returning home, but reflection had kept him to his journey if it had in no way eased his mind.

Yesterday he had observed a smoky haze spreading slowly northward on the lightest of breezes; and it was coming across the Reservation. It was early June, and the prairie was too young and green to burn yet.

The haze was still hanging in the bright morning air. It had spread right across his path in the night, and a strong smell of burning greeted him as he rode out.

He urged his horse and rode faster than he had ridden the day before. There was a silent sympathy between horse and rider which displayed itself in the alertness of the animal's manner; he was traveling with head held high, nostrils distended, as though sniffing at the smell of burning in some alarm. And his gait, too, had become a little uneven, which, in a horse, means that his attention is distracted.

Before an hour had passed the man's look changed to one of some apprehension. Smoke was rising in a new direction. He had no need to turn to see it, it was on his left front, far away beyond the horizon, but somewhere where the railroad track, linking the East with Beacon Crossing, cut through the plains of Nebraska. Suddenly his horse leapt forward into a strong swinging gallop. He had felt the touch of the spur. Seth pulled out a great silver timepiece and consulted it.

"I ken make it in two hours an' a haf from now," he muttered. "That'll be haf past eight. Good! Put it along, Buck."

The last was addressed to the horse; and the dust rose in great heavy clouds behind them as the willing beast stretched out to his work.

Beacon Crossing is called a city by those residents who have lived in it since the railway brought it into existence. Chance travelers, and those who are not prejudiced in its favor, call it a hole. It certainly has claims in the latter direction. It is the section terminal on the railway; and that is the source of its questionable prosperity.

There is a main street parallel to the railroad track with some stores facing the latter. It has only one sidewalk and only one row of buildings; the other side of the street is given up to piles of metal rails and wooden ties and ballast for the track. The stores are large fronted, with a mockery which would lead the unenlightened to believe they are two-storied; but this is make-believe. The upper windows have no rooms behind them. They are the result of overweening vanity on the part of the City Council and have nothing to do with the storekeepers.

The place is unremarkable for anything else, unless it be the dirty and unpaved condition of its street. True there are other houses, private residences, but these are set indiscriminately upon the surrounding prairie, and have no relation to any roads. A row of blue gum trees marks the front of each, and, for the most part, a clothes-line, bearing some articles of washing, indicates the back. Beacon Crossing would be bragged about only by those who helped to make it.

The only building worth consideration is the hotel, opposite the depot. This has a verandah and a tie-post, and there are always horses standing outside it, and always men standing on the verandah, except when it is raining, then they are to be found inside.

It was only a little after eight in the morning. Breakfast was nearly over in the hotel, and, to judge by the number of saddle-horses at the tie-post, the people of Beacon Crossing were very much astir. Presently the verandah began to fill with hard-faced, rough-clad men. And most of them as they came were filling their pipes, which suggested that they had just eaten.

Nevil Steyne was one of the earliest to emerge from the breakfast room. He had been the last to go in, and the moment he reappeared it was to survey swiftly the bright blue distance away in the direction of the Indian Reservations, and, unseen by those who stood around, he smiled ever so slightly at what he beheld. The two men nearest him were talking earnestly, and their earnestness was emphasized by the number of matches they used in keeping their pipes alight.

"Them's Injun fires, sure," said one, at the conclusion of a long argument.

"Maybe they are, Dan," said the other, an angular man who ran a small hardware store a few yards lower down the street. "But they ain't on this side of the Reservation anyway."

The significant selfishness of his last remark brought the other round on him in a moment.

"That's all you care for, eh?" Dan said witheringly. "Say. I'm working for the 'diamond P's,' and they run their stock that aways. Hev you been through one o' them Injun risings?"

The other shook his head.

"Jest so."

Another man, stout and florid, Jack McCabe, the butcher, joined them.

"Can't make it out. There ain't been any Sun-dance, which is usual 'fore they get busy. Guess it ain't no rising. Big Wolf's too clever. If it was spring round-up or fall round-up it 'ud seem more likely. Guess some feller's been and fired the woods. Which, by the way, is around Jason's farm. Say, Dan Lawson, you living that way, ain't it right that Jason's got a couple of hundred beeves in his corrals?"

"Yes," replied Dan of the "diamond P's." "He bought up the 'flying S' stock. He's holding 'em up for rebrandin'. Say, Nevil," the cowpuncher went on, turning to the wood-cutter of White River, "you oughter know how them red devils is doin'. Did you hear or see anything?"

Nevil turned with a slight flush tingeing his cheeks. He didn't like the other's tone.

"I don't know why I should know or see anything," he said shortly.

"Wal, you're kind o' livin' ad-jacent, as the sayin' is," observed Dan, with a shadowy smile.

The other men on the verandah had come around, and they smiled more broadly than the cowpuncher. It was easy to see that they were not particularly favorable toward Nevil Steyne. It was as Dan had said; he lived near the Reservation, and, well, these men were frontiersmen who knew the ways of the country in which they lived.

Nevil saw the smiling faces and checked his anger. He laughed instead.

"Well," he said, "since you set such store by my opinions I confess I had no reason to suspect any disturbance, and, to illustrate my faith in the Indians' peaceful condition, I am going home at noon, and to-morrow intend to cut a load or two of wood on the river."

Dan had no more to say. He could have said something but refrained, and the rest of the men turned to watch the white smoke in the distance. Decidedly Steyne had scored a point and should have been content; but he wasn't.

"I suppose you fellows think a white man can't live near Indians without 'taking the blanket,'" he pursued with a sneer.

There was a brief silence. Then Dan answered him slowly.

"Jest depends on the man, I guess."

There was a nasty tone in the cowpuncher's voice and trouble seemed imminent, but it was fortunately nipped in the bud by Jack McCabe.

"Hello!" the butcher exclaimed excitedly, "there's a feller pushin' his plug as tho' them Injuns was on his heels. Say, it's Seth o' White River Farm, and by the gait he's travelin', I'd gamble, Nevil, you don't cut that wood to-morrow. Seth don't usually ride hard."

The whole attention on the verandah was centred on Seth, who was riding toward the hotel from across the track as hard as his horse could lay foot to the ground.

In a few moments he drew up at the tie-post and flung off his horse. And a chorus of inquiry greeted him from the bystanders.

The newcomer raised an undisturbed face to them, and his words came without any of the excitement that the pace he had ridden in at had suggested.

"The Injuns are out," he said, and bent down to feel his horse's legs. They seemed to be of most interest to him at the moment.

Curiously enough his words were accepted by the men on the verandah without question. That is, by all except Steyne. No doubt he was irritated by what had gone before, but even so, it hardly warranted, in face of the fires in the south, his obstinate refusal to believe that the Indians were out on the war-path. Besides, he resented the quiet assurance of the newcomer. He resented the manner in which the others accepted his statement, disliking it as much as he disliked the man who had made it. Nor was the reason of this hatred far to seek. Seth was a loyal white man who took his life in his own hands and fought strenuously in a savage land for his existence, a bold, fearless frontiersman; while he, Nevil, knew in his secret heart that he had lost that caste, had thrown away that right — that birthright. He had, as these men also knew, "taken the blanket." He had become a white Indian. He lived by the clemency of that people, in their manner, their life. He was one of them, while yet his skin was white. He was regarded by his own race as an outcast. He was a degenerate. So he hated — hated them all. But Seth he hated most of all because he saw more of him, he lived near him. He knew that Seth knew him, knew him down to his heart's core. This was sufficient in a nature like his to set him hating, but he hated him for yet another reason. Seth was as strong, brave, honest as he was the reverse. He belonged to an underworld which nothing could ever drag a nature such as Seth's down to.

He knocked his pipe out aggressively on the wooden floor of the verandah.

"I don't believe it," he said loudly, in an offensive way.

Seth dropped his broncho's hoof, which he had been examining carefully, and turned round. It would be impossible to describe the significance of his movement. It suggested the sudden rousing of a real fighting dog that had been disturbed in some peaceful pursuit. He was not noisy, he did not even look angry. He was just ready.

"I guess you ought to know, Nevil Steyne," he said with emphasis. Then he turned his head and looked away down the street, as the clatter of hoofs and rattle of wheels reached the hotel. And for the second time within a few minutes, trouble, such as only Western men fully understand, was staved off by a more important interruption.

A team and buckboard dashed up to the hotel. Dan Somers, the sheriff, and Lal Price, the Land Agent, were in the conveyance, and as they drew up, one of the horses dropped to the ground in its harness. The men, watching these two plainsmen scrambling from the vehicle, knew that life and death alone could have sent them into town at a pace sufficient to kill one of their horses.

"Boys!" cried the sheriff at once. "Who's for it? Those durned Injuns are out; they're gittin' round Jason's place. I'm not sure but the woods are fired a'ready. They've come from the south, I guess. They're Rosebuds. Ther's old man Jason and his missis; and ther's the gals—three of 'em. We can't let 'em——"

Seth interrupted him.

"And we ain't going to," he observed. He knew, they all knew, what the sheriff would have said.

Seth's interruption was the cue for suggestions. And they came with a rush, which is the way with men such as these, all eager and ready to help in the rescue of a white family from the hands of a common foe. There was no hesitation, for they were most of them old hands in this Indian business, and, in the back recesses of their brains, each man held recollections of past atrocities, too hideous to be contemplated calmly.

Those who were later with their breakfast now swelled the crowd on the verandah. The news seemed to have percolated through to the rest of the town, for men were gathering on all sides, just as men gather in civilized cities on receipt of news of national importance. They came at once to the central public place. The excitement had leapt with the suddenness of a conflagration, and, like a conflagration, there would be considerable destruction before it died down. The Indians in their savage temerity might strike Beacon Crossing. Once the Indians were loose it was like the breaking of a tidal wave on a low shore.

The sheriff was the man they all looked to, and, veteran warrior that he was, he quickly got a grip on things. One hard-riding scout, a man as wily as the Indian himself, he despatched to warn all outlying settlers. He could spare no more than one. Then he sent telegraphic messages for the military, whose fort a progressive and humane government had located some two hundred miles away. Then he divided his volunteers, equipped with their own arms, and all the better for that, and detailed one party for the town's defence, and the other to join him in the work of rescue.

These things arranged, then came the first check. It was discovered that the driver of the only locomotive in the place was sick. The engine itself, a rusty looking ancient machine, was standing coldly idle in the yards.

A deputation waited upon the sick man, while others went and coupled up some empty trucks and fired the engine. Seth was among the latter. The deputation returned. It was fever; and the man could not come. Being ready campaigners, their thoughts turned on their horses.

The sheriff was a blank man for the moment. It was a question of time, he knew. He was standing beside the locomotive which had already begun to snort, and which looked, at that moment, in the eyes of those gathered round it, despite its rustiness, a truly magnificent proposition. He was about to call for volunteers to replace the driver, when Seth, who all the time had been working in the cab, and who had heard the news of the trouble, leant over the rail that protected the foot-plate.

"Say, Dan," he said. "If none of the boys are scared to ride behind me, and I don't figger they are, I'll pump the old kettle along. Guess I've fired a traction once. I don't calc'late she'll have time to bust up in forty miles. I'll take the chances if they will."

The sheriff looked up at the thoughtful face above him. He grinned, and others grinned with him. But their amusement was quite lost on

Seth. He was trying to estimate the possible result of putting the "kettle," as he called the locomotive, at full steam ahead, disregarding every other tap and gauge on the driving plate, and devoting himself to heaping up the furnace. These things interested him, not as a source of danger, but only in the matter of speed.

"Good for you, Seth," cried Dan Somers. "Now, boys, all aboard!"

And Seth turned to the driving plate and sounded a preliminary whistle.

CHAPTER IV

ROSEBUD

It is nearly midday, and the Indians round the blazing woods on the southern spur of the Black Hills are in full retreat. Another desperate battle, such as crowd the unwritten history of the United States, has been fought and won. The history of the frontiersman's life would fill a record which any soldier might envy. It is to the devotion of such men that colonial empires owe their being, for without their aid, no military force could bring peace and prosperity to a land. The power of the sword may conquer and hold, but there its mission ends. It is left to the frontiersman to do the rest.

The battle-field is strewn with dead and dying; but there are no white faces staring blankly up at the heavens, only the painted, seared features of the red man. Their opponents are under cover. If they have any dead or dying they are with the living. These men fight in the manner of the Indian, but with a superior intelligence.

But though the white men have won the battle their end is defeated. For the blazing woods have swept across the homestead of "old man" Jason, for years a landmark in the country, and now it is no more. A mere charred skeleton remains; smoking, smouldering, a witness to the white man's daring in a savage country.

The blazing woods are approachable only on the windward side, and even here the heat is blistering. It is still impossible to reach the ruins of the homestead, for the wake of the fire is like a superheated oven. And so the men who came to succor have done the only thing left for them. They have fought and driven off the horde of Indians, who first sacked the ranch and then fired it. But the inmates; and amongst them four women. What of them? These rough plainsmen asked themselves this question as they approached the conflagration; then they shut their teeth hard and meted out a terrible chastisement before pushing their inquiries further. It was the only way.

A narrow river skirts the foot of the hills, cutting the homestead off from the plains. And along its bank, on the prairie side, is a scattered brush such as is to be found adjacent to most woods. The fire has left it untouched except that the foliage is much scorched, and it is here that the victors of an unrecorded battle lie hidden in the cover. Though the enemy is in full retreat, and the rearmost horsemen are fast diminishing against the horizon, not a man has left his shelter. They are men well learned in the craft of the Indians.

Dan Somers and Seth are sharing the same cover. The sheriff is watching the last of the braves as they desperately hasten out of range. At last he moves and starts to rise from his prone position. But Seth's strong hand checks him and pulls him down again.

"Not yet," he said.

"Why?"

But the sheriff yielded nevertheless. In spite of his fledgling twenty-two years, Seth was an experienced Indian fighter, and Dan Somers knew it; no one better. Seth's father and mother had paid the life penalty seventeen years ago at the hands of the Cheyennes. It was jokingly said that Seth was a white Indian. By which those who said it meant well but put it badly. He certainly had remarkable native instincts.

"This heat is hellish!" Somers protested presently, as Seth remained silent, gazing hard at a rather large bluff on the river bank, some three hundred yards ahead. Then he added bitterly, "But it ain't no use. We're too late. The fire's finished everything. Maybe we'll find their bodies. I guess their scalps are elsewhere."

Seth turned. He began to move out of his cover in Indian fashion, wriggling through the grass like some great lizard.

"I'll be back in a whiles," he said, as he went. "Stay right here."

He was back in a few minutes. No Indian could have been more silent in his movements.

"Well?" questioned the sheriff.

Seth smiled in his own gradual manner. "We're going to draw 'em, I guess," he said. "Fill up."

And the two men recharged the magazines of their Winchesters.

Presently Seth pointed silently at the big bluff on the river bank. The next moment he had fired into it, and his shot was followed at once by a perfect hail of lead from the rest of the hidden white men. The object of his recent going was demonstrated.

For nearly two minutes the fusilade continued, then Seth's words were proved. There was a rush and scrambling and breaking of brush. Thirty mounted braves dashed out of the hiding and charged the white men's cover. It was only to face a decimating fire. Half the number were unhorsed, and the riderless ponies fled in panic in the direction of those who had gone before.

But while others headed these howling, painted fiends Seth's rifle remained silent. He knew that this wild rush was part of a deliberate plan, and he waited for the further development. It came. His gun leapt to his shoulder as a horse and rider darted out of the brush. The man made eastward, attempting escape under cover of his staunch warriors' desperate feint. Seth had him marked down. He was the man of all whom he had looked for. But the aim had to be careful, for he was carrying a something that looked like woman's clothes in his arms, and, besides, this man must not go free. Seth was very deliberate at all times; now he was particularly so. And when the puff of smoke passed from the muzzle of his rifle it was to be seen that the would-be fugitive had fallen, and his horse had gone on riderless.

Now the few remaining braves broke and fled, but there was no escape for them. They had defeated their own purpose by approaching too close. Not one was left to join the retreating band. It was a desperate slaughter.

The fight was done. Seth left his cover, and, followed by the sheriff, went across to where the former's victim had fallen.

"Good," exclaimed Somers, as they came up. "It is Big Wolf——What?" He broke off and dropped to his knees.

But Seth was before him. The latter had dragged the body of the great chief to one side, and revealed, to the sheriff's astonished eyes, the dainty clothing, and what looked like the dead form of a white girl child. They both held the same thought, but Somers was the first to put it into words.

"Tain't Jason's. They're all grown up," he said.

Seth was looking down at the child's beautiful pale face. His eyes took in the thick, fair ringlets of flowing hair all matted with blood. He noted even the texture of the clothes. And, suddenly stooping, he gathered her into his arms.

"She's mine now," he said. Then his thoughtful, dark eyes took on their slow smile again. "And she ain't dead, though pretty nigh, I'm thinking."

"How'd you know?" asked Somers curiously.

"Can't say. I've jest a notion that aways."

The others came up, but not another word passed Seth's lips. He walked off in the direction of the track where the engine was standing at the head of its trucks. And by the time he reached his destination he was quite weighted down, for this prize of his was no infant but a girl of some years. He laid her tenderly in the cab of the engine, and quickly discovered a nasty scalp wound on the back of her head. Just for a moment he conceived it to be the result of his own shot, then he realized that the injury was not of such recent infliction. Nevertheless it was the work of a bullet; which discovery brought forth a flow of scathing invective upon the head of the author of the outrage.

With that care which was so characteristic of this thoughtful plainsman, he fetched water from the tank of the locomotive, tore off a large portion of his own flannel shirt, and proceeded to wash the wound as tenderly as might any devoted mother. He was used to a rough treatment of wounds, and, by the time he had bandaged the pretty head, he found that his supply of shirt was nearly exhausted. But this in no way disturbed him.

With great resource he went back to the prairie and tore out great handfuls of the rank grass, and so contrived a comparatively luxurious couch for his foundling on the foot-plate of the engine.

By this time the men were returning from their search for the bodies at the ruins of the ranch. The story was quickly told. The remains had been found, as might have been expected, charred cinders of bone.

There was no more to be done here, and Somers, on his return to the track, sounded the true note of their necessity.

"We must git back. Them durned Injuns 'll make tracks fer Beacon Crossing, or I'm a Dago."

Then he looked into the cab where the still form of the prairie waif lay shaded by a piece of tarpaulin which Seth had found on the engine. He observed the bandage and the grass bed, and he looked at the figure bending to the task of firing.

"What are you goin' to do with her?" he asked.

Seth worked on steadily.

"Guess I'll hand her over to Ma Sampson," he said, without turning.

"Maybe she has folks. Maybe ther's the law."

Seth turned now.

"She's mine now," he cried over his shoulder. Then he viciously aimed a shovelful of coal at the open furnace door.

All his years of frontier life had failed to change a naturally tender heart in Seth. Whatever he might do in the heat of swift-rising passion it had no promptings in his real nature. The life of the plains was his in all its varying moods, but there was an unchanging love for his kind under it all. However, like all such men, he hated to be surprised into a betrayal of these innermost feelings, and this is what had happened. Somers had found the vulnerable point in his armor of reserve, but, like the sensible man he was, he kept his own counsel.

At the saloon in Beacon Crossing the men were less careful. Their curiosity found vent in questionable pleasantries, and they chaffed Seth in a rough, friendly way.

On their arrival Seth handed the still unconscious child over to the wife of the hotel-keeper for an examination of her clothes. He did this at Dan Somers' suggestion, as being the most legal course to pursue, and waited with the sheriff and several others in the bar for the result.

Good news had greeted the fighting party on their return. The troops were already on the way to suppress the sudden and unaccountable Indian rising. Eight hundred of the hard-riding United States cavalry had left the fort on receipt of the message from Beacon Crossing. The hotel-keeper imparted the news with keen appreciation; he had no desire for troublesome times. Plainsmen had a knack of quitting his execrable drink when there was fighting to be done—and Louis Roiheim was an Israelite.

A silence fell upon the bar-room on the appearance of Julie Roiheim. She saw Seth, and beckoned him over to her.

"There are initials on the little one's clothing. M. R.," she said. And Seth nodded.

"Any name?" he asked.

The stout old woman shook her greasy head.

"But she's no ordinary child, Seth. Not by a lot. She belongs East, or my name's not Julie. That child is the girl of some millionaire in Noo York, or Philadelphy. She's got nothing on her but what is fine lawn and *real* lace!"

"Ah!" murmured the plainsman, without any responsive enthusiasm, while his dark eyes watched the triumphant features of the woman to whom these things were of such consequence. "And has the Doc. got around?"

"He's fixin' her up," Julie Roiheim went on. "Oh, yes, you were right, she's alive, but he can't wake her up. He says if she's to be moved, it had best be at once."

"Good." Just for one brief instant Seth's thoughtful face lit up. He turned to old Louis. "Guess I'll borrow your buckboard," he went on. "I'll need it to take the kiddie out."

The hotel-keeper nodded, and just then Nevil Steyne, who at that moment had entered the bar, and had only gleaned part of the conversation, made his way over to where Seth was standing.

"Who is she?" he asked, fixing his cold blue eyes eagerly on the face of the man he was addressing.

"Don't know," said Seth shortly. Then as an afterthought, "Clothes marked M. R."

The blue eyes lowered before the other's steady gaze.

"Ah," murmured Nevil. Then he, too, paused. "Is she alive?" he asked at last. And there was something in his tone which suggested a dry throat.

"Yes, she is," replied Seth. "And," he said, with unusual expansiveness, "I guess she'll keep right on doing that same."

Seth had again betrayed himself.

Nevil seemed half inclined to say more. But Seth gave him no chance. He had no love for this man. He turned on his heel without excuse and left the hotel to attend to the preparation of the buckboard himself.

On his way home that afternoon, and all the next day, the Indians were in his thoughts only so far as this waif he had picked up was concerned. For the most part he was thinking of the child herself, and those to whom he was taking her. He pictured the delight with which his childless foster-parents would receive her. The bright-faced little woman whom he affectionately called "Ma"; the massive old plainsman, Rube, with his gurgling chuckle, gruff voice and kindly heart. And his thoughts stirred in him an emotion he never would have admitted. He thought of the terrible lot he had saved this child from, for he knew only too well why she had been spared by the ruthless Big Wolf.

All through that long journey his watchfulness never relaxed. He looked to the comfort of his patient although she was still unconscious. He protected her face from the sun, and kept cool cloths upon her forehead, and drove only at a pace which spared the inanimate body unnecessary jolting. And it was all done with an eye upon the Reservations and horizon; with a hearing always acute on the prairie, rendered doubly so now, and with a loaded rifle across his knees.

It was dusk when he drove up to the farm. A certain relief came over him as he observed the peaceful cattle grazing adjacent to the corrals, the smoke rising from the kitchen chimney, and the great figure of Rube smoking reflectively in the kitchen doorway.

He did not stop to unhitch the horses, just hooking them to the corral fence. Then he lifted the child from the buckboard and bore her to the house.

Rube watched him curiously as he came with his burden. There was no greeting between these two. Both were usually silent men, but for different reasons. Conversation was a labor to Rube; a twinkling look of his deep-set eyes, and an expressive grunt generally contented him. Now he removed his pipe from his lips and stared in open-mouthed astonishment at the queer-looking bundle Seth was carrying.

"Gee!" he muttered. And made way for his foster son. Any questions that might have occurred to him were banished from his slow-moving thoughts.

Seth laid his charge upon the kitchen table, and Rube looked at the deathlike face, so icy, yet so beautiful. A great broad smile, not untouched with awe, spread over his bucolic features.

"Where's Ma?" asked Seth.

Rube indicated the ceiling with the stem of his pipe.

"Ma," cried Seth, through the doorway, up the narrow stairs which led to the rooms above. "Come right down. Guess I've kind o' got a present for you."

"That you, Seth?" called out a cheery voice from above.

"Guess so."

A moment later a little woman, with gray hair and a face that might have belonged to a woman of thirty, bustled into the room.

"Ah, Seth," she cried affectionately, "you jest set to it to spoil your old mother." Then her eyes fell on the figure on the kitchen table. "La sakes, boy, what's—what's this?" Then as she bent over the unconscious child. "Oh, the pore—pore little beauty!"

Rube turned away with a chuckle. His practical little wife had been astonished out of her wits. And the fact amused him immensely.

"It's a gal, Ma," said Seth. He too was smiling.

"Gracious, boy, guess I've got two eyes in my head!"

There was a long pause. Ma fingered the silken curls. Then she took one of the cold hands in hers and stroked it softly.

"Where—where did you git her?" she asked at last.

"The Injuns. I shot Big Wolf yesterday. They're on the war-path."

"Ah." The bright-eyed woman looked up at this tall foster son of hers.

"War-path—you shot Big Wolf?" cried Rube, now roused to unwonted speech. "Then we'd best git busy."

"It's all right, father," Seth reassured him. "The troops are on the trail."

There was another considerable pause while all eyes were turned on the child. At last Mrs. Sampson looked up.

"Who is she?" she asked.

Seth shook his head.

"Don't know. Maybe she's yours—an' mine."

"Don't you know wher' she come from?"

Again Seth shook his head.

"An'—an' what's her name?"

"Can't say—leastways her initials are M. R. You see I got her from—there that's it. I got her from the Rosebuds. That's her name. Rosebud!"

CHAPTER V

A BIRTHDAY GIFT

Rosebud struggled through five long months of illness after her arrival at White River Farm. It was only the untiring care of Rube and his wife, and Seth, that pulled her through. The wound at the base of the skull had affected her brain as well as body, and, until the last moment when she finally awoke to consciousness, her case seemed utterly without hope.

But when at last her convalescence came it was marvelously rapid. It was not until the good old housewife began to question her patient that the full result of the cruel blow on her head was realized. Then it was found that she had no recollection of any past. She knew not who she was, her name, her age, even her nationality. She had a hazy idea of Indians, which, as she grew stronger, became more pronounced, until she declared that she must have lived among Indians all her life.

It was this last that roused Seth to a sense of what he conceived to be his duty. And with that deliberateness which always characterized him, he set about it at once. From the beginning, after his first great burst of pitying sorrow for the little waif, when he had clasped her in his arms and almost fiercely claimed her for his own, his treasure trove, he had realized that she belonged to some other world than his own. This thought stayed with him. It slumbered during the child's long illness, but roused to active life when he discovered that she had no knowledge of herself. Therefore he set about inquiries. He must find out to whom she belonged and restore her to her people.

There was no one missing for two hundred miles round Beacon Crossing except the Jasons. It was impossible that the Indians could have gone farther afield, for they had not been out twenty-four hours when Rosebud was rescued. So his search for the child's friends proved unavailing.

Still, from that day on he remained loyal to her. Any clue, however frail, was never too slight for him to hunt to its source. He owed it to her to restore her to her own, whatever regret it might cost him to lose her. He was not the man to shirk a painful duty, certainly not where his affections were concerned.

During the six years, while Rosebud was growing to womanhood, Seth's hands were very full. Those wonderful violet eyes belonged to no milk and water "miss." From the very beginning the girl proved herself spirited and wilful. Not in any vicious way. A "madcap" best describes her. She had no thought of consequences; only the delight of the moment, the excitement and risk. These were the things that plunged her into girlish scrapes from which it fell to the lot of Seth to extricate her. All her little escapades were in themselves healthy enough, but they were rarely without a smack of physical danger.

She began when she learned to ride, a matter which of course devolved upon Seth.

Once she could sit a wild, half-tamed broncho her career in the direction of accident became checkered. Once, after a day's search for her, Seth brought her home insensible. She had been thrown from her horse, an animal as wildly wilful as herself.

A little private target practice with a revolver resulted in the laming of a cow, and the killing of a chicken, and in nearly terminating Rube's career, when he ran out of the house to ascertain the meaning of the firing. Once she was nearly drowned in the White River, while bathing with the Indian children after service at the Mission. She was never free from the result of childish recklessness. And this feature of her character grew with her, though her achievements moderated as the years passed.

It was by these wild means that she endeared herself to the folks on the farm. Seth's love grew apace. He made no attempt to deceive himself. He loved her as a child, and that love changed only in its nature when she became a woman. He made no attempt to check it. He knew she was not for him; never could be. He, a rough, half-educated plainsman; she, a girl who displayed, even in her most reckless moods, that indelible stamp which marked the disparity between the social worlds to which they belonged. He was convinced, without disparaging himself, that to attempt to win her would be an outrage, an imposition on her. Worse, it would be rankly dishonest.

So the man said nothing. All that lay within his heart he kept hidden far out of sight. No chance word or weak moment should reveal it. No one should ever know, least of all Rosebud.

But in all this Seth reckoned without his host. Such glorious eyes, such a charming face as Rosebud possessed were not likely to belong to a girl devoid of the instincts of her sex. As she grew up her perspective changed. She saw things in a different light. Seth no longer appealed to her as a sort of uncle, or even father. She saw in him a young man of medium good looks, a strong, fine figure. A man who had no idea of the meaning of the word fear; a man who had a way of saying and doing things which often made her angry, but always made her glad that he said and did them. Furthermore, she soon learned that he was only twenty-eight. Therefore, she resented many things which she had hitherto accepted as satisfactory. She made up her wilful mind that it didn't please her to call him "Daddy" Seth any longer.

Those six years brought another change; a change in the life of the wood-cutter of White River. He still lived in his log hut, but he had taken to himself a wife, the beautiful orphaned daughter of Big Wolf, and sister of the reigning chief, Little Black Fox. Whatever may have been Nevil Steyne's position before, he was completely ostracized by his fellows now, that is by all but the folk at White River Farm. Men no longer suggested that he had "taken the blanket"; they openly asserted it.

The reason of Nevil Steyne's toleration by the White River Farm people was curious. It was for Rosebud's sake; Rosebud and Wanaha, the wife of the renegade wood-cutter. The latter was different from the rest of her race. She was almost civilized, a woman of strong, honest character in spite of her upbringing. And between Rosebud and this squaw a strong friendship had sprung up. Kindly Rube and his wife could not find it in their hearts to interfere, and even Seth made no attempt to check it. He looked on and wondered without approval; and wonder with him quickly turned into keen observation.

And it is with this strange friendship that we have to deal now.

Inside the log hut on the White River, Wanaha was standing before a small iron cook-stove preparing her husband's food. It was the strangest sight imaginable to see her cooking in European fashion. Yet she did it in no uncertain manner. She learned it all because she loved her white husband, just as she learned to speak English, and to dress after the manner of white women. She went further. With the assistance of the missionary and Rosebud she learned to read and sew, and to care for a house. And all this labor of a great love brought her the crowning glory of legitimate wifehood with a renegade white man, and the care of a dingy home that no white girl would have faced. But she was happy. Happy beyond all her wildest dreams in the smoke-begrimed tepee of her father.

Nevil Steyne had just returned from Beacon Crossing, whither he had gone to sell a load of cord-wood, and to ask for mail at the post-office. Strange as it may seem, this man still received letters from England. But to-day he had returned with only a packet of newspapers.

He entered the hut without notice or greeting for Wanaha, who, in true Indian fashion, waited by the cook-stove for her lord to speak first.

He passed over to the bedstead which occupied the far end of the room, and sat himself down to a perusal of his papers. He was undoubtedly preoccupied and not intentionally unkind to the woman.

Wanaha went steadily on with her work. For her this was quite as it should be. He would speak presently. She was satisfied.

Presently the man flung his papers aside, and the woman's deep eyes met his as he looked across at her.

"Well, Wana," he said, "I've sold the wood and got orders for six more cords. Business is booming."

The man spoke in English. Yet he spoke Wanaha's tongue as fluently as she did herself. Here again the curious submissive nature of the woman was exampled. He must speak his own tongue. It was not right that he should be forced to use hers.

"I am much happy," she said simply. Then her woman's thought rose superior to greater issues. "You will eat?" she went on.

"Yes, Wana. I'm hungry—very."

"So." The woman's eyes smiled into his, and she eagerly set the food on a table made of packing cases.

Steyne began at once. He was thoughtful while he ate. But after a while he looked up, and there was a peculiar gleam in his blue eyes as they rested on the warm, rich features of his willing slave.

"Pretty poor sort of place—this," he said. "It's not good enough for you, my Wana."

The woman had seated herself on a low stool near the table. It was one of her few remaining savage instincts she would not give up. It was not fitting that she should eat with him.

"How would you like a house, a big house, like—White River Farm?" he went on, as though he were thinking aloud. "And hundreds, thousands, of steers and cows? And buggies to ride in? And farm machinery? And—and plenty of fine clothes to wear, like—like Rosebud?"

The woman shook her head and indicated her humble belongings.

"This—very good. Very much good. See, you are here. I want you."

The man flushed and laughed a little awkwardly. But he was well pleased.

"Oh, we're happy enough. You and I, my Wana. But—we'll see."

Wanaha made no comment; and when his meat was finished she set a dish of buckwheat cakes and syrup before him.

He devoured them hungrily, and the woman's eyes grew soft with delight at his evident pleasure.

At last his thoughtfulness passed, and he put an abrupt question.

"Where's your brother, now?"

"Little Black Fox is by his tepee. He goes hunting with another sun. Yes?"

"I must go and see him this afternoon."

Steyne pushed his plate away, and proceeded to fill his pipe.

"Yes?"

The expressive eyes of the woman had changed again. His announcement seemed to give her little pleasure.

"Yes, I have things to pow-wow with him."

"Ah. Rosebud? Always Rosebud?"

The man laughed.

"My Wana does not like Little Black Fox to think of Rosebud, eh?"

Wanaha was silent for a while. Then she spoke in a low tone.

"Little Black Fox is not wise. He is very fierce. No, I love my brother, but Rosebud must not be his squaw. I love Rosebud, too."

The blue eyes of the man suddenly became very hard.

"Big Wolf captured Rosebud, and would have kept her for your brother. Therefore she is his by right of war. Indian war. This Seth kills your father. He says so. He takes Rosebud. Is it for him to marry her? Your brother does not think so."

Wanaha's face was troubled. "It was in war. You said yourself. My brother could not hold her from the white man. Then his right is gone. Besides— —"

"Besides— —?"

"A chief may not marry a white girl."

"You married a white man."

"It is different."

There was silence for some time while Wanaha cleared away the plates. Presently, as she was bending over the cook-stove, she spoke again. And she kept her face turned from her husband while she spoke.

"You want Rosebud for my brother. Why?"

"I?" Nevil laughed uneasily. Wanaha had a way of putting things very directly. "I don't care either way."

"Yet you pow-wow with him? You say 'yes' when he talks of Rosebud?"

It was the man's turn to look away, and by doing so he hid a deep cunning in his eyes.

"Oh, that's because Little Black Fox is not an easy man. He is unreasonable. It is no use arguing with him. Besides, they will see he never gets Rosebud." He nodded in the direction of White River Farm.

"I have said he is very fierce. He has many braves. One never knows. My brother longs for the war-path. He would kill Seth. For Seth killed our father. One never knows. It is better you say to him, 'Rosebud is white. The braves want no white squaw.'"

But the man had had enough of the discussion, and began to whistle. It was hard to understand how he had captured the loyal heart of this dusky princess. He was neither good-looking nor of a taking manner. His appearance was dirty, unkempt. His fair hair, very thin and getting gray at the crown, was long and uncombed, and his moustache was ragged and grossly stained. Yet she loved him with a devotion which had made her willing to renounce her people for him if necessary, and this means far more in a savage than it does amongst the white races.

Steyne put on his greasy slouch hat and swung out of the house. Wanaha knew that what she had said was right, Nevil Steyne encouraged Little Black Fox. She wondered, and was apprehensive. Nevertheless, she went on with her work. The royal blood of her race was strong in her. She had much of the stoicism which is, perhaps, the most pronounced feature of her people. It was no good saying more than she had said. If she saw necessity she would do, and not talk.

She was still in the midst of her work when a sound caught her ear which surely no one else could have heard. In response she went to the door. A rider, still half a mile away, was approaching. She went back to her washing-up, smiling. She had recognized the rider even at that distance. Therefore she was in nowise surprised when, a few minutes later, she heard a bright, girlish voice hailing her from without.

"Wana, Wana!" The tone was delightfully imperious. "Why don't you have some place to tie a horse to?"

It was Rosebud. Wanaha had expected her, for it was the anniversary of her coming to White River Farm, and the day Ma Sampson had allotted for her birthday.

Wanaha went out to meet her friend. This greeting had been made a hundred times, on the occasion of every visit Rosebud made to the woman's humble home. It was a little joke between them, for there was a large iron hook high up on the wall, just out of the girl's reach, set there for the purpose of tying up a horse. The squaw took the girl's reins from her hands, and hitched them to the hook.

"Welcome," she said in her deep voice, and held out a hand to be shaken as white folk shake hands, not in the way Indians do it.

"What is it I must say to you?" she went on, in a puzzled way. "Oh, I know. 'Much happy return.' That is how you tell me the last time you come."

The squaw's great black eyes wore their wonderful soft look as they gazed down upon her visitor. It was a strange contrast they made as they stood there in the full light of the summer afternoon sun.

Both were extremely handsome of figure, though the Indian woman was more natural and several inches taller. But their faces were opposite in every detail. The squaw was dark, with clear velvety skin, and eyes black and large and deeply luminous; she had a broad, intelligent forehead over which her straight black hair fell from a natural centre parting, and was caught back from her face at about the level of her mouth with two bows of deep red braid. Her features might have been chiseled by a sculptor, they were so perfectly symmetrical, so accurately proportioned. And there were times, too, when, even to the eyes of a white man, her color rather enhanced her beauty; and this was when her slow smile crept over her face.

Rosebud had no classical regularity of feature, but she had what is better. Her face was a series of expressions, changing with almost every moment as her swift-passing moods urged her. One feature she possessed that utterly eclipsed anything the stately beauty of the other could claim. She had large, lustrous violet eyes that seemed like wells of ever-changing color. They never looked at you with the same shade in their depths twice. They were eyes that madden by reason of their inconsistency. They dwarfed in beauty every other feature in the girl's face. She was pretty in an irregular manner, but one never noticed anything in her face when her eyes were visible. These, and her masses of golden hair, which flowed loosely about her head in thick, rope-like curls, were her great claims to beauty.

Now, as she stood smiling up into the dark face above her, she looked what she was; a girl in the flush of early womanhood, a prairie girl, wild as the flowers which grow hidden in the lank grass of the plains, as wayward as the breezes which sweep them from every point of the compass.

"Mayn't I come in?" asked Rosebud, as the woman made no move to let her pass.

Wanaha turned with some haste. "Surely," she said. "I was thinking. What you call 'dreaming.'"

She eagerly put a stool for the girl to sit upon. But Rosebud preferred the table.

"Well, Wana," said the girl, playfully, "you said you wanted me particularly to-day, so, at great inconvenience to myself, and mother, I have come. If it isn't important you'll get into grave trouble. I was going to help Seth hoe the potatoes, but — —"

"Poor Seth." Wanaha had caught something of the other's infectious mood.

"I don't think he needs any pity, either," said Rosebud, impulsively. "Seth's sometimes too much of a good thing. He said I ought to learn to hoe. And I don't think hoeing's very nice for one thing; besides, he always gets angry if I cut out any of the plants. He can just do it himself."

"Seth's a good man. He killed my father; but he is good, I think."

"Yes." For the moment Rosebud had become grave. "I wonder what would have——" She broke off and looked searchingly into her friend's face. "Wana," she went on abruptly, "why did you send for me to-day? I can't stay. I really can't, I must go back and help Seth, or he'll be so angry."

Rosebud quite ignored her own contradictions, but Wanaha didn't.

"No, and it is not good to make Seth angry. He—what-you-call—he very good by you. See, I say come to me. You come, and I have—ah—ah," she broke off in a bewildered search for a word. "No—that not it. So, I know. Birthday pre—sent."

Wanaha gave a triumphant glance into Rosebud's laughing face and went to a cupboard, also made of packing cases, and brought forth a pair of moose-hide moccasins, perfectly beaded and trimmed with black fox fur. She had made them with her own hands for her little friend, a labor of love into which she had put the most exquisite work of which she was capable.

Rosebud's delight was unfeigned. The shoes were perfect. The leather was like the finest kid. It was a present worthy of the giver. She held out her hands for them, but the Indian laughed and shook her head.

"No," she said playfully. "No, you white woman! Your folk not carry things so," and she held the tiny shoes out at arm's length. "You put paper round, so." She picked up one of her husband's newspapers and wrapped the present into a clumsy parcel. "There," she exclaimed, handing it to the girl, "I wish you much happy!"

As she put the parcel into the outstretched hands, Rosebud sprang from the table and flung her arms round the giver's neck, and kissed her heartily.

"You're the dandiest thing in the world, Wana," she cried impulsively, "and I love you."

CHAPTER VI

A NEWSPAPER

Seth was bending over his work among the potatoes. It was a large order, for there were more than five acres of it. Every time he stood erect to ease his back he scanned the distance in the direction of the White River. Each time he bent again over his hoe, it was with a dissatisfied look on his sunburnt face. He made up his mind that Rosebud was playing truant again. He cared nothing for the fact of the truancy, but the direction in which his eyes turned whenever he looked up displayed his real source of dissatisfaction. Rosebud had been out since the midday dinner, and he guessed where she was. The mosquitoes worried him to-day, which meant that his temper was ruffled.

Suddenly he paused. But this time he didn't look round. He heard the sound of galloping hoofs racing across the prairie. Continuing his work, he roughly estimated the distance the rider was away.

He gave no sign at all until Rosebud's voice called to him.

"Seth, I've come to help you hoe," she said.

The man saw that the horse was standing pawing the ground among the potatoes.

"I take it friendly of you," he said, eyeing the havoc the animal was creating. "Guess that horse o' yours has intentions that aways too. They're laud'ble, but misplaced."

The girl checked the creature, and turned him off the patch. Then she quietly slid to the ground and removed her saddle and bridle, and drove him off out on the prairie for a roll.

"I'm so sorry, Seth! I'm afraid he's made a mess of these plants."

Rosebud stooped and tried to repair the damage her horse had done. She did not look in Seth's direction, but her smiling face conveyed nothing of her regret. Presently she stood up and stepped gingerly along the furrows toward the man.

"Did you bring a hoe out for me?" she asked innocently.

But her companion was used to the wiles of this tyrant.

"Guess not," he said quietly. "Didn't reckon you'd get back that soon. Say, Rosebud, you'd best git out o' those fixin's if you're going to git busy with a hoe. Ma has her notions."

"Ye-es. Do you think I'm getting any better with a hoe?"

The eyes that looked up into Seth's face were candidly inquiring. There was not a shadow of a smile on the man's face when he answered.

"I've a notion you have few equals with a hoe."

"I was afraid — —"

"Ah, that's always the way of folks wi' real talent. Guess you're an eddication with a hoe."

Seth went on with his work until Rosebud spoke again. She was looking away out across the prairie, and her eyes were just a trifle troubled.

"Then I'd best get my things changed and—bring out a hoe. How many rows do you think I could do before tea?"

"That mostly depends on how many p'tater plants git in your way, I guess."

The girl's face suddenly wreathed itself in smiles.

"There, you're laughing at me, and—well, I was going to help you, but now I shan't. I've been down to see my Wanaha. Seth, you ought to have married her. She's the sweetest creature—except Ma—I know. I think it's a pity she married Nevil Steyne. He's a queer fellow. I never know what to make of him. He's kind to her, and he's kind to me—which I'm not sure I like—but I somehow don't like his eyes. They're blue, and I don't like blue eyes. And I don't believe he ever washes. Do you?"

Seth replied without pausing in his work. He even seemed to put more force into it, for the hoe cut into the earth with a vicious ring. But he avoided her direct challenge.

44

"Guess I haven't a heap of regard for no Injuns nor squaws. I've no call to. But I allow Wanaha's a good woman."

Just for a moment the girl's face became very serious.

"I'm glad you say that, Seth. I knew you wouldn't say anything else; you're too generous. Wanaha is good. Do you know she goes to the Mission because she loves it? She helps us teach the little papooses because she believes in the 'God of the white folks,' she says. I know you don't like me to see so much of her, but somehow I can't help it. Seth, do you believe in foreboding?"

"Can't say I'd gamble a heap that aways."

"Well, I don't know, but I believe it's a good thing that Wanaha loves me—loves us all. She has such an influence over people."

Seth looked up at last. The serious tone of the girl was unusual. But as he said nothing, and simply went on with his work, Rosebud continued.

"Sometimes I can't understand you, Seth. I know, generally speaking, you have no cause to like Indians, while perhaps I have. You see, I have always known them. But you seem to have taken exception only to Little Black Fox and Wanaha as far as I am concerned. You let me teach the Mission children, you even teach them yourself, yet, while admitting Wanaha's goodness, you get angry with me for seeing her. As for Little Black Fox, he is the chief. He's a great warrior, and acknowledged by even the agent and missionary to be the best chief the Rosebuds have ever had. Quite different from his father."

"Guess that's so."

"Then why—may I not talk to them? And, oh, Seth"—the girl's eyes danced with mischief—"he is such a romantic fellow. You should hear him talk in English. He talks—well, he has much more poetry in him than you have."

"Which is mostly a form of craziness," observed Seth, quite unruffled.

"Well, I like craziness."

"Ah!"

Seth's occasional lapses into monosyllables annoyed Rosebud. She never understood them. Now there came a gleam of anger into her eyes, and their color seemed to have changed to a hard gray.

"Well, whether you like it or not, you needn't be so ill-tempered about it."

Seth looked up in real astonishment at this unwarrantable charge, and his dark eyes twinkled as he beheld Rosebud's own evident anger.

He shook his head regretfully, and cut out a bunch of weeds with his hoe.

"Guess I'm pretty mean," he said, implying that her assertion was correct.

"Yes." Rosebud's anger was like all her moods, swift rising and as swift to pass. Now it was approaching its zenith. "And to show you how good Wanaha is, look at this." She unfolded her parcel and threw the paper down, disclosing the perfect moccasins the Indian had made for her. "Aren't they lovely? She didn't forget it was my birthday, like—like——"

"Ah, so it is." Seth spoke as though he had just realized the fact of her birthday.

"Aren't they lovely?" reiterated the girl. Her anger had passed. She was all smiles again.

"Indian," said Seth, with a curious click of the tongue, which Rosebud was quick to interpret into an expression of scorn.

"Yes," she exclaimed, firing up again, and her eyes sparkling. "And I like Indian things, and I like Indian people, and I like Little Black Fox. He's nice, and isn't always sneering. And I shall see them all when I like. And—and you can do the hoeing yourself."

She walked off toward the house without the least regard for the potatoes, which now suffered indiscriminately. Her golden head was held very high, but she had less dignity than she thought, for she stumbled in the furrows as she went.

She went straight into the house and up to her room; but she could not fling herself upon her bed and cry, as she probably intended to do. Three large parcels occupied its entire narrow limits. Each was addressed to her, wishing her all happiness on her birthday, and the biggest of the three was from Seth. So, failing room anywhere else, she sat in her rocking-chair, and, instead of an angry outburst, she shed a few quiet, happy tears.

Meanwhile Seth continued his work as though nothing had interrupted him. It was not until supper-time, and he was making his way to the house, that he happened to observe the newspaper which Rosebud had left lying among the potatoes. He stepped across the intervening furrows and picked it up. Newspapers always interested him, he saw so few.

This one, he saw at once, was an English paper. And from London at that. He glanced at the date, and saw that was nearly a month old, and, at the same time, he saw that it was addressed to Nevil Steyne, and beside the address was a note in blue pencil, "Page 3."

His curiosity was aroused, and he turned over to the page indicated. There was a long paragraph marked by four blue crosses. It was headed—

"The Estate of the Missing Colonel Raynor."

Seth read the first few lines casually. Then, as he went on, a curious look crept into his dark eyes, his clean-shaven face took on an expression of strained interest, and his lips closed until they were lost in a straight line which drew down at the corners of his mouth. He read on to the end, and then quietly folded up the paper, and stuffed it into the bosom of his shirt. Once he turned and looked away in the direction in which Nevil Steyne's hut lay tucked away on the river bank. Then he shouldered his hoe and strolled leisurely homeward.

CHAPTER VII

AN INDIAN POW-WOW

Nevil Steyne was indifferent to such blessings as a refreshing thunder-shower at sundown on a hot summer's day. It is doubtful if he would have admitted the beneficence of Providence in thus alleviating the parching heat of the day. He had no crops to think of, which made all the difference. Now, as he walked along through the brush on the north bank of the White River, in the direction of the log bridge, with the dripping trees splashing all round him, and his boots clogging with the heavy, wet loam, he openly cursed the half-hour's drenching. His vindictiveness was in no way half-measured. He cursed those who were glad of it, and who, when in direst necessity, occasionally remembered to offer up prayers for it.

This man had no love for the woods; no love even for the prairie, or his life on it. He lived a grudging existence. From his manner nothing in life seemed to give him real joy. But there is no doubt but that he had purpose of a sort which had much to do with his associations with his Indian neighbors. With him purpose served for everything else, and made existence tolerable.

There was purpose in his movements now. He could just as easily have made his way to the bridge through the open, but he chose the woods, and put up with the wet while he railed at it. And there was some haste in his slouching, loose-jointed gait which gave to his journey a suggestion of furtiveness.

At the bridge he paused, gave a quick look round, and then crossed it more rapidly still. For at this point he was in full view of the prairie. Once on the Indian Reservation, which began beyond the bridge, he again took to the cover the park-like land afforded him. Nor did he appear again in the open until he had passed the Mission and the Agency.

Once clear of these, however, he gave no more heed to secrecy, and walked boldly along open paths in the full, bright evening light. He passed in and out among the scattered tepees, speaking a word here and there to the men as he passed, or nodding a greeting. The latter being the more frequent of the two, for the Indian is a silent man.

The life amidst which he was walking was too familiar to cause such a man as he any unusual interest. Perhaps it was because he felt he had a certain underhand power with these people; like a person who loses interest in the thing which he has mastered. Certain it is that the busy homes he beheld were all unnoticed. The smoke-begrimed tepees with their great wooden trailers propped against them; the strings of drying meats stretching along under the boughs of adjacent trees. The bucks huddled, in spite of the warmth of summer, in their parti-colored blankets, gazing indolently at their squaws pounding the early berries into a sort of muddy preserve, or dressing a skin for manufacture into leggings, moccasins, or buckskin shirt. He gave no heed to the swarms of papooses, like so many flies buzzing round the tepees, whooping in imitation of their father braves, or amusing themselves with the pursuit of one of the many currish camp dogs, which, from their earliest years, they love to persecute to the limits of the poor beasts' endurance. The totem poles with their hideous carved heads had no meaning for him, just as the dried scalps which hung from the tepee poles might have been rabbit skins for all he thought of them.

Just now his purpose was to reach the house of Little Black Fox, and this he came to at last. It was a large building; next to the Mission and Agency it was by far the largest house on the Reservation. It was built of logs and thatch and plaster, and backed into a thick clump of shady maple trees. The son was more lavish than the father. Big Wolf had always been content to live in a tepee. He was an older type of chief. The son moved with the times and was given to display.

Nevil raised the latch of the door and walked in, and his manner was that of a privileged visitor. He entered the spacious living-room without word for those he beheld gathered there. He walked to a certain vacant place, and sat down upon the mud floor. It was at once plain that he had been expected. More, it was evident that he belonged by right to that gathering.

Despite the display in the dimensions of Little Black Fox's house the interior revealed the old savage. There was nothing civilized about the council-chamber. There was the central fire of smouldering logs, without which no Indian can exist in summer or winter. The smoke passed out through a square chimney in the middle of the roof.

In a large circle the chief's councilors sat perched upon their haunches and swathed in their blankets. There was not a seat or table there. They sat in their councils as their forefathers had done before them, their leader in their midst with nothing but his youth to distinguish him from those who were his subjects.

The debate proceeded in its spasmodic fashion. There was no haste, no heat like in the debates of civilized folk. Each man was listened to in respectful silence, which might have served as an example to modern legislatures. Nevil spoke like the rest in their low, musical tongue. Whenever he spoke it was noticeable that the great, wild eyes of the chief were turned upon him with interest. But even he seemed a mere unit in the debate, no more and no less, unless it were that Little Black Fox was more influenced by what he said than by what was said by the others.

At length, well on into the night, the meeting drew to a close. The business in hand had been threshed out and a decision arrived at. The warriors and the men of "medicine" filed slowly out. Even in this there was a certain formality and precedence. Each man addressed his chief, shook hands, and passed through the door. And no two went out together.

When the last had gone Nevil and the chief remained alone in the bare room. Little Black Fox rose from his pile of skins and stood erect. He was a mere youth, but of such shape and appearance that one could easily understand the epithet "romantic" Rosebud had applied to him. He stood at least four inches over six feet, and dwarfed even Nevil's height. But it was in the perfect symmetry of his lithe, sinuous body, and the keen, handsome, high-caste face where his attractions lay.

His eyes were the eyes of the untamed savage, but of a man capable of great thought as well as great reckless courage. There was nothing sinister in them, but they were glowing, live eyes which might blaze or soften in two succeeding moments, which exactly expresses the man's character. He was handsome as Indian men go. Not like the women. They are often beautiful in a way that appeals to any artistic eye, but the men are a type for study before they can be appreciated.

This chief was in the first flush of manhood, and had attained nothing of the seared, bloated appearance which comes to the Indian later in life. His face was almost as delicately chiseled as his sister's, but it was strong as well as high caste. The eagle beakishness of his nose matched the flashing black eyes. His mouth was sensitive and clean-cut. His forehead was high and broad, and his cheeks were delicately round.

Nevil became a wretched, unkempt type of manhood in comparison. In form, at least, this chief of twenty-one years was a veritable king.

He smiled on his white councilor when the last of his own people had departed. He thrust out a slim, strong hand, and the two men shook hands heartily.

"It is slow with many in council," the chief said, in his own smooth-flowing tongue. "You, white man, and I can settle matters quickly. Quicker than these wise men of my father."

There was a flash of impatience in his speaking eyes. Nevil nodded approval.

"They think much before they speak," he replied, in the language in which he had been addressed. He, too, smiled; and in their manner toward each other it was plain the excellent understanding they were on.

"Sit, my white brother, we have many things for talk. Even we, like those others, must sit if we would pow-wow well. It is good. Sit." Little Black Fox laughed shortly, conceiving himself superior in thought to the older generation of wise men. He was possessed of all the vanity of his years.

They both returned to the ground, and the chief kicked together the embers of the council-fire.

"Tell me, brother, of Wanaha," this still unproved warrior went on, in an even, indifferent voice; "she who was the light of our father's eyes; she who has the wisdom of the rattlesnake, and the gentle heart of the summer moon."

"She is well." Nevil was not expansive. He knew the man had other things to talk of, and he wanted him to talk.

"Ah. And all the friends of my white brother?"

The face smiled, but the eyes were keenly alight.

"They are well. And Rosebud — —"

"Ah."

"She grows fairer every day."

There was a truly Indian pause. The fire sputtered and cast shadows upon the dark, bare walls. The two men gazed thoughtfully into the little flame which vauntingly struggled to rear itself in the dense atmosphere. At last the Indian spoke.

"That man who killed my father is a great brave."

"Yes," nodded Nevil, with a reflective smile in his pale eyes. "And Rosebud is a ripe woman. Beautiful as the flower which is her name."

"Hah!" Then the Indian said slowly with an assumed indifference, "She will be his squaw. This white brave."

"That is how they say." It might have puzzled Nevil to apply names to those represented by "they." "He is a great brave, truly. He fought for her. He killed your father. That is how these things go. She is for him surely."

A frown had settled on the fierce young chief's face.

"My father was old," he said.

Nevil glanced at the speaker out of the corner of his eyes, and then continued his watch on the flame still struggling so ardently to devour the half-green wood. He knew when to hold his tongue.

"Yes," the young man went on. "My father was a wise chief, but he was old — too old. Why did he keep the white girl alive?"

"He took her for you. You only had fifteen summers. The white girl had eleven or thereabouts. He was wise. It was good med'cine."

Then the chief stirred himself. And Nevil, who lost no movement on the other's part, detected the restless action of one who chafes under his thought. Little Black Fox prefixed his next remark with another short laugh.

"My people love peace now. It is good. So good that your people come and teach us. They show our squaws how to make things like the white squaws make. And the papooses forget our tongue, and they make words out of strange drawings which the white med'cine man makes on a board. Tchah! We forget our fathers. We feed when your people give us food, and our young men are made to plough. We only hunt when we are told to hunt. Our life is easy, but it is not a brave's life."

Nevil nodded, and chose his reply carefully.

"So," he said, "it is a life of ease. You choose your life. And naturally you choose a life where you have all you want, and do not have to trouble. After all, what is the old life? A life of much danger, and little ease. You fight, you kill, or you are killed. You risk much and gain little. But you are men, brave men, great warriors, I grant you. And the squaws like brave men—even white squaws. But I say it is wise, though not brave, to live in the tepee. It is so easy. Your braves have their squaws always with them. They grow fat till their sides shake. They no longer care to hunt. Why should they? Many papooses come, and they grow up like their fathers. There are no Sun-Dances to make braves, because none want to be braves. There are no Ghost-Dances, because the white men keep the Evil Spirits away, and there is no need. So. The Indian lies upon his blankets, and he lives with the squaw always. They all become squaw-men. Never was there such peace for the Indian."

Nevil had drawn his peaceful picture with care; also the tail of his eye told him that his companion was listening. And his movements, every now and then, had in them something of the spasmodic movements of a chained wild beast. This lithe youth had certain resemblance to the puma. He seemed to burn with a restless craving spirit. The puma never ceases to seek his prey. This man would be the same were he once to begin.

"Yes. You say well," he observed moodily, "we are all squaw-men. The white squaws love braves, you say. I know all squaws love braves. The squaws of our people will soon spit in our faces."

"You have no squaw to do that," observed Nevil, bending over and pushing the fire together.

"No."

"You are chief. You should have many."

"Yes."

"Then give the word to your people and you can have them."

"I do not want them—yet."

Nevil looked round. The chief turned to the fire uncertainly. His fierce eyes were half veiled.

"This Rosebud, she was for me," he went on. "She is fair as the summer sky. Her eyes are like the stars, and her laugh is like the ripple of the waters when the sun and the wind make play with them. She is so fair that no squaw can compare with her. Even Wanaha is as night to day."

"You cannot have her. She is for the man who killed your father."

The young chief leapt to his feet with a cry that told of a spirit which could no longer be restrained. And he towered threateningly over the undisturbed wood-cutter.

"But I will!" he cried vehemently, while his eyes flashed in the dying light of the fire. "You are my white brother, and to you I can say what is in my thoughts. This squaw, I love her. I burn for her! She is with me night and day. I will have her, I tell you! There shall be no peace till my father is avenged. Ha, ha!" And the ferocity of that laugh brought a smile to the hidden lips of the listening man.

He looked up now, and his words came thoughtfully.

"You are a great chief, Little Black Fox," he said. "But, see, there is no need to go on the war-path. Sit, like those wise councilors of yours. It is good to pow-wow."

The headstrong youth sat down again, and the pow-wow went forward. It was daylight again when Nevil returned to Wanaha. For Indian pow-wows are slow moving, ponderous things, and Little Black Fox was no better than the rest of his race when deliberations of grave import were on.

CHAPTER VIII

SETH WASHES A HANDKERCHIEF

Seth was not in the habit of making very frequent visits to Beacon Crossing. For one thing there was always plenty to do at the farm. For another the attractions of the fledgling city were peculiarly suited to idle folk, or folk who had money to spend. And this man was neither the one nor the other.

White River Farm was a prosperous farm, but it was still in that condition when its possibilities were not fully developed, and, like the thrifty, foresighted farmers Rube and his adopted son were, they were content to invest every available cent of profit in improvements. Consequently, when the latter did find his way to Roiheim's hotel it was always with a definite purpose; a purpose as necessary as any of his duties in his day's labor.

Riding into the township one evening he made straight for the hotel, and, refusing the stablehand's offer of care for his horse, sat down quietly on the verandah and lit his pipe. Beyond the loungers in the saloon and old Louis Roiheim no one worth any remark approached him. He sat watching the passers-by, but went on smoking idly. There were some children playing a sort of "King-of-the-Castle" game on a heap of ballast lying beside the track, and these seemed to interest him most. The sheriff stopped and spoke to him, but beyond a monosyllabic reply and a nod Seth gave him no encouragement to stop. An Indian on a big, raw-boned broncho came leisurely down the road and passed the hotel, leaving the township by the southern trail.

Seth waited until the sun had set. Then he stepped off the verandah and tightened the cinches of his saddle, and readjusted the neatly rolled blanket tied at the cantle. The proprietor of the hotel was lounging against one of the posts which supported the verandah.

"Goin'?" he asked indifferently. Seth was not a profitable customer.

"Yes."

"Home?"

"No. So long."

Seth swung into the saddle and rode off. And he, too, passed out of the town over the southern trail.

Later he overhauled the Indian. It was Jim Crow, the chief of the Indian police.

"Where do we sleep to-night?" he asked, after greeting the man.

Jim Crow, like all his race who worked for the government, never spoke his own language except when necessary. But he still retained his inclination to signs. Now he made a movement suggestive of three rises of land, and finished up with the word "Tepee."

"I must get back the day after to-morrow," Seth said. "Guess I'll hit back through the Reservations. I want to see Parker."

"Good," said the Indian, and relapsed into that companionable silence which all prairie men, whether Indian or white, so well understand.

That night the two men sheltered in the tepee belonging to Jim Crow. It was well off the Reservation, and was never pitched in the same place two nights running. Jim Crow's squaw looked after that. She moved about, acting under her man's orders, while the scout went about his business.

After supper a long talk proceeded. Seth became expansive, but it was the Indian who gave information.

"Yes," he said, in answer to a question the white man had put. "I find it after much time. Sa-sa-mai, my squaw. She find it from old brave. See you. Big Wolf and all the braves who come out this way, you make much shoot. So. They all kill. 'Cep' this one ol' brave. He live quiet an' say nothing. Why? I not say. Some one tell him say nothing. See? This Big Wolf. Before you kill him maybe. So he not say. Bimeby Sa-sa-mai, she much 'cute. She talk ol' brave. Him very ol'. So she learn, an' I go. I show you. You give me fi' dollar, then I, too, say nothing."

"Ah." Seth pulled out a five-dollar bill and handed it to the scout, and went on smoking. Presently he asked, "Have you been there?"

"No." Jim Crow smiled blandly. He had the truly Indian ambiguity of expression.

"Then you don't know if there's any traces, I guess."

"See. I go dis place. Little Black Fox hear. He hear all. So. There are devils on the Reservation. Jim Crow much watched. So. They know. These red devils."

Seth noted the man's air of pride. He was keenly alive to his own importance and exaggerated it, which is the way of his class. Jim Crow was a treacherous rascal, but it paid him to work for the white folk. He would work for the other side just as readily if it paid him better.

"That's so," observed Seth, seriously; but it was his pipe that absorbed his attention. "Wal, to-morrow, I guess," he added after a while. And, knocking his pipe out, he rolled over on his blanket and slept.

On the morrow the journey was continued, and at sundown they neared the great valley of the Missouri. Their route lay over a trail which headed southeast, in the direction of Sioux City. The sun had just dropped below the horizon when Jim Crow suddenly drew rein. Whatever character he might bear as a man he was a master scout. He had a knowledge and instinct far greater than that of a bloodhound on a hot scent. He glanced around him, taking in the lay of the land at every point of the compass. Then he finally pointed at a brush growing a few hundred yards from the trail.

"The bluff," he said. "It may be what we look for. Sa-sa-mai, she tell me. Ow."

The last was a grunt which expressed assurance.

The horses left the trail for the prairie. The eyes of both men were turned upon the ground, which is the habit of such men when out on the trail. It is the soil over which the prairie man passes which is the book. The general scene is only the illustration.

At the bluff the men dismounted. Seth now took the lead. He did not plunge haphazard into his search. He still studied the brush and the ground. But it was the scout whose trained instincts were the first to discover the signs they sought. And he found it in the dead, broken twigs which marked the course of a wagon.

The two followed the lead; followed it unerringly. With every foot of the way the task became easier. Once they had turned the cover the book had become the simplest reading. In a few minutes they came to a clearing well screened from the road. Now they parted company. The scout went on toward the water further on, but the white man turned to the clearing. Herein was displayed the difference in the men. Seth had come to the point where imagination served him. The other was only a craftsman.

The grass was tall in the clearing. There was a low scrub too, but it was a scrub that might be trodden under foot. In two minutes Seth was stooping examining a tent-peg, discolored by weather, but intact, and still holding in the earth where it had been driven. It was but four yards from this to a place where two distinct piles of human bones were lying hidden in the rank grass.

Seth was on his knees pulling the grass aside, but he did not touch the bones. The skeletons were far from complete. Fortunately the skulls were there, and he saw that they were those of a man and a woman. While he contemplated the ghastly remains his thoughts conjured up many scenes. He saw the bullet hole through the woman's skull, and the horrid rift in the man's. The absence of many of the bones of the extremities made him think of the coyotes, those prairie scavengers who are never far off when death stalks the plains.

After a few moments he was searching the long grass in every direction. He looked for remnants of clothing; for anything to give him a sign. In his search he was joined by the scout who had returned from the water, where he had discovered further traces of an encampment.

At last the examination was completed. There was nothing left to indicate the identity of the bones.

The two men now stood by the bones of the unfortunate man and woman. Seth was staring out at the surrounding brush.

"I guess the Injuns cleaned things up pretty well," he said, while his eyes settled on one little bush apart from the rest.

The scout shook his head.

"That's not Injuns' work," he said.

"No?" Seth queried casually.

"No. Everything gone. So. That not like Injun."

Seth made no response, but walked over to the bush he had been looking at. The scout saw him thrust a hand in amongst the branches and withdraw it holding something.

"What you find?" he asked, when Seth came back.

"Only a rag."

Then, a moment later, Seth asked suddenly: "How far from here to — Jason's old place?"

"Six—eight—nine hour," Jim Crow said, with his broad smile that meant nothing.

Seth looked long and thoughtfully at the split skull on the ground. Then his eyes sought the bullet hole in the woman's skull. But he said nothing.

A little later the two men went back to the horses and mounted.

"Guess I'll git on to see the Agent," Seth observed, while the horses moved away from the bluff.

"You go by Reservation?"

"Yes."

Jim Crow surveyed the prospect in silence. They reached the trail, and their horses stood preparatory to parting company.

"S'long," said Seth.

The Indian turned and looked away to the north. It was the direction in which lay the great Reservations. Then he turned back, and his black, slit-like eyes shot a sidelong glance at his companion.

"You go—alone?" he asked.

The other nodded indifferently.

"Then I say sleep little and watch much—I, Jim Crow."

The two men parted. The scout moved off and his hand went to the pocket of his trousers where his fingers crumpled the crisp five-dollar bill he had received for his services. Nothing else really mattered to him. Seth rode away humming a tune without melody.

All the way to the Agent's house he carried out the scout's advice of watchfulness; but for a different reason. Seth had no personal fear of these stormy Indians. His watchfulness was the observation of a man who learns from all he sees. He slept some hours on the prairie while his horse rested, and arrived at the Agency the next day at noon.

Jimmy Parker, as he was familiarly called, greeted him cordially in his abrupt fashion.

"Ah, howdy," he said. "Prowling, Seth?" His words were accompanied by a quick look that asked a dozen questions, all of which he knew would remain unanswered. Seth and he were old friends and understood one another.

"Takin' a spell off," replied the farmer.

"Ah. And putting it in on the Reservation."

The Agent smiled briefly. His face seemed to have worn itself into a serious caste which required effort to change.

"Many huntin' 'passes' these times?" Seth inquired presently.

"None. Only Little Black Fox says he's going hunting soon." The Agent's eyes were fixed on the other's face.

"See you've got Jim Crow workin' around—south." Seth waved an arm in the direction whence he had come.

"Yes." Again came the Agent's swiftly passing smile. "We're a good distance from the southern boundary. Jim Crow's smart enough. How did you know?"

"Saw his tepee."

"Ah. You've been south?"

"Yes. There's a fine open country that aways."

They passed into the Agency, and Parker's sister and housekeeper brought the visitor coffee. The house was very plain, roomy, and comfortable. The two men were sitting in the office.

"Seen anything of Steyne around?" asked Seth, after a noisy sip of his hot coffee.

"Too much. And he's very shy."

Seth nodded. He quite understood.

"Guess suthin's movin'," he said, while he poured his coffee into his saucer and blew it.

"I've thought so, too, and written to the colonel at the fort. What makes you think so?"

"Can't say. Guess it's jest a notion." Seth paused. Then he went on before the other could put in a word. "Won't be just yet. Guess I'll git on."

The two men passed out of the house, and Seth remounted.

"Guess you might let me know if Black Fox gits his 'pass,'" he said, as he turned his horse away.

"I will."

Parker watched the horseman till he disappeared amongst the bushes. A moment later he was talking to his sister.

"Wish I'd telegraphed to the fort now," he said regretfully. "I can't do it after writing, they'd think—I believe Seth came especially to convey warning, and to hear about Black Fox's pass. It's a remarkable thing, but he seems to smell what these Indians are doing."

"Yes," said his sister. But she felt that when two such capable men discussed the Indians there was no need for her to worry, so she took out Seth's cup and retired to her kitchen.

In the meantime Seth had reached the river. Here he again dismounted, but this time for no more significant reason than to wash out the rag he had rescued from the bush south of the Reservations. He washed and rewashed the cotton, till it began to regain something of its original color. Then he examined it carefully round the hem.

It was a small, woman's handkerchief, and, in one corner, a name was neatly written in marking ink. The name was "Raynor."

CHAPTER IX

THE ADVENTURES OF RED RIDING HOOD

It is Sunday. The plaintive tinkle of the schoolroom bell at the Mission has rung the Christianized Indians to the short service which is held there.

"Indian Mission." The name conveys a sense of peace. Yet the mission histories of the Indian Reservations would make bloody reading. From the first the Christian teacher has been the pitiable prey of the warlike savage. He bears the brunt of every rising. It is only in recent years that his work has attained the smallest semblance of safety. The soldier fights an open foe. The man in charge of an Indian mission does not fight at all. He stands ever in the slaughter-yard, living only at the pleasure of the reigning chief. He is a brave man.

The service is over. It is perforce brief. The grown men and women come out of the building. The spacious interior is cleared of all but the children and a few grown-up folk who remain to hold a sort of Sunday-school.

There are Wanaha and Seth. Rosebud, too, helps, and Charlie Rankin and his young wife, who have a farm some two miles east of White River Farm. Then there is the missionary, Mr. Hargreaves, a large man with gray hair and rugged, bearded face, whose blue eyes look straight at those he is addressing with a mild, invincible bravery. And the Agent, James Parker, a short, abrupt man, with a bulldog chest and neck, and a sharp, alert manner.

These are the workers in this most important branch of the civilizing process. They are striking at the root of their object. The children can be molded where the parents prove impossible. Once these black-eyed little ones have mastered the English language the rest is not so difficult. They have to be weaned from their own tongue if their Christian teachers would make headway. A small, harmless bribery works wonders in this direction. And all these children have learned to speak and understand the English language.

Seth attempts no Bible instruction, and his is a class much in favor. His pockets always contain the most home-made taffy. He has a method purely his own; and it is a secular method. Only to the brightest and most advanced children is the honor of promotion to his class awarded.

He is holding his class outside the building. His children sit round him in a semicircle. He is sitting on an upturned box with his back against the lateral logs of the building. There is a pleasant shade here, also the pungent odor from the bright green bluff which faces him. The Indian children are very quiet, but they are agog with interest. They have noted the bulging pockets of Seth's Sunday jacket, and are more than ready to give him their best attention in consequence. Besides they like his teaching.

Seth's method is quite simple. Last Sunday he told them a little, old-fashioned children's fairy story with a moral. Now he takes each child in turn, and questions him or her on the teaching he then conveyed. But in this direction they are not very apt, these little heathens.

The singing inside the Mission had died out, and the last chords on the small organ had wheezed themselves into silence. Seth, having finished his preliminaries, began serious business.

He deposited a large packet of treacle taffy upon the ground at his feet, cut the string of it with his sheath-knife, opened it, and examined the contents with a finely critical air. Having satisfied himself he set it down again and smiled on his twelve pupils, all ranging from ten to twelve years of age, sitting round him. He produced a well-thumbed volume from his pocket, and, opening it, laid it upon his knee. It was there in case he should stumble, for Seth was not a natural born teacher. He did it for the sake of the little ones themselves.

Next he handed each child a piece of taffy, and waited while it was adjusted in the cheek.

"Guess you've all located your dollops o' candy?" he said, after a while. "I allow you ken get right at it and fix it in. This camp ain't goin' to be struck till the sweet food's done. Guess you'll mostly need physic 'fore you're through, sure. Howsum, your mam's 'll see to it."

The last remarks were said more to himself than to the children, who sat staring up into his dark, earnest face with eyes as solemn as those of the moose calf, and their little cheeks bulging dangerously. Seth cleared his throat.

"Guess you ain't heard tell o' that Injun gal that used to go around in a red blanket same as any of you might. I'm jest going to tell you about her. Ah, more candy?" as a small hand was held out appealingly toward him. "Guess we'll have another round before I get going right." He doled out more of the sticky stuff, and then propped his face upon his hands and proceeded.

"Wal, as I was goin' to say, that little squaw lived away there by the hills in a snug tepee with her gran'ma. They were jest two squaws by themselves, an old one, and a young one. And they hadn't no brave to help 'em, nor nothin'. The young squaw was jest like any of you. Jest a neat, spry little gal, pretty as a picture and real good.

"She kind o' looked after her gran'ma who was sick. Sick as a mule with the botts. Did the chores around that tepee, bucked a lot of cord-wood, fixed up moccasins, an' did the cookin', same as you gals 'll mebbe do later on. She was a slick young squaw, she was. Knew a caribou from a jack-rabbit, an' could sit a bucking broncho to beat the band. Guess it was doin' all these things so easy she kind o' got feelin' independent—sort o' wanted to do everything herself. And she just used to go right down to the store for food an' things by herself.

"Now I don't know how it rightly come about, but somewheres around that tepee a wolf got busy. A timber wolf, most as big as—as—the Mission house. An' he was savage. Gee, but he was real savage! Guess he was one o' them fellers always ready to scare squaws an' papooses an' things. Ther's lots o' that sort around."

Wanaha, quite unobserved by Seth, had come round the corner of the building, and stood watching the earnest face of the man who was so deliberately propounding his somewhat garbled version of Little Red Riding Hood. While she listened to his words she smiled pensively.

"Yes, they git themselves up fancy an' come sneakin' around, an' they're jest that fierce there ain't no chance for you. Say, them things would eat you right up, same as you've eaten that taffy. Wal, this young squaw was goin' off on her broncho when this timber wolf comes up smilin', an' he says, 'Good-day.' An' he shakes hands with her same as grown folks do. All them timber wolves are like that, 'cause they think you won't see they're going to eat you then. You see he was hungry. He'd been out on the war-path—which is real bad—an' he'd been fightin', and the folks had beaten him off, and he couldn't get food, 'cause he'd left the Reservation where there's always plenty to eat an' drink, and there was none anywhere else.

"Wal, he sizes up that squaw, and sees her blanket's good an' thick, and her moccasins is made of moose hide, and her beads is pretty, and he thinks she'll make a good meal, but he thinks, thinks he, he'll eat the squaw's sick gran'ma first. So he says 'Good-bye,' an' waits till she's well away on the trail, and then hurries back to the tepee an' eats up the old squaw. Say wolves is ter'ble—'specially timber wolves.

"Now, when that squaw gits home— —" Seth paused and doled out more taffy. The children were wonderfully intent on the story, but the sweets helped their attention. For there was much of what he said that was hard on their understandings. The drama of the story was plain enough, but the moral appealed to them less.

"When that squaw gits home she lifts the flap of the tepee, and she sees what she thinks is her gran'ma lying covered up on the skins on the ground. The fire is still burnin', and everything is jest as she left it. She feels good an' chirpy, and sits right down by her gran'ma's side. And then she sees what she thinks looks kind o' queer. Says she, 'Gee, gran'ma, what a pesky long nose you've got!' You see that wolf had come along an' eaten her gran'ma, and fixed himself up in her clothes an' things, and was lying right there ready to eat her, too, when she come along. So master timber wolf, he says, 'That's so I ken smell out things when I'm hunting.' Then that squaw, bein' curious-like, which is the way with wimminfolk, says, 'Shucks, gran'ma, but your tongue's that long you ain't room for it in your mouth.' That wolf gits riled then. Says he, 'That's so I ken taste the good things I eat.' Guess the squaw was plumb scared at that. She'd never heard her gran'ma say things like that. But she goes on, says she, 'Your teeth's fine an' long an' white, maybe you've cleaned 'em some.' Then says the wolf, 'That's so I ken eat folks like you right up.' With that he springs out of the blankets an' pounces sheer on that poor little squaw and swallows her up at one gulp, same as you ken swaller this taffy."

Seth suddenly sprang from his seat, held the bag of candy out at arm's length, and finally dropped it on the ground in the midst of the children. There was a rush; a chorus of childish glee, and the whole twelve fell into a struggling heap upon the ground, wildly fighting for the feast.

With a gentle smile Seth looked on at the fierce scramble. To judge from his manner it would have been hard to assert which was the happier, the children or their teacher. Though Seth found them a tax on his imaginative powers, and though he was a man unused to many words, he loved these Sunday afternoons with his young charges.

His thoughtful contemplation was broken by Wanaha. Her moccasins gave out no sound as she stepped up to him from behind and touched him on the shoulder. Her grave smile had passed; and when he turned he found himself looking into a pair of steady, serious, inscrutable eyes. No white woman can hide her thoughts behind such an impenetrable mask as the squaw. Surely the Indian face might well have served as a model for the Sphinx.

"The white teacher makes much happy," she said in her labored English.

Seth promptly answered her in her own tongue.

"The papooses of the Indian make the white man happy," he said simply.

There was a long pause. Suddenly one dusky urchin rose with a whoop of delight, bearing aloft the torn paper with several lumps of sweet stuff, discolored with dirt, sticking to it. With one accord the little mob broke. The triumphant child fled away to the bluff pursued by the rest of her howling companions. The man and the squaw were left alone.

"The white man tells a story of a wolf and a squaw," Wanaha said, returning to her own language. The children were still shrieking in the distance.

Seth nodded assent. He had nothing to add to her statement.

"And the wolf eats the squaw," the woman went on, quite seriously. It sounded strange, her literal manner of discussing this children's story.

A look of interest came into the man's thoughtful eyes. But he turned away, not wishing to display any curiosity. He understood the Indian nature as few men do.

"There was no one by to warn the squaw?" she went on in a tone of simple inquiry. "No brave to help her?"

"No one to help," answered the man.

There was another pause. The children still inside the Mission house were helping to chant the Doxology, and the woman appeared to listen to it with interest. When it was finished she went on— —

"Where the wolf is there is much danger for the squaw. Indian squaw—or white. I, too, learn these things. I learn from much that I hear—and see."

"I know," Seth nodded.

"You know?"

"Yes."

"Wanaha is glad. The white brave will watch over the young squaw." The woman smiled again. Seth thought he detected a sigh of relief. He understood this woman as well as it is given to man to understand any woman—even an Indian woman.

"This wolf won't bother about the gran'ma," said Seth, looking straight into Wanaha's eyes. "He's after the young squaw."

"And he will have the young squaw soon."

Wanaha abruptly turned away and hurried round to the entrance of the Mission. The sound of people moving within the building told her that the Sunday-school was over. Her silent going suggested that she had no wish to be seen talking in private to Seth.

Seth remained where he was. His delay may have been intentional, yet he had the appearance of deep preoccupation. He quite understood that Wanaha's presence during his story had been deliberate. She had left her own class on some trifling excuse and come out to warn him, knowing that he would be alone with his children. There was no smile on his face while he stood thinking, only a pucker between his dark brows, and an odd biting of his under-lip.

At last he shook himself as though he found the shade chilly, and, a moment later, sauntered round to the front of the building in time to meet the others coming out.

He joined the group which included Wanaha, and they talked a few minutes with the Agent and Mr. Hargreaves. Then Mrs. Rankin and Rosebud moved off to the two waiting buckboards, and Wanaha disappeared down a by-path through the trees. Seth and Charlie Rankin followed their womenfolk.

Seth was the only silent member of the party, but this was hardly noticeable, for he rarely had much to say for himself.

On the way home Rosebud at last found reason to grumble at his silence. She had chattered away the whole time in her light-hearted, inconsequent fashion, and at last asked him a question to which she required more than a nod of the head in reply. And she had to ask it three times, a matter which ruffled her patience.

"Why are you so grumpy with me, Seth?" she asked, with a little frown. She always accused Seth of being "grumpy" when he was more than usually silent.

"Eh?" The man turned from the contemplation of the horses' tails.

"I asked you three times if you saw the Agent talking to two of his scouts—Jim Crow and Rainmaker—before service."

Seth flicked his whip over the backs of the horses.

"Sure," he said indifferently.

"Jim Crow is the head of his Indian police."

The girl spoke significantly, and Seth glanced round at her in surprise.

"I know," he observed.

"Do you think there is anything—moving? Oh, look, Seth, there's a lovely jack-rabbit." Rosebud pointed ahead. A large jack-rabbit was loping slowly out of the way of the buckboard. Seth leant forward with unnecessary interest, and so was saved a direct answer to the girl's question.

CHAPTER X

SETH ATTEMPTS TO WRITE A LETTER

It is not usually a remarkable event in one's life, the writing of a letter. In these days of telephone, however, it soon will be. In Seth's case it nearly was so, but for a different reason. Seth could write, even as he could read. But he was not handy at either. He abominated writing, and preferred to read only that which Nature held out for his perusal. However, after some days of deep consideration, he had decided to write a letter. And, with characteristic thoroughness, he intended it to be very long, and very explicit.

After supper one evening, when Rube had gone out for his evening smoke, and that final prowl round necessary to see that all was prepared for the morrow's work, and the stock comfortable for the night, and Ma Sampson and Rosebud were busy washing up, and, in their department, also seeing things straight for the night, Seth betook himself to the parlor, that haven of modest comfort and horsehair, patchwork rugs and many ornaments, earthen floor and low ceiling, and prepared for his task. He had no desire to advertise the fact of that letter, so he selected this particular moment when the others were occupied elsewhere.

His ink and paper were on the table before him, and his pen was poised while he considered. Then the slow, heavy footfall of old Rube sounded approaching through the kitchen. The scribe waited to hear him pass up-stairs, or settle himself in an armchair in the kitchen. But the heavy tread came on, and presently the old man's vast bulk blocked the doorway.

"Ah! Writin'?"

The deep tone was little better than a grunt.

Seth nodded, and gazed out of the window. The parlor window looked out in the direction of the Reservation. If he intended to convey a hint it was not taken. Old Rube had expected Seth to join him outside for their usual smoke. That after-supper prowl had been their habit for years. He wanted to talk to him.

"I was yarnin' with Jimmy Parker s'afternoon," said Rube.

Seth looked round.

The old man edged heavily round the table till he came to the high-backed, rigid armchair that had always been his seat in this room.

"He says the crops there are good," he went on, indicating the Reservation with a nod of his head toward the window.

"It'll be a good year all round, I guess," Seth admitted.

"Yes, I dare say it will be," was the answer.

Rube was intently packing his pipe, and the other waited. Rube's deep-set eyes had lost their customary twinkle. The deliberation with which he was packing his pipe had in it a suggestion of abstraction. Filling a pipe is a process that wonderfully indicates the state of a man's mind.

"Jimmy's worried some. 'Bout the harvest, I guess," Rube said presently, adjusting his pipe in the corner of his mouth, and testing the draw of it. But his eyes were not raised to his companion's face.

"Injuns ain't workin' well?"

"Mebbe."

"They're a queer lot."

"Ye-es. I was kind o' figgerin'. We're mostly through hayin'."

"I've got another slough to cut."

"That's so. Down at the Red Willow bluff." The old man nodded.

"Yes," assented Seth. Then, "Wal?"

"After that, guess ther's mostly slack time till harvest. I thought, mebbe, we could jest haul that lumber from Beacon Crossing. And cut the logs. Parker give me the 'permit.' Seems to me we might do wuss."

"For the stockade?" suggested Seth.

"Yes."

"I've thought of that, too." The two men looked into each other's eyes. And the old man nodded.

"Guess the gals wouldn't want to know," he said, rising and preparing to depart.

"No—I don't think they would."

The hardy old pioneer towered mightily as he moved toward the door. In spite of his years he displayed none of the uneasiness which his words might have suggested. Nothing that frontier life could show him would be new. At least, nothing that he could imagine. But then his imagination was limited. Facts were facts with him; he could not gild them. Seth was practical, too; but he also had imagination, which made him the cleverer man of the two in the frontiersman's craft.

At the door Rube looked round.

"Guess you was goin' to write some?"

He passed out with a deep gurgle, as though the fact of Seth's writing was something to afford amusement.

Seth turned to the paper and dipped his pen in the ink. Then he wiped it clean on his coat sleeve and dipped it again. After that he headed his paper with much precision. Then he paused, for he heard a light footstep cross the passage between the parlor and the kitchen. He sighed in relief as it started up-stairs. But his relief was short-lived. He knew that it was Rosebud. He heard her stop. Then he heard her descend again. The next moment she appeared in the doorway.

"What, Seth writing?" she exclaimed, her laughing eyes trying to look seriously surprised. "I knew you were here by the smell of the smoke."

"Guess it was Rube's." Seth's face relaxed for a moment, then it returned to its usual gravity.

"Then it must have been that pipe you gave him the other night," she returned quick as thought.

Seth shook his head.

"Here it is," he said, and drew a pipe from his pocket. "He 'lowed he hadn't no nigger blood in him."

"Too strong?"

"Wal—he said he had scruples."

Rosebud laughed, and came and perched herself on the edge of Seth's table. He leant back in his chair and smiled up at her. Resignation was his only refuge. Besides—

"So you're writing, Seth," the girl said, and her eyes had become really serious. They were deep, deep now, the violet of them was almost black in the evening light. "I wonder— —"

Seth shook his head.

"Nobody yet," he said.

"You mean I'm to go away?" Rosebud smiled, but made no attempt to move.

"Guess I ain't in no hurry."

"Well, I'm glad of that. And you're not grumpy with me either, are you? No?" as Seth shook his head. "That's all right, then, because I want to talk to you."

"That's how I figgered."

"You're always figuring, Seth. You figure so much in your own quiet way that I sometimes fancy you haven't time to look at things which don't need calculating upon. I suppose living near Indians all your life makes you look very much ahead. I wonder—what you see there. You and Rube."

"Guess you're side-tracked," Seth replied uneasily, and turning his attention to the blank paper before him.

The girl's face took on a little smile. Her eyes shone again as she contemplated the dark head of the man who was now unconscious of her gaze. There was a tender look in them. The old madcap in her was taming. A something looked out of her eyes now which certainly would not have been there had the man chanced to look up. But he didn't. The whiteness of the paper seemed to absorb all his keenest interest.

"I rather think you always fancy I'm side-tracked, Seth," the girl said at last. "You don't think I have a serious thought in my foolish head."

Seth looked up now and smiled.

"Guess you've always been a child to me," he said. "An' kiddies ain't bustin' with brain—generly. However, I don't reckon you're foolish. 'Cep' when you git around that Reservation," he added thoughtfully.

There was a brief silence. The man avoided the violet eyes. He seemed afraid to look at them. Rosebud's presence somehow made things hard for him. Seth was a man whom long years of a life fraught with danger had taught that careful thought must be backed up by steady determination. There must be no wavering in any purpose. And this girl's presence made him rebel against that purpose he had in his mind now.

"That has always been a trouble between us, hasn't it?" Rosebud said at last. And her quiet manner drew her companion's quick attention. "But it shan't be any more."

The man looked up now; this many-sided girl could still astonish him.

"You're quittin' the Reservation?" he said.

"Yes,—except the sewing and Sunday classes at the Mission," Rosebud replied slowly. "But it's not on your account I'm doing it," she added hastily, with a gleam of the old mischief in her eyes. "It's because—Seth, why do the Indians hate you? Why does Little Black Fox hate you?"

The man's inquiring eyes searched the bright earnest face looking down upon him. His only reply was a shake of the head.

"I know," she went on. "It's on my account. You killed Little Black Fox's father to save me."

"Not *to* save you," Seth said. He was a stickler for facts. "*And* saved you."

"Oh, bother! Seth, you are stupid! It's on that account he hates you. And, Seth, if I promise not to go to the Reservation without some one, will you promise me not to go there without me? You see it's safer if there are two."

Seth smiled at the naïve simplicity of the suggestion. He did not detect the guile at first. But it dawned on him presently and he smiled more. She had said she was not going to visit the Reservation again.

"Who put these crazy notions into your head, Rosebud?" he asked.

"No one."

The girl's answer came very short. She didn't like being laughed at. And she thought he was laughing at her now.

"Some one's said something," Seth persisted. "You see Little Black Fox has hated me for six years. There is no more danger for me now than there was when I shot Big Wolf. With you it's kind o' different. You see—you're grown——"

"I see." Rosebud's resentment had passed. She understood her companion's meaning. She had understood that she was "grown" before. Presently she went on. "I've learned a lot in the last few days," she said quietly, gazing a little wistfully out of the window. "But nobody has actually told me anything. You see," with a shadowy smile, "I notice things near at hand. I don't calculate ahead. I often talk to Little Black Fox. He is easy to read. Much easier than you are, Seth," she finished up, with a wise little nod.

"An' you've figgered out my danger?" Seth surveyed the trim figure reposing with such unconscious grace upon the table. He could have feasted his eyes upon it, but returned to a contemplation of his note-paper.

"Yes. Will you promise me, Seth—dear old Seth?"

The man shook his head. The wheedling tone was hard to resist.

"I can't do that," he said. "You see, Rosebud, ther's many things take me there which must be done. Guess I git around after you at times. That could be altered, eh?"

"I don't think you're kind, Seth!" The girl pouted her disappointment, but there was some other feeling underlying her manner. The man looked up with infinite kindness in his eyes, but he gave no sign of any other feeling.

"Little Rosebud," he said, "if ther's a creetur in this world I've a notion to be kind to, I guess she ain't more'n a mile from me now. But, as I said, ther's things that take me to the Reservation. Rube ken tell you. So——"

The man broke off, and dipped his pen in the ink. Rosebud watched him, and, for once in her wilful life, forgot that she had been refused something, and consequently to be angry. She looked at the head bending over the paper as the man inscribed, "Dear sirs," and that something which had peeped out of her eyes earlier in their interview was again to be seen there.

She reached out a hand as she slid from the table and smoothed the head of dark hair with it.

"All right, Seth," she said gently. "We'll have no promises, but take care of yourself, because you are my own old—'Daddy.'"

At the door she turned.

"You can write your letter now," she said, with a light laugh. The next moment she was gone.

CHAPTER XI

THE LETTER WRITTEN

But Seth's trials were not yet over. The two interviews just passed had given Ma Sampson sufficient time to complete her household duties. And now she entered her parlor, the pride of her home.

She came in quite unaware of Seth's presence there. But when she observed him at the table with his writing materials spread out before him, she paused.

"Oh," she exclaimed, "I didn't know you were writin', Seth!"

The man's patience seemed inexhaustible, for he smiled and shook his head.

"No, Ma," he said with truth.

The little old woman came round the table and occupied her husband's chair. If Seth were not writing, then she might as well avail herself of the opportunity which she had long wanted. She had no children of her own, and lavished all her motherly instincts upon this man. She was fond of Rosebud, but the girl occupied quite a secondary place in her heart. It is doubtful if any mother could have loved a son more than she loved Seth.

She had a basket of sewing with her which she set upon the table. Then she took from it a bundle of socks and stockings and began to overhaul them with a view to darning. Seth watched the slight figure bending over its work, and the bright eyes peering through the black-rimmed glasses which hooked over her ears. His look was one of deep affection. Surely Nature had made a mistake in not making them mother and son. Still, she had done the next best thing in invoking Fate's aid in bringing them together. Mrs. Sampson looked no older than the day on which Rosebud had been brought to the house. As Seth had once told her, she would never grow old. She would just go on as she was, and, when the time came, she would pass away peacefully and quietly, not a day older than she had been when he first knew her.

But Seth, understanding so much as he did of the life on that prairie farm, and the overshadowing threat which was always with them, had yet lost sight of the significance of the extreme grayness of this woman's hair. Still her bright energy and uncomplaining nature might well have lulled all fears, and diverted attention from the one feature which betrayed her ceaseless anxiety.

"I kind o' tho't sech work was for young fingers, Ma," Seth observed, indicating the stockings.

"Ah, Seth, boy, I hated to darn when I was young an' flighty."

The man smiled. His accusations had been made to ears that would not hear. He knew this woman's generous heart.

"I reckon Rosebud'll take to it later on," he said quietly.

"When she's married."

"Ye-es."

Seth watched the needle pass through and through the wool on its rippling way. And his thoughts were of a speculative nature.

"She's a grown woman now," said Mrs. Sampson, after a while.

"That's so."

"An' she'll be thinkin' of 'beaus,' or I'm no prophet."

"Time enough, Ma."

"Time? I guess she's goin' on eighteen. Maybe you don't know a deal o' gals, boy."

The bright face looked up. One swift glance at her companion and she was bending over her work again.

"I had 'beaus' enough, I reckon, when I was eighteen. Makes me laff when I think o' Rube. He's always been like what he is now. Jest quiet an' slow. I came nigh marryin' a feller who's got a swell horse ranch way up in Canada, through Rube bein' slow. Guess Rube was the man for me, though, all through. But, you see, I couldn't ask him to marry me. Mussy on us, he was slow!"

"Did you have to help him out, Ma?"

"Help him? Did you ever know a gal who didn't help her 'beau' out? Boy, when a gal gets fixed on a man he's got a job if he's goin' to get clear. Unless he's like my Rube—ter'ble slow."

"That's how you're sizin' me now," said Seth, with a short laugh.

Ma Sampson worked on assiduously.

"Maybe you're slow in some things, Seth," she ventured, after a moment's thought.

"See here, Ma, I've always reckoned we'd get yarnin' like this some day. It 'ud please you an' Rube for me to marry Rosebud. Wal, you an' me's mostly given to talkin' plain. An' I tell you right here that Rosebud ain't for the likes o' me. Don't you think I'm makin' out myself a poor sort o' cuss. 'Tain't that. You know, an' I know, Rosebud belongs to mighty good folk. Wal, before ther's any thought of me an' Rosebud, we're goin' to locate those friends. It's only honest, Ma, and as such I know you'll understand. Guess we don't need to say any more."

Mrs. Sampson had ceased working, and sat peering at her boy through her large spectacles. Seth's look was very determined, and she understood him well.

She shook her head.

"Guess you're reckoning out your side." She laughed slyly and went on darning. "Maybe Rosebud won't thank you a heap when you find those friends. They haven't made much fuss to find her."

"No, Ma. An' that's just it."

"How?" The darning suddenly dropped into Mrs. Sampson's lap.

"Maybe they were killed by the Injuns."

"You're guessin'."

"Maybe I am. But——"

"What do you know, boy?" The old woman was all agog with excitement.

"Not a great deal, Ma," Seth said, with one of his shadowy smiles. "But what I do makes me want to write a letter. And a long one. An' that sort of thing ain't easy with me. You see, I'm 'ter'ble slow.'"

Seth's manner was very gentle, but very decided, and Ma Sampson did not need much explanation. She quietly stood up and gathered her belongings together.

"You get right to it, boy. What you do is right for me. I'll say no more. As my Rube says, ther' ain't nothin' like livin' honest. An' so I says. But if that letter's goin' to lose you Rosebud, I'd take it friendly of Providence if it would kind o' interfere some. I'll go an' sit with Rube, an' you can write your letter."

At last Seth turned to his letter in earnest. He first pulled out a piece of newspaper from his pocket and unfolded it. Then he laid it on the table, and carefully read the long paragraph marked by four blue crosses. He wanted to make no mistake. As he had said himself, letter-writing wasn't easy to him. He read thoughtfully and slowly.

"THE ESTATE OF THE LOST COLONEL RAYNOR

"Once more we are reminded of the mysterious disappearance of that distinguished cavalry officer, Colonel Landor Raynor. This reminder comes in the form of the legal proceedings relating to his estate.

"For the benefit of our readers, and also in the gallant officer's own interests, we give here a recapitulation of the events surrounding his sudden disappearance.

"On May 18th, 18—, Colonel Raynor returned from service in Egypt, on six months' leave, and rented a shooting-box in the Highlands. Hardly had he settled down when he suddenly declared his intention of crossing the Atlantic for a big game shoot in the Rockies. This purpose he carried out within four days of his announcement, accompanied by Mrs. Raynor and their little daughter Marjorie, aged eleven, a golden-haired little beauty with the most perfect violet eyes, which is a very rare and distinguishing feature amongst women. It has been clearly proved that the party arrived safely in New York, and proceeded on their way to the Rockies. Since that time nothing has been heard of any of the three.

"There is no definite pronouncement as to the administration of Colonel Raynor's estate. He owns large property, valued roughly at nearly a quarter of a million sterling. It has come to light that he leaves a will behind him, but whether this will be executed or not remains to be seen. There are no near relations, except the colonel's brother, Stephen, who was disinherited by their father in favor of the colonel, and who, it is believed, left this country at the time, and went to the United States. His whereabouts are also unknown, in spite of advertisement during the last six years.

"We publish these details, even at this late hour, in the faint hope that some light may yet be thrown on the mystery which enshrouds the fate of the gallant colonel and his family, or, at least, that they may assist in discovering the whereabouts of his brother. Theories have been put forward. But the suggestion which seems most feasible comes from the New York police. They think he must have met with some accident in the obscurer mountains, for he was a daring climber, and that, unaccompanied as they were by any servants, his wife and daughter, left helpless, were unable to get back to civilization. There is a chance that misfortune of some other character overtook him, but of what nature it is impossible to estimate. It has been asserted by one of the officials at the railway station at Omaha that a party alighted from a transcontinental train there answering the description of Colonel Raynor's party. These people are supposed to have stayed the night at a hotel, and then left by a train going north. Inquiry, however, has thrown no further light in this direction, and so the police have fallen back on their original theory."

Seth laid the cutting aside, and thoughtfully chewed the end of his pen. There were many things he had to think of, but, curiously enough, the letter he had to compose did not present the chief item. Nor did Rosebud even. He thought chiefly of that railway official, and the story which the police had so easily set aside. He thought of that, and he thought of the Indians, who now more than ever seemed to form part of his life.

Finally he took a fresh piece of paper and headed it differently. He had changed his mind. He originally intended to write to the New York police. Now he addressed himself to the Editor of the — —,

London, England. And his letter was just the sort of letter one might have expected from such a man, direct, plain, but eminently exact.

As he finally sealed it in its envelope there was no satisfaction in the expression of his face. He drew out his pipe and filled it and lit it, and smoked with his teeth clenching hard on the mouthpiece. He sat and smoked on long after Rube had looked in and bade him good-night, and Ma had come in for a good-night kiss, and Rosebud had called out her nightly farewell. It was not until the lamp burnt low and began to smell that he stole silently up to his bed. But, whatever thought had kept him up to this hour, he slept soundly, for he was a healthy-minded man.

CHAPTER XII

CROSS PURPOSES

Seth was out haying. It was noon, and his dinner hour. He and his old collie dog, General, were taking their leisure on the slope of Red Willow slough, while the horses, relieved of their bits and traces, were nibbling at the succulent roots of the grass over which the mower had already passed.

General possessed a sense of duty. His master was apparently sleeping, with his prairie hat drawn over his face. The dog crouched at his feet, struggling hard to keep his eyes open, and remain alert while the other rested from his labors. But the sun was hot, the scent of the grass overpowering, and it was difficult.

At last the man roused and sat up. The dog sprang to his feet. His ears were pricked, and he raced off across the slough. As he went, the sound of wheels became distinctly audible. Rosebud, seated in a buckboard, and driving the old farm mare, Hesper, appeared on the opposite side of the slough. She was bringing Seth his dinner.

A moment later the girl drew rein and sprang out of the vehicle. The heat in no way weighed upon her spirits. She looked as fresh and cool in her white linen dress and sun-hat as if it were an early spring day. Her laughing face was in marked contrast to the man's dark, serious countenance. Her dazzling eyes seemed to be endowed with something of the brilliancy of the sunlight that was so intensely pouring down upon them.

"Oh, Seth, I'm so sorry!" she cried, in anything but a penitent tone, "but just as I was starting Wana came up with a note for you, and I'm afraid we stopped and talked, and you know what a dozy old mare Hesper is, and she just went slower than ever, and I hadn't the heart to whack her, she's such a dear, tame old thing, and so I'm ever so late, and I'm afraid your dinner's all spoiled, and you'll be horribly angry."

But Seth displayed no anger; he only held out his hand.

"An' the note?"

Rosebud thought for a moment. "Whatever did I do with it?" she said, looking about her on the ground. Seth watched her a little anxiously.

"Who was it from?" he asked.

"Oh, just the old Agent. I don't suppose it was important, but I know I put it somewhere."

"Guess so."

Seth lifted the dinner-box out of the buckboard. Suddenly Rosebud's face cleared.

"That's it, Seth. I put it in there. In with the dinner. Oh, and, Seth, I got Ma to let me bring my dinner out, so we can have a picnic, you and I, and General."

Seth was bending over the box.

"Then I guess your dinner's kind o' spoiled too," he said.

"Oh, that doesn't matter so long as yours isn't. You see it's my own fault, and serves me right. If it's very nasty we can give it all to General; so it won't be wasted."

"No, it won't be wasted."

Rosebud watched her companion remove the things from the box, and wondered if he were glad or sorry that she was going to have her dinner with him. She had been wildly delighted at the thought of springing this surprise on him, but now she felt doubtful, and a certain shyness kept her usually busy tongue silent. She would have given much to know what Seth thought. That was just where she found the man so unsatisfactory. She never did know what he really thought about anything.

Seth found the note, and put it in his pocket. Now he set their meal on the newly cut grass. Rosebud, with a thoughtfulness hardly to be expected of her, turned Hesper loose. Then she sat down beside General and put the tin dishes straight, according to her fancy. In silence she helped Seth to a liberal portion of lukewarm stew, and cut the bread. Then she helped the dog, and, finally, herself.

"Ma's a dear!" she suddenly exclaimed, when the silence had become irksome to her. "She's making me a new dress. It's a secret, and I'm not supposed to know."

"Ah! An' how d' you find out?"

"Oh, I asked Pa," Rosebud laughed. "I knew it was something for me. So when he went to look at the new litter of piggies this morning I went with him, and just asked him. I promised not to give him away. Isn't she a dear?"

"Sure. Guess you like dress fixin's."

"Love them."

"Most gals do, I reckon."

"Well, you see, Seth, most girls love to look nice. Mrs. Rankin, even, says that she'd give the world to get hold of a good dressmaker, and she's married. Do you know even Wana likes pretty things, and that's just what I'd like to talk to you about. You see, I've got twenty dollars saved, and I just thought I would get Wana a nice dress, like white people wear. I mean a good one. Do you know what store I could send to in Sioux City, or Omaha, or even New York?"

"I ain't much knowledge o' stores an' things. But I 'lows it's a good notion."

The man's brown eyes looked over at the girl as she plied her knife and fork.

"Maybe," he went on, a moment later, "ther' ain't no need to spend them twenty dollars. I've got some. Say, you talk to Ma an' fix the letter an' I'll mail it."

The girl looked up. Seth's kindness had banished the ready laugh for the moment. If her tongue remained silent her eyes spoke. But Seth was concerned with his food and saw nothing. Rosebud did not even tender thanks. She felt that she could not speak thanks at that moment. Her immediate inclination was a childish one, but the grown woman in her checked it. A year ago she would have acted differently. At last Seth broke the silence.

"Say, Rosebud," he said. "How'd you like a heap o' dollars?"

But the girl's serious mood had not yet passed. She held out her plate to General, and replied, without looking at her companion.

"That depends," she said. "You see, I wouldn't like to marry a man with lots of money. Girls who do are never happy. Ma said so. The only other way to have money is by being clever, and writing, or painting, or play-acting. And I'm not clever, and don't want to be. Then there are girls who inherit money, but——"

"That's jest it," broke in Seth.

"Just what?" Rosebud turned from the dog and eyed her companion curiously.

"Why, s'pose it happened you inherited them dollars?"

"But I'm not likely to."

"That's so. But we know your folks must a' been rich by your silk fixin's. Guess you ain't thought o' your folks."

The girl's sunburnt face took on a confident little smile as she looked out from under the wide brim of her hat.

"Oh, yes, I have. I've thought a lot. Where are they, and why don't they come out and look for me? I can't remember them, though I try hard. Every time I try I go back to Indians—always Indians. I know I'm not an Indian," she finished up naïvely.

"No." Seth lit his pipe. "Guess if we did find 'em you'd have to quit the farm."

There was a short silence.

"Seth, you're always looking for them, I know. Why do you look for them? I don't want them." Rosebud was patting the broad back of General. "Do you know, sometimes I think you want to be rid of me. I'm a trouble to you, I know."

"'Tain't that exactly."

Seth's reply sounded different to what he intended. It sounded to the girl as if he really was seeking her parents to be rid of her. And his manner was so deliberate, so short. She scrambled to her feet without a word, and began to gather up the dishes. Seth smoked on for a moment or two. But as Rosebud showed no sign of continuing the conversation he, too, rose in silence, and went over to Hesper and hitched her to the buckboard. Then he came back and carried the dinner-box to the vehicle, while Rosebud mounted to the driving-seat.

"Seth," she said, and her face was slightly flushed, and a little sparkle of resentment was in her eyes, "when you find them I'll go away. I never looked at it as you do. Yes, I think I should like that heap of dollars."

Seth smiled slowly. But he didn't quite understand her answer.

"Wal, you see, Rosebud, I'm glad you take it that aways. You see it's better you should go. Yes, much better."

His thoughts had turned on the Reservations, that one direction in which they ever seemed to turn. Rosebud was thinking in another direction. Seth wanted to be rid of her, and was meanly cloaking his desire under the guise of her worldly welfare. The angry flush deepened, and she sat very erect with her head held high as she drove off. Nor did she turn for her parting shot.

"I hope you'll find them; I want to go," she said.

Seth made no answer. He watched her until the vehicle dropped down behind the brow of the farther slope. The girl's attitude was as dignified as she could make it while she remained in view. After that it was different. And Seth failed to realize that he had not made his meaning plain. He saw that Rosebud was angry, but he did not pause to consider the cause of her anger.

He stood where she had left him for some time. He found his task harder than ever he had thought it would be. But his duty lay straight before him, and, with all his might, he would have hurried on his letter to England if he could. He knew he could see far ahead in the life of his little world as it affected himself and those he loved. He might be a dull-witted lover, but he was keen and swift to scent danger here on the plains; and that was what he had already done. Cost him what it might, Rosebud must be protected, and this protection meant her removal.

He sighed and turned back to his work, but before he went on with it he opened and read the note which Rosebud had thought so unimportant.

He read it twice over.

"Little Black Fox applied for 'pass' for hunting. He will probably leave the Reservation in three weeks' time. He will take a considerable number of braves with him; I cannot refuse.

"J. P."

CHAPTER XIII

THE DEVOTION OF WANAHA

Nevil Steyne's day's labor, of whatever it consisted, was over. Wanaha had just lit the oil lamp which served her in her small home.

The man was stretched full length upon the bed, idly contemplating the dusky beauty who acknowledged his lordship, while she busied herself over her shining stove. His face wore a half smile, but his smile was in nowise connected with that which his eyes rested on.

Yet the sight he beheld was one to inspire pleasurable thoughts. For surely it falls to the lot of few men, however worthy, to inspire one woman with such a devotion as Wanaha yielded to him. Besides, she was a wonderful picture of beauty, colored it is true, but none the less fair for that. Her long black, braided hair, her delicate, high-bred face so delightfully gentle, and her great, soft black eyes which had almost, but not quite, lost that last latent glimmer of the old savage. Surely, she was worth the tenderest thought.

But Nevil's thoughts were not with her, and his smile was inspired by his thoughts. The man's mean, narrow face had nothing pleasant in it as he smiled. Some faces are like this. He was a degenerate of the worst type; for he was a man who had slowly receded from a life of refinement, and mental retrogression finds painful expression on such a face. A ruffian from birth bears less outward trace, for his type is natural to him.

Wanaha always humored her husband's moods, in which, perhaps, she made a grave error. She held silent until he chose to speak. And when she turned at last to arrange the supper table, he was so moved. The smile had died out of his thin face, and his pale blue eyes wore a look of anxious perplexity when he summoned her attention.

"Wana," he said, as though rousing himself from a long worrying thought, "we must do something, my Wana. And—I hardly know what."

The black eyes looked straight into the blue ones, and the latter shifted to the table on which the woman's loving hands had carefully set the necessaries for supper.

"Tell me," she said simply, "you who are clever—maybe I help."

"That's just it, my Wana. I believe you can. You have a keen brain. You always help me."

Nevil relapsed into silence, and bit nervously at his thumb nail. The woman waited with the stoical patience of her race. But she was all interest, for had not the man appealed to her for help?

"It's your brother," Nevil said at last. "Your brother, and the white girl at the farm, Rosebud."

"Yes."

The dark eyes suddenly lit. Here was a matter which lay very near her heart. She had thought so much about it. She had even dared at other times to speak to her husband on the subject, and advise him. Now he came to her.

"Yes," the man went on, still with that look of perplexity in his shifty eyes; "perhaps I have been wrong. You have told me that I was. But, you see, I looked on your brother as a child almost. And if I let him talk of Rosebud, it was, as I once told you, because he is headstrong. But now he has gone far enough—too far. It must be stopped. The man is getting out of hand. He means to have her."

Wanaha's eyes dilated. Here indeed was a terrible prospect. She knew her brother as only a woman can know a man. She had not noted the melodramatic manner in which her husband had broken off.

"You say well. It must be stop. Tell your Wana your thought. We will pow-wow like great chiefs."

"Well, that's just it," Nevil went on, rising and drawing up to the table. "I can't see my way clearly. We can't stop him in whatever he intends. He's got some wild scheme in his head, I know; and I can't persuade him. He's obstinate as a mule."

"It is so. Little Black Fox is fierce. He never listen. No. But you think much. You, who are clever more than all the wise men of my race."

Wanaha served her husband with his food. Whatever might be toward, her duty by him came first. Nevil sat eating in what appeared to be a moody silence. The velvety eyes watched his every expression, and, in sympathy, the woman's face became troubled too.

"Well, of course we must warn—some one," Nevil went on at last. "But the question is, who? If I go to the Agent, it'll raise trouble. Parker is bullheaded, and sure to upset Black Fox. Likely he'll stop his going hunting. If I warn old Rube Sampson it'll amount to the same thing. He'll go to the Agent. It must be either Seth or Rosebud."

"Good, good," assented the Indian woman eagerly. "You say it to Seth."

Nevil ate silently for some minutes, while the woman looked on from her seat beside the stove. Whatever was troubling the man it did not interfere with his appetite. He ate coarsely, but his Indian wife only saw that he was healthily hungry.

"Yes, you're right again, my Wana," Nevil exclaimed, with apparent appreciation. "I'd prefer to tell Seth, but if I did he'd interfere in a manner that would be sure to rouse your brother's suspicions. And you know what he is. He'd suspect me or you. He'd throw caution to the devil, and then there'd be trouble. It's a delicate thing, but I can't stand by and see anything happen to your chum, my Wana."

"No; I love the paleface girl," replied Wanaha, simply.

"It comes to this," Nevil went on, with something like eagerness in his manner. "We must warn her, and trust to her sense. And mind, I think she's smart enough."

"How?"

The woman's dark eyes looked very directly into the man's. Nevil was smiling again. His anxiety and perplexity seemed suddenly to have vanished, now that he had come to his point; as though the detailing of his fears to her had been the real source of his trouble.

"Why, I think it will be simple enough."

The man left the table and came to the woman's side. He laid one hand caressingly on her black hair, and she responded with a smiling upward glance of devotion. "See, you must tell her I want to speak with her. I can't go to her. My presence at the farm is not welcome for one thing," he said bitterly, "and, for another, in this matter I must not be seen anywhere near her. I've considered this thing well. She mustn't come here either. No."

He spoke reflectively, biting his long, fair moustache in that nervous way he so often betrayed.

"You, my Wana, must see her openly at the farm. You must tell her that I shall be in the river woods just below the bridge, cutting wood at sundown on Monday. That's three days from now. She must come to me without being seen, and without letting any one know of her visit. The danger for me, for us, my Wana, is great, and so you must be extra careful for all our sakes—and so must she. Then I will tell her all, and advise her."

The woman's eyes had never left his face. The trust and confidence her look expressed were almost touching. She did not question. She did not ask why she could not give the girl her warning. Yes, she understood. The proceeding appealed to her nature, for there is no being in the world to compare with the Indian when native cunning is required. She could do this thing. Was it not for Rosebud? But, above all, was it not for him? The honest man rarely puts faith in a woman's capacity outside her domestic and social duties. The rascal is shrewder.

"It is a good way," she said, in her deep, soft voice, after much thought. "And I go—yes. I tell her. I say to her that she must not speak. And she say 'yes.' I know Rosebud. She clever too. She no child." She paused, and the man moved away to his seat. She looked over at him and presently went on. "Rosebud, she love Seth. I know."

Nevil suddenly swung round. Only the blind eyes of love could have failed to detect the absolute look of triumph which had leapt to the man's face. Wanaha mistook the look for one of pleasure, and went on accordingly, feeling that she had struck the right note.

"Yes. And Seth, he love too. They are to each as the Sun and the Moon. But they not know this thing. She think Seth think she like sister. Like Black Fox and your Wana. But I know. I love my man, so I see with live eyes. Yes, these love. So." And the dark eyes melted with a consuming love for the man she was addressing.

Nevil sprang from his seat, and, crossing to the dark princess, kissed her with unwonted ardor.

"Good, my Wana; you are a gem. You see where I am blind." And for once he was perfectly sincere.

"It good?" she questioned. Nevil nodded, and at once the woman went on. "So. I know much. Rosebud tell me much. She much angry with Seth. She say Seth always—always look for find her white folks. She not want them—these white folks. She love Seth. For her he is the world. So. She say Seth angry, and want her go away. Wana listen. Wana laugh inside. Wana love too. Seth good. He love her much—much. Then she say she think Seth find these white folks."

"Seth has found Rosebud's—folk?"

The man's brows had drawn together over his shifty blue eyes, and a sinister look had replaced the look of triumph that had been there before.

"She say she think."

"Ah! She only thinks." Nevil's thumb was at his mouth again.

"Yes."

Wanaha finished. The change in the man's face had checked her desire to pursue the subject. She did not understand its meaning, except that her talk seemed no longer to please him; so she ceased. But Nevil was more interested than she thought.

"And what made her think so?" he asked sharply.

"She not say."

"Ah, that's a pity."

The room became silent. The yellow light of the lamp threw vague shadows about, and these two made a dark, suggestive picture. The woman's placid and now inscrutable face was in marked contrast to

95

her husband's. His displayed the swift vengeful thoughts passing behind it. His overshot jaws were clenched as closely as was physically possible, while his pallid eyes were more alight than Wanaha had ever seen them. As he sat there, biting his thumb so viciously, she wondered what had angered him.

"I don't see how he could have found them," he said at last, more to himself than to her. But she answered him with a quiet reassurance, yet not understanding why it was necessary.

"She only think," she said.

"But he must have given her some cause to think," he said testily. "I'm afraid you're not as cute as I thought."

Wanaha turned away. His words had caused her pain, but he did not heed. Suddenly his face cleared, and he laughed a little harshly.

"Never mind," he said; "I doubt if he'll lose her through that."

The ambiguity of his remark was lost upon the Indian. She heard the laugh and needed no more. She rose and began to clear the table, while Nevil stood in the open doorway and gazed out into the night.

Standing there, his face hidden from Wanaha, he took no trouble to disguise his thoughts. And from his expression his thoughts were pleasant enough, or at least satisfactory to him, which was all he could reasonably expect.

His face was directed toward White River Farm, and he was thinking chiefly of Seth, a man he hated for no stronger reason than his own loss of caste, his own degeneracy, while the other remained an honest man. The deepest hatreds often are founded on one's own failings, one's own obvious inferiority to another. He was thinking of that love which Wanaha had assured him Seth entertained for Rosebud, and he was glad. So glad that he forgot many things that he ought to have remembered. One amongst them was the fact that, whatever he might be, Wanaha was a good woman. And honesty never yet blended satisfactorily with rascality.

CHAPTER XIV

THE WARNING

"Ma," exclaimed Rosebud, after a long and unusual silence while she was washing up the breakfast things, and Mrs. Sampson was busy with some cleaning at the other side of the kitchen, "do you ever get tired of your work here? Your life, I mean?"

It was early morning. Already the heat in the kitchen was intense. Ma looked hot, but then she was stooping and polishing, and the flies were provoking. Rosebud, in linen overall, still looked cool. Her face was serious enough, which seemed to be the result of some long train of thought. Ma suddenly stopped working to look up, and waved a protesting hand at the swarming flies. She found the girl's violet eyes looking steadily into hers. There was an earnestness in their depths as unusual as the seriousness of her face. The old woman had been about to answer hastily, but she changed her mind.

"Why should I, child?" she said, as though such a contingency were out of all reason. "It's all ours, I guess. It's jest ours to make or mar. Ther' isn't a stick on this farm that we haven't seen set ther', Rube an' me. Tired of it? Guess the only tire I'll feel'll come when I can't set foot to the ground, an' ain't the strength to kindle a stove or scrub a floor. Tired? No, child. What fixed you to get askin' that?"

The plates clattered under Rosebud's hands as she went on with her work. Ma eyed the stack of dishes in some doubt. She thought there might be some excuse for the girl being a little tired of domestic duties. She often wondered about this. Yet she had never heard Rosebud complain; besides, she had a wise thought in the back of her head about the girl's feelings toward at least one of their little family circle.

"I don't quite know, Ma," the girl said at last. Then she added quickly, feeling, of a sudden, that her question had suggested something she did not intend. "Don't think I am. I was wondering over something else." She laughed a little uncertainly. "It's Seth. He's always harping on my going away. Always thinking of the time when my people are to be found. And I just wondered if he thought I was tired of the farm and wanted to be away. He's so kind and good to me, and I thought he might, in a mistaken way, believe I'd be happier in—well, with those people who have forgotten my very existence. I love the farm, and—and all of you. And I don't want to go away."

Ma turned again to her work with a wise little smile in her twinkling eyes.

"Seth's a far-seein' boy, an' a good boy in 'most everything," she said, in a tone indicating wholehearted affection; "but he's like most folks with head-pieces, I guess. He don't stop at things which it is given to men to understand. Ef I wus a man I'd say of Seth, he's li'ble to git boostin' his nose into places not built fer a nose like his. Seein' I'm his 'Ma,' I'd jest say he ain't no call to git figgerin' out what's good fer wimminfolk."

"That's just what I think," exclaimed Rosebud, with a quick laugh. "He made me quite angry some time ago. He means to get me off the farm somehow. And—and—I could just thump him for it." The girl's seriousness had passed, and she spoke lightly enough now.

"Men-folk do rile you some," nodded Ma. But the twinkle had not left her eyes. "But, my girl, I shouldn't be surprised if Seth's got mighty good reason. An' it ain't to do with his personal feelin's."

Rosebud went on with her washing without speaking. She was thinking of that picnic she had taken with Seth and General nearly three weeks ago. It had almost developed into a serious quarrel. It would have done so, only Seth refused to quarrel.

"He said, one day, he thought it was better I should go. Much better," she said, presently. "Well, it made me angry. I don't want to go, and I don't see why Seth should be allowed to order me to go. The farm doesn't belong to him. Besides——"

"Well, y' see, Rosebud, you're forgettin' Seth brought you here. He's a kind of father to you." Ma smiled mischievously in the girl's direction, but Rosebud was too busy with her own thoughts to heed it.

"He's not my father, or anything of the kind. He's just Seth. He's not thirty yet, and I am eighteen. Pa's a father to me, and you are my mother. And Seth—Seth's no relation at all. And I'm just not going to call him 'Daddy' ever again. It's that that makes him think he's got the right to order me about," she added, as a hasty afterthought.

Further talk was interrupted at that moment by a knock at the back door. Rosebud passed out into the wash-house to answer the summons, and Ma Sampson heard her greet the Indian woman, Wanaha. The old farmwife muttered to herself as she turned back to her work.

"Guess Seth ain't got the speed of a jibbin' mule," she said slowly and emphatically.

The girl did not return, and Ma, looking out of the window, saw the two women walking together, engaged in earnest conversation. She looked from them to the breakfast things, and finally left her own work and finished the washing up herself. It was part of her way to spare Rosebud as much as she could, and the excuse served her now.

While Rosebud was receiving a visit from Wanaha at the back of the house, the men-folk, engaged in off-loading pine logs from a wagon, were receiving visitors at the front of it. The Indian Agent and Mr. Hargreaves had driven up in a buckboard. The Agent's team was sweating profusely, a fact which the sharp eyes of Seth were quick to detect; also he noted that Parker was driving a team and not the usual one horse.

"Kind o' busy?" questioned Seth, in answer to the two men's greetings.

The Agent glanced at the steaming horses and nodded.

"Going into Beacon Crossing," he said.

"Ah," said Rube, in his heavy, guttural fashion. "Gettin' fixin's?"

The Agent smiled, and nodded at the minister beside him.

"Yes, of a sort; we both are."

"How?"

It was Seth who spoke, and a shade more sharply than usual.

"Well, I want to send a wire over the line, and wait a reply. We shan't be out again until Tuesday, and that's why we came over.

The Watchers of the Plains: A Tale of the Western Prairies

There'll be no sewing class on Monday. You see, Mr. Hargreaves is going with me. We are driving instead of riding, because we're going to bring out some small arm ammunition. We're both getting short of it."

The Agent's manner was casual enough, but the minister's face was grave. The former endeavored to pass lightly over the matter of the ammunition.

A brief silence followed. It was broken at last by the Agent again.

"Getting on with the logs?" he said.

"Yes. We're fixin' a big corral right round the farm."

It was Rube who explained; and the old man glanced from Seth with a comprehensive survey of the proposed enclosure.

"By the way," said Mr. Hargreaves, "I shouldn't let Rosebud come to the Mission on Sunday. I shan't be there, but Jackson from Pine Ridge will hold the service. You see, there's—well——" The churchman broke off, and turned appealingly to the Agent.

"The fact is," Parker said, in his quick, abrupt manner, "Jim Crow and some of the other boys have warned me that these red heathens are 'making med'cine.' I don't know what it means—yet. I wish to goodness the troops were nearer."

The Agent's hard face was very set. His final wish was the key-note of his life. His was truly an unsmiling existence.

"So you're jest goin' in to sound the warnin'," observed Seth. The other nodded.

"I'd like to cancel Little Black Fox's pass on Monday," Parker went on, "but it would be a bad policy. Anyway, if he goes out for a month the others will likely keep quiet until he comes back, unless of course this pass of his has another meaning. I shall have him tracked. But—well, we'd best get on. I should give some slight word of this to the Rankin people and old Joe Smith, north of you, and any one else you have time to—I mean the men-folk. You know, the usual thing, pass it on."

After a few more remarks the buckboard drove off and Rube and Seth returned to their work. The silence between them was broken at last by Rube.

"Seems to me ther's something to that pass."

"Yes," said Seth, thoughtfully. Then, with an impatient gesture, "Guess I'll go into Beacon myself to-day. There's a thing or two for me to do. Keep an eye on the wimminfolk. Guess I'll git goin' now."

Seth's announcement was received without question by Rube, for there was perfect understanding between these men.

Half an hour later Seth was leading his horse from the barn ready saddled for the journey. As he moved out he saw Rosebud coming toward him from the house. He waited, and she came up in something of a flutter of confusion. She had an unusual color, and her eyes were sparkling. Seth noted these things while he appeared to be arranging the contents of his saddle-bags.

"Pa says you're going into Beacon Crossing, Seth," she said without preamble, as she stood at the horse's head and idly smoothed its velvety muzzle with her soft brown hand.

"That's so," the man answered.

"I've written a letter to New York for a store price list. Will you mail it?"

"Sure."

There was an odd smile in Seth's dark eyes. He knew this was not the girl's object in coming to him. He always called in at the house to ask for letters at the last moment before starting. There was a slight awkwardness while he waited for the girl to go on.

Suddenly Rosebud stooped and ran her hands down the horse's fore-legs. Her face was thus concealed.

"Seth, I used to think you wanted to get rid of me. You remember? Well, I—I think I know differently now. I'm sure I do. And I want to say I'm sorry for being angry and nasty about it that time. What beautiful clean legs Buck has got."

"Ye-es." A soft light shone in the man's steady eyes as he gazed upon the girl's still bent figure. One of his hands was resting on the cantle of his saddle, and for a moment it gripped tight. He was suddenly swept by a passionate longing that was hard to resist, and his answer came in a slightly husky tone. "You see, Rosie, when I want to be quit of you, it ain't for anything you do or say, it's — — Guess I must be goin'."

Rosebud had abruptly straightened up, and her bright eyes were smiling into his face. At that moment Seth could not support the flashing inquiry of them, so he sought safety in flight. He vaulted into the saddle almost as he spoke, and, with a wave of his hand, rode off, leaving her undeniably mistress of the situation.

She followed him with her eyes as he rode to the kitchen door and hailed Ma. Her smile was still wreathing her pretty features when he finally headed away for the trail. It became more and more tender as horse and rider receded, and at last she turned away with a sigh.

"I wonder what he'd say if he knew what I've promised Wana?" she said to herself. Then she laughed a sudden, wilful laugh as she remembered that she hadn't given him her letter.

But Seth was not quite free to go his way. Another interruption occurred about half a mile from the farm, where the trail dipped so that he was completely hidden from view. He overtook Wanaha. The Indian had been walking steadily on, but, since the sound of his horse's hoofs reached her, she had been waiting at the roadside.

He greeted her and would have passed on, but she stopped him, addressing him in her soft, flowery, native tongue.

"It is of Rosebud," she said, her dark eyes looking solemnly up into his. "My brother, the great chief, he love her, and in his love is danger for her. I come. And I tell her these things. You love her. So, it is good. You know Indian as no other knows, 'cep' my man. He learn this danger, and he send me for warning. I tell her to-day. You I tell too, for you have much knowledge and you watch. So."

"What danger? What is it?" Seth's questions came very sharply.

"I not know. It is so. My man he not know. He say only 'danger.' He say Black Fox leave Reservation. So, watch. An' I tell you. You must speak no word, or there danger for my man too, and for Wanaha. It is all."

Seth nodded.

"All right. I understand. You're a good squaw, Wanaha."

He passed on, for Wanaha waited for no questions. She had done what she thought best. Had not Nevil seen the gravity of the matter? But of her own accord she had gone further than her instructions. She had warned Seth, whom Nevil had said must not be told. For once in her life Wanaha had exercised her own judgment in defiance of her husband's.

The squaw passed down the deep prairie furrow while Seth held to the trail. And the man's thoughts went back to the interview he had had with Rosebud that morning. So it was Wanaha who had caused her to come to him.

CHAPTER XV

THE MOVEMENTS OF LITTLE BLACK FOX

The woodlands on the northern side of the great Reservations of Dakota amount almost to a forest. From Beacon Crossing, after entering the Pine Ridge Reservation, a man might travel the whole length of the Indian territory without the slightest chance of discovery, even by the Indians themselves; that is, provided he be a good woodsman. And this is what Seth accomplished. He did it without any seeming care or unusual caution. But then he was consummate in the necessary craft which is to be found only amongst the sons of the soil, and, even then, rarely outside the few who have been associated with Indians all their lives.

It was soon after sunrise on Monday morning that Seth found himself in the neighborhood of the principal Indian camp of the Rosebuds. Yet none had seen him come. He was hidden in the midst of a wide, undergrown bluff. Directly in front of him, but with at least four hundred yards of uninterrupted view intervening, was the house of Little Black Fox.

Seth was not usually a hard rider—he was far too good a horseman—but when necessity demanded it he knew how to get the last ounce out of his horse. He had left the farm on Saturday morning, and at midnight had roused the postmaster of Beacon Crossing from his bed. Then, at the hotel of Louis Roiheim, he had obtained a fresh horse, and, by daylight on Monday morning, after traveling the distance through nothing but mazy woodland, had reached the locality of Little Black Fox's abode. Thus he had covered something like one hundred and seventy miles in less than forty-eight hours. Nor had he finished his work yet.

Now he lay on the ground in the shadow of the close, heavy-foliaged brush, watching with alert, untiring eyes. Something of the Indian seemed to have grown into the nature of this uncultured product of the prairie world. He had smothered the only chance of betrayal by blindfolding his horse, now left in the well-trained charge of the dog, General. For himself he gave no sign. Not a leaf moved, nor a twig stirred where he lay. If he shifted his position it must have been done in the manner of the Indians themselves, for no sound resulted. He knew that a hundred pairs of eyes would infallibly detect his presence at the least clumsy disturbance of the bush. For the Indian is like the bear in his native woods. He may be intent in another direction, but the disturbance of the leaves, however slight, in an opposite direction, will at once attract his attention.

The squaws were astir at daylight. Now, as the sun rose, it became apparent that there were many preparations going forward in the chief's quarters. There was a gathering of ponies in a corral hard by. Also the long "trailers," already packed with tepee-poles and great bundles of skins and blankets, were leaning against the walls of the corral.

To Seth's practised eyes these things denoted an early departure; and, by the number of ponies and the extent of the equipment, it was evidently to be the going of a large party. But time went on, and no further move was made. Only all those who came and went seemed busy; not on account of what they did, but from their manner and movement. Through the greater part of the day Seth kept his sleepless watch. Only once did he abandon his post, and then merely to return to his horse to secure food from his saddle-bags. When he rose to go thither it was to be seen that he was fully armed, which had not been the case when he left the farm.

Seth's arguments were as simple and straightforward as he was himself, and none the less shrewd. The position was this. The Indians were in a state of ferment, to which, of course, the chief was party. Second, the chief was going off on a hunting trip, and apparently abandoning his people at a critical time. Third, he had received warning of Rosebud's danger from one whose knowledge and good-will could be relied on. Fourth, the warning had come to them, indirectly, from the one man who he now had every reason to suspect had no very good-will toward Rosebud; but he also saw, or thought he saw, the reason of that warning. It was that this man might clear himself should the chief's plans go wrong. These were Seth's arguments, and he intended to prove them by remaining on Little Black Fox's trail until he was assured that the danger to

Rosebud no longer existed. It was in the nature of the man that he had sought no outside aid, except that of his faithful General.

The story the watcher read as he observed the Indians' movements was a long one. The climax of it did not come until late in the afternoon, and the conclusion not until an hour later.

The climax was reached when he saw a tall figure coming up from the direction of the bridge. A grim pursing of the lips lent a curious expression to the smile that this appearance brought to his face. The man was clad in a blanket, and his gait was the gait of an Indian. There was nothing to give any other impression to the casual observer. But Seth was very intent, and he saw the color of the man's face. It was then that his lips shut tight and his smile developed something tigerish in its appearance.

However, he remained quite still, and saw the man pass into the chief's house. He did not reappear for a full half-hour. When at last he came out he departed at once the way he had come. Half an hour later the chief's ponies, a number of squaws, and the baggage, set out accompanied by half a dozen mounted bucks. Another half-hour and Little Black Fox appeared and vaulted to the back of his waiting pony. A dozen warriors joined him almost at the same moment, gathering from different directions, and the chief rode off at their head.

Then it was that Seth rose from his hiding-place. He stood watching the going of these men until he had made sure of the direction they were taking. They were making for the river ford, and he instantly ran back to his horse and mounted. Just for a second he hesitated. Then he set off for the wagon bridge as fast as he could urge his horse.

It was late the same afternoon that Charlie Rankin rode up to the River Farm and greeted Rube, who was hard at work upon the stockade. He was a large, cheery Britisher, with a florid face and ready laugh. He drew up with a jerk, sprang to the ground, and began talking with the perfect freedom of long friendship.

"I've passed the word, Rube," he said, without any preamble. "It's gone the round by this time. I thought I'd run over and consult you about the womenfolk. I'm new to this work. You are an old bird. I thought of sending the missis into Beacon."

Rube paused in his work and surveyed the horizon, while, in his slow way, he wiped the perspiration from his weather-furrowed face.

"Howdy, Charlie," he said, without displaying the least concern. "Wal, I don't know. Y' see this thing's li'ble to fizzle some. We've had 'em before. Guess my missis an' the gal'll stay right here by us. I 'low I feel they're safer wi' us. Mebbe it's jest a notion. If things gits hummin' I'd say come right along over an' share in wi' us. Y' see if it's a case of git, we'd likely do better in a party. Seth's away jest now."

The old man's quiet assurance was pleasant to the less experienced farmer. There was soundness in his plans too. Charlie nodded.

"That's good of you. Of course, we've got the warning, but we don't know how far things are moving. Do you?"

"Wal, no. But I don't think ther's anything to worry over fer a week or two."

"I thought there couldn't be, because I saw your Rosebud riding down toward the river as I came along. And yet — —"

But Rube broke in upon him vehemently.

"Goin' to the river?" he cried. Then his usual slow movements suddenly became electrical. He strode away to the barn, and left Charlie to follow.

"What's up?" the latter asked, as he paused in the doorway.

"Up? Up? What's up?" The old man was saddling a big raw-boned mare with almost feverish haste. "She's no right goin' that aways. An' I promised Seth, too. I didn't know but what she wus in the kitchen. Here, fix that bridle while I get into the house. Ha' y' got your gun?"

"Yes; but why?"

"Wal—y' never can figger to these durned Injuns when they're raisin' trouble."

The old man was off like a shot, while Charlie fixed the great mare's bridle. He returned almost immediately armed with a brace of guns.

"Say, ken y' spare an hour or so?"

As Charlie looked into the old farmer's face when he made his reply he read the answer to all he would have liked to ask him. Rube was consumed with an anxiety that no words, delivered in his slow fashion, could have conveyed to any one but Seth.

"Certainly, as long as you like."

"Good boy," said Rube, with an air of relief. "I wouldn't ask you, but it's fer her." And the two men rode off hastily, with Rube leading.

"By-the-way," said Charlie, drawing his horse up alongside the dun-colored mare, "Joe Smith, north of us, says some neighbor of his told him there were tents on the plains further north. I was wondering. The troops haven't been sent for, have they?"

"Can't say," said Rube, without much interest. Then he asked hastily, "Which way was she headin'?"

The question showed the trend of his whole thought.

"Why, straight down."

"Ah, Nevil Steyne's shack."

"He lives that way, doesn't he?"

"Yes."

The two men rode on in silence. This was the first time Charlie had ever seen Rube disturbed out of his deliberate manner. He made a mental resolve to bring his wife and children into White River Farm at the first sign of actual danger.

CHAPTER XVI

GENERAL DISTINGUISHES HIMSELF

Never since her first coming to the farm had Rosebud been forced to keep her goings and comings secret. But Wanaha had made it imperative now. It went sorely against the girl's inclination, for she hated deception of any kind; and she knew that what she meditated was a deception against those she loved. Consequently she was angry; angry with Wanaha, angry with the Indians, but most of all with herself. Wanaha had asked for a secret visit to Nevil Steyne, who was cutting wood below the bridge.

But in spite of her anger, as she made the necessary detour for concealment in one of those deep troughs amid the billows of grass-land, there was a sparkle of anticipation and excitement in her violet eyes. Before she was half-way to the woods that lined the river the last shadow of her brief anger had passed from her face. After all, she told herself in weak excuse, what she was doing was only a very little matter, and, perhaps—who could tell?—she might learn something that would be useful to Seth, who cared for nothing and nobody in the world but the Indians. So she rode on quite fearless, with no graver qualms than the very slightest twinge of conscience.

As she rode she debated with herself the manner in which she was to conceal her destination from chance observers. Wilful and irresponsible as Rosebud always appeared to be, there was yet something strongly reliant in her nature. She was, as so many girls are, a child in thought and deed until some great event, perchance some bereavement, some tragedy, or some great love, should come to rouse the dormant strength for good or ill which lies hidden for years, sometimes for life, in nearly every daughter of Eve.

The result of her debate was a decision to head for the ford when once she was out of view of the farm. She argued, if Nevil Steyne were cutting wood below the bridge, as Wanaha had told her, then by entering the woods at the ford she could make her way through them until she came to him. Thus she would not show herself near his hut, or near where he might be known to be working.

So, in the waning daylight, she cantered over the scented grass without a thought of the danger which Wanaha had hinted to her. She was defenceless, unarmed, yet utterly fearless. Her spirit was of the plains, fresh, bright, strong. Life to her was as the rosy light of dawn, full of promise and hope. Her frail figure, just budding with that enchanting promise of magnificent womanhood, swaying to the light gait of her broncho, was a sight to stir the pulse of any man. It was no wonder that the patient, serious Seth watched over her, shielding her with every faculty alert, every nerve straining, all his knowledge of that living volcano over which they lived brought into service.

Some such thoughts as these may have passed through Charlie Rankin's mind when he saw her as he passed on his way to the farm. For men are like this. Married or single they always have an eye for feminine beauty, only when they are married they generally keep their observations to themselves—if they be wise.

The sun was almost upon the horizon when the girl reached the ford. The rift in the woods, which formed a wagon trail, was very narrow, and even though the sun had not yet set, the spot was dark and sombre by reason of the wall of pine trees which lined it upon each side.

Just for a second Rosebud experienced the dark moody influence of the gloomy pine canopy beneath which she was to plunge. Like all high-spirited creatures she had no love for any form of gloom. And there is nothing in nature that can compare with the American pinewoods for gloom. Stately, magnificent, if you will, but funereal in their gloom.

Something of her surroundings now found reflection in the expression of her fair face as she plunged down the solemn aisles of black, barren tree trunks, like columns supporting the superstructure of some Gothic cathedral.

Her broncho was forced to take his way carefully, and thus his gait was reduced to little better than a walk. Further in, the tree-trunks gave way occasionally to patches of undergrowth. Then they became mixed with other growths. Maple and spruce held place and made her course more awkward, and further hindered her. The blue gums crowded so closely that frequently she was driven to considerable detour. Gradually the maze began to confuse her. She started to reckon the whereabouts of the river, a process which confused her more. But she kept on, her whole attention concentrated, —so much so that even her object was almost forgotten.

So engrossed was she that she failed to notice that her horse had suddenly become very alert. His large, low-bred ears, that weathercock of the horseman, were pricked up, and he looked inquiringly from side to side as he picked his way. Once he gave a short, suppressed whinny.

The girl's perplexity, however, was strong upon her. She did not hear it, or, if she did, it conveyed nothing to her. Her brows were puckered, and she gazed only ahead. Had she paused she must have heard that which had drawn her horse's attention. But she kept on, struggling with the maze about her, and so heard no sound of the breaking brush upon either side of her.

She was more than half-way to the bridge, when, to her intense relief, she saw daylight ahead through the overshadowing foliage. She pushed on urgently, and sighed her relief; it was a clearing. That opening meant more to her than she would have admitted. To see the sky again, to breathe air that was fresh, free from the redolence of the forest underlay, was all she desired.

The clearing was fringed with a low, thorny brush, which, as she came to it, caught her skirt, and forced her to draw rein, and stoop to release it.

While thus occupied her broncho threw up his head and gave a tremendous neigh. The sound startled her, as these things will startle the strongest when all is profoundly silent. But what followed was more startling still. Not one, but half a dozen echoes at least responded, and, with a thrill, the girl sat up. The next moment she had spurred her horse and charged, regardless of the thorns, into the midst of the clearing.

As she came a wave of horror swept over her. Simultaneous with her entry a mounted Indian appeared from the opposite side. Others appeared, each from a different direction, silent, but with automatic precision. To her right she saw them; to her left; and behind her, too.

111

A deliberate ring of silent sentries had formed themselves about her, almost in the twinkling of an eye.

The girl's first terror was almost overwhelming, and her impulse was to shriek aloud. But the shock of that ghostly appearance passed, not because the danger appeared to lessen, but because her nerves were healthy, and she somehow possessed sympathy with the red men. Mechanically she noticed, too, that they were blanketed, as in peace. They had donned no feathers or paint. Nor could she see aught of any firearms. So her courage returned, but she did not attempt to move or speak.

She was not long left in doubt. With crude, dramatic effect Little Black Fox suddenly appeared from the adjacent woods. He rode into the ring on his black pony, sitting the sleek beast in that haughty manner which is given to the Indian alone, and which comes from the fact that he uses no saddle, and sits with the natural pose of a lithe figure that is always carried erect.

He wore no blanket. He was clad from head to foot resplendent in beaded buckskin, his long black hair flowing beneath his crown of feathers and falling upon his shoulders. His handsome face was unscarred by any barbaric markings such as many of his warriors displayed. He was fresh and young; his eyes were flashing with deep emotion, and lit up his dusky countenance with a smile that had nothing gentle in it. He was every inch a chief. Nor was there any mistaking the barbaric lover that looked out of his eyes.

Rosebud unconsciously drew herself up. There was no responsive smile upon her face. She knew there was mischief looming, and the woman in her was stirred to the depths. Young as she was she realized that that ring of sentries about her could mean but one thing. Now, when it was too late, she recalled Seth's many warnings, and bitterly repented her unutterable folly in ever going near this wild, untried young chieftain.

She kept silent. But the seconds that passed as the man rode up were trying. He rode to within six inches of her, and their horses stood head to tail. Then he spoke in his native Sioux tongue, which so lends itself to the expression of ardent passion.

"The sun has no brightness like the eyes of the paleface princess," he said, his proud face serious, and his eyes steady and flashing. There was almost a flush under the dusky skin of his cheeks. "The waters of the great lakes are deep, but the depth is as nothing to the blue of the princess's eyes. She is queen of her race, as Little Black Fox is king of his race. The king would wed the queen, whose eyes make little the cloudless summer sky. He loves her, and is the earth beneath her feet. He loves her, and all his race shall be her servants. He loves her, and all that is his is hers. So there shall be everlasting peace with her people and his. His heart is swept with a passion which is like to the fiercest blizzard of the plain. But its blast is hot; hotter and swifter than the fiercest heats of earth. There is no peace for him without the white princess. He is ever at war. The body fights with the brain, and his heart is torn. So he would wed the princess."

Even in her extremity something of the real passion of this wild youth found a chord of sympathy in Rosebud's heart. His sincerity, his splendid personality, savage though he was, made her listen attentively. The woman in her was not insensible to his address, but the very truth of his passion roused her fears again to the topmost pitch. There was no mistaking those horsemen surrounding her. She gave one little helpless glance around at them that surely would have melted the heart of any white man. But the impassive faces held out no hope to her. She was at this man's mercy.

Now, oddly enough, when she might have been expected to cry out in her terror, her anger rose. That quick rising anger which Seth understood so well and smiled at. And she spoke without a shadow of fear in her tone. Her use of the Sioux tongue was not perfect, and her words gained force therefrom.

"The princess cannot wed the chief," she said. "It is not according to the law of the palefaces. Go—go back to your tepees, and the squaws of your race. Leave me to go in peace. I have to go back to my people."

There was a moment's pause, during which a dog's yelp might have been heard by any less occupied. The sound was such as is the yelp of a foxhound drawing a cover. The chief's face had changed its expression; his passion was subservient to his native ferocity, and his face displayed it.

"I have asked," he said, "I, Little Black Fox, who am chief. I have said come to me. The paleface girl treats me like any dog. So. I have done. The spirit of Big Wolf, my father, enters my body. Like him, who took the princess and held her for his son, I will take that for which I have asked. There shall be no peace with your race."

He raised an arm to seize her by the waist. The girl saw his intention, and a wild fear dilated her eyes. But she did not lose her head. She suddenly spurred her broncho with a little vicious stab. The animal, already on his mettle, charged forward desperately, taking the pony of the Indian facing it in the chest and throwing it back upon its haunches. But the chief was round like lightning. He saw nothing, heeded nothing but the possible escape of this white girl, and that he had no intention of permitting. Had he been less engrossed he would have seen a dog rush madly into the clearing, and, in the manner of a cattle dog, incontinently begin a savage assault on the heels of the Indians' ponies. No human intelligence could have conceived a more effective plan, for the braves were thrown into utter confusion.

Little Black Fox came up with the fugitive, and, leaning over, caught the girl in his strong young arms. He meant to lift her from the saddle, but he held her thus only for a bare second. There was the sharp crack of a revolver, and Rosebud felt his grasp relax. He sat up on his horse and looked about him fiercely, then he reeled and clutched his pony's mane, while Seth, shouting encouragement to the terrified girl, came at him from out of the woods.

He came with such a cry of rage and fury that his voice was almost unrecognizable. His face, usually so calm, was flaming. His smoking revolver was raised aloft and, as his horse charged into that of the wounded chief, it fell crashing on to the befeathered head, and the man went down like a log.

"You gol durned black heathen!" Seth cried. Then his rage died out before the greater emergency. "Ride, Rosebud! The woods, and turn left. Ride like hell!"

It was all he had time for. He turned again in time to empty another chamber of his gun into the stomach of an Indian, who came at him with an upraised axe. Then, as the man rolled from his horse, he saw that the rest had discarded their blankets—their wearing of which had probably saved him—and now meant battle to the death.

He fully realized that he had no chance of escape, but he meant to give them all he could before the end came. One Indian raised a queer old rifle at him, but he let it drop before it was discharged. Another bullet had found its billet in the pit of the man's stomach.

General, who had taken himself off when Rosebud departed, now returned to the scene. He came with his fierce, canine worrying just as the rest of the Indians charged their solitary adversary. His diversion helped to check their onslaught, but only for a second. They had abandoned their firearms in favor of their native weapons as they came.

Seth was powerless against such odds. There was no hope. His revolver cracked and more than one man fell, but they closed with him, and, as his last barrel was emptied, he felt the flesh of his left shoulder rip under the slashing blow of an axe. His horse reared and for the moment took him clear of the horde, and at the same instant, he heard the deep tones of Rube's voice shouting to him. The Indians heard it, too. They turned, and the fire of revolvers from this new direction greeted them. They could murder one man, but reinforcements were different. It was enough. As Rube and Charlie Rankin galloped into the clearing they broke and fled.

"Rosebud?" cried Rube in a voice of agonized suspense.

Seth had swung his horse round and led the way out of the clearing in the track the girl had taken.

"Come on!" he cried. And, in a moment, the battle ground was deserted by all but the wounded Indians.

CHAPTER XVII

THE LETTER FROM ENGLAND

"La, child, an' why did you go for to do it?"

Ma was bending over Seth, bathing the ugly flesh wound in his shoulder. Her old eyes were pathetically anxious behind her spectacles, but her touch was sure and steady. Her words were addressed to Rosebud, who was standing by with a handful of bandages. The girl made no reply, and her eyes were fixed on this result of her escapade. She was pale, and her young face looked drawn. The violet of her eyes was noticeably dull, and it was easy to see that she was struggling hard to keep tears back. She simply could not answer.

Seth took the task upon himself. He seemed to understand, although he was not looking her way.

"Don't worrit the gal, Ma," he said, in his gentle fashion, so that Rosebud felt like dropping the bandages and fleeing from the room. "Say, jest git right to it an' fix me up. I 'low ther's li'ble to be work doin' 'fore this night's out."

"God a-mussy, I hope not, Seth, boy!" the old woman said, with a deep intake of breath. But her busy fingers hastened. She tenderly laid the wool, saturated in carbolic oil, upon the gash. Seth bore it without flinching. "More'n six year," she added, taking the bandages from Rosebud and applying them with the skill of long experience, "an' we've had no trouble, thank God. But I knew it 'ud come sure. Rube had it in his eye."

"Wher's Rube now?" asked Seth, cutting her short.

"Doin' guard out front."

The bandage was adjusted, and Seth rose and was helped into his coat.

"Guess I'll git out to him."

He found it hard, for once, to sit in there with the womenfolk. His feeling was one common to men of action.

"You're feelin' easy?" Ma asked him anxiously, as he moved to the door.

"Dead right, Ma."

The old woman shook her head doubtfully, and Rosebud's troubled eyes followed him as he moved away. She had scarcely spoken since they returned to the house. Her brain was still in a whirl and she was conscious of a weak, but almost overpowering, inclination to tears. The one thing that stood out above all else in her thoughts was Seth's wound.

No one had questioned her; no one had blamed her. These simple people understood her feelings of the moment too well. Later they knew they would learn all about it. For the present there was plenty to be done.

Rube had been making preparations. Their plans needed no thinking out. Such an emergency as the present had always been foreseen, and so there was no confusion. Charlie Rankin had gone on to old Joe Smith, and that individual would be dispatched post-haste in the direction of the white tents that had been seen on the plains. For the rest the horses in the barn were ready harnessed, and Ma could be trusted to get together the household things ready for decamping. There was nothing to do but to keep a night-long watch.

Seth had crossed the passage, and was passing through the parlor, out of which the front door opened. Rosebud hesitated. Then with something almost like a rush she followed him. She was at his side in a moment, and her two small hands were clasping his rough, strong right hand.

"Seth," she whispered, tearfully. "I— —"

"Don't, little Rosie!" the man interrupted, attempting to draw his hand gently from her grasp. "Guess ther' ain't no need to say anything. Mebbe I know."

But Seth had misinterpreted her action. He thought she meant to explain. She kept hold of his hand, and tears were in her lovely eyes as she looked up into his dark face, now little more than a shadow in the faint light that came from the passage.

"Oh, Seth, Seth, it was all my fault!" she cried, in her distress. "Your poor shoulder! Oh, what should I do if you were to die! Oh——" And the girl fell on her knees at his side and kissed the hand she was clinging to. The long threatened tears had come at last, and her voice was choked with sobs.

Seth had been unprepared for this outburst. It took him quite aback, and he felt a great lump rise in his throat. Unconsciously he almost roughly released his hand. But the next moment it was laid tenderly upon the bowed head.

"Git up, little gal," he said. And there was a world of tenderness in his voice. His effort at self-restraint was great, but his feelings found a certain amount of expression in spite of him, for he was stirred to the depths of his loyal heart. He was face to face with a scene such as he had never even pictured. His sense of duty was powerless just then before his deep, strong love for the girl. "Little Rosebud," he went on, and he struggled hard to make his words rough, "ther's things to do. Go right back to Ma an' help her. I must go out to Rube. He's doin' all the work, an' so is she."

The girl made no move to rise. Her sobs were heart-breaking. Seth turned sharply and left her where she was. He simply dared not stay there another moment.

Outside General was lying a few yards away from the house, crouched alertly, and gazing out prairiewards. He called the dog to him.

"Injuns, boy," he said, in a low tone. "S-seek 'em!"

The dog responded with a low growl, and then moved off out into the darkness, with the prowling gait of a puma stalking its prey.

"He'll keep us posted," Seth observed quietly to Rube.

"You kind o' understan' him."

"He understands Injuns," the dog's master returned significantly. No more was said for a while, and the two men peered out into the darkness with eyes trained to such watchfulness.

"'Bout them tents?" said Rube later on.

"They're the troops. The postmaster told me they were comin' hard."

"Kind o' handy."

It was very dark. The moon had not yet risen. Presently Seth fetched a chair. The older man watched him seat himself a little wearily.

"Hurt some?" he said.

"Jest a notion," Seth replied in his briefest manner.

"Say, you got around jest in time."

"Yup. Wanaha put me wise after I left here, so I came that aways. Say, this is jest the beginnin'."

"You think — —"

"Ther's more comin'. Guess the troops 'll check it some. But—say, this feller's worse'n his father. Guess he's jest feelin' his feet. An' he's gettin' all the Pine Ridge lot with him—I located that as I came along."

They talked on for some time longer, in their slow, short way discussing their plans. The one topic they did not discuss was Rosebud. They tacitly ignored her share in the evening's work like men who knew that certain blame must attach to her and refused to bestow it.

The night dragged slowly on. Rube wanted Seth to go in and rest, but Seth sat in his chair with dogged persistence. So they shared the vigil.

Rube, by way of variation, occasionally visited the stables to see to the horses. And all the time the dog was out scouting with an almost human intelligence. After once being dispatched he did not appear again. Seth had brought him up to this Indian scouting, and the beast's natural animosity to the Indians made him a perfect guard.

The moon rose at midnight. There was no sign of disturbance on the Reservation. All was quiet and still. But then these men knew that the critical time had not yet arrived. Dawn would be the danger. And by dawn they both hoped that something might result from Charlie Rankin's journey.

Rube was sitting in a chair at Seth's side. The clock in the kitchen had just cuckooed three times. The old man's eyes were heavy with sleep, but he was still wide awake. Neither had spoken for some time. Suddenly Seth's right hand gripped the old man's arm.

"Listen!"

There was a faint, uneasy whine far out on the prairie. Then Seth's straining ears caught the sound of horses galloping. Rube sprang to his feet, and his hands went to the guns at his waist. But Seth checked him.

"Easy," he said. "Guess it ain't that. General only whined. He mostly snarls wicked for Injuns."

They listened again. And soon it became apparent that those approaching were coming out of the north.

"Charlie's located 'em." Seth's tone was quietly assuring, and old Rube sighed his relief.

Then the dog suddenly reappeared. He, too, seemed to understand that friends were approaching.

And so it proved. The night of long suspense was over. A few minutes later a squad of United States cavalry, in charge of a dapper, blue-coated lieutenant, rode up to the farm. And when they arrived Seth was there by himself to receive them.

"Rube Sampson's farm?" inquired the lieutenant, as he swung from his steaming horse.

"Right." Seth shook hands with the man.

"Trouble over there," observed the other, indicating the Reservation with a nod of the head.

"Yup. Come right in. Guess your boys had best make their plugs snug in the barn. Come right in, and I'll rouse Ma."

Those last two hours before morning were the hardest part of all to Rube and Seth, for, in the parlor, they had to detail all the events of the preceding day to Lieutenant Barrow and his sergeant. And neither of them was good at explaining.

Breakfast was partaken of; after which, since the soldiers had accepted all responsibility, Ma packed her men-folk off to bed. Seth had not seen a bed since Friday night, and this was Tuesday.

The neighborhood of the farm, and, in fact, all along the north side of the river presented an unusual sight when Seth and Rube reappeared at noon. Two regiments of United States cavalry had taken up their position ready for any emergency.

The midday meal was a little late, so that Seth's shoulder might be properly dressed. And when at last the family sat down to it, it threatened to be more than usually silent. All were weary, and the women overwrought. Ma was the only one who made any attempt to rouse the drooping spirits about her. The men knew that they were confronted with no ordinary Indian rising. There was something far more threatening to them personally.

As the meal dragged on Ma abandoned her efforts entirely, and a long silence ensued. Finally Rube pushed back his chair and rose from the table. Then it was that Seth spoke for the first time.

He looked from Rube to Ma. He was trying to look unconcerned, and even smiled.

"Say," he observed, "guess I was fergittin'. I got a bit of a letter from—England."

Rube dropped back into his chair, and his eyes were questioning. Ma was staring through her spectacles at her boy. She, too, was asking a mute question. But hers was merely a quiet curiosity, while Rube's, slow old Rube's, was prompted by Seth's manner, which, instinctively, he knew to be a false one.

Rosebud was patting General's head as he sat at her side. She continued her caressing, but her eyes, swift and eager but tenderly grave, watched Seth as he drew out the letter from his pocket and smoothed it upon the table. There was just the slightest tremor in her hand as it rested on the dog's head.

"Yup," Seth went on, with a great assumption of unconcern which deceived nobody. "It's a feller—jest one o' them law fellers. He's comin' right along to the farm. I 'low he must be nigh here now. He was goin' to git here Tuesday the 16th—that's to-day."

He was intent on the letter. Nor did he once raise his eyes while he was speaking. Now he turned the paper as though in search of some detail of interest.

"Ah," he went on. "Here it is. Says he's hit the trail o' some gal as was lost. Guesses he'd like to see—Rosebud, an' ask a few questions."

"Seth!"

Ma had risen, and somehow her chair overturned behind her. Her exclamation was a gasp. Rube stared; he had no words just then. Rosebud continued to caress the dog, who whined his pleasure at the unusual attention. At last she turned. For an instant her eyes met Seth's.

"May I read that letter, Seth?" she asked quietly.

"Sure." Seth rose from the table. "Rube," he said, "I'd take it friendly if you'd fill my pipe." Then he moved across to the window.

Rosebud looked up from reading the letter. She came round to him and handed it back.

"So my name's Marjorie Raynor?" she said with a queer smile.

Seth nodded.

"And all this money is what you once spoke about?"

Again came Seth's affirmation.

"And how long have you known—that I'm not Rosebud?"

"Got that bit of a letter Saturday."

"But you guessed it long before that—when we were out at the slough?"

"I'd a notion."

The girl glanced round. Ma's face was still in a condition of florid perplexity. Rube was quietly whittling a match with his tobacco knife. Rosebud's eyes were very soft as she looked from one to the other.

"And I'm to go away from—here?" she said at last, and her lips were trembling.

"Guess when a 'stray' comes along we mostly git it back home."

Seth found a lot to interest him in the blank wall of the barn outside the window.

"But it seems I'm a stray without a home. My father and mother must be dead."

"Ther's aunts an' things—an' the dollars."

The girl also surveyed the wall of the barn.

"Yes, I forgot the—dollars."

Suddenly she turned away. Just for a moment she seemed in some doubt of her own purpose. Then she walked over to Ma and put her arms about her neck and kissed her. Then she passed round to Rube and did the same. Finally she opened the door, and stood for a second looking at Seth's slim back.

"Farewell, friends. The heiress must prepare for her departure."

There was something harsh and hysterical about the laugh which accompanied her mocking farewell, but she was gone the next instant, and the door slammed behind her.

Ma stepped up to her boy, and forgetful of his wounded shoulder rested her hand upon it. Seth flinched and drew away; and the old woman was all sympathy at once.

"I'm real sorry, boy, I kind o' forgot."

"It's nothin', Ma; it jest hurts some."

CHAPTER XVIII

SETH'S DUTY ACCOMPLISHED

"It's a great country. It astonishes me at every turn, madam; but it's too stirring for me. One gets used to things, I know, but this," with a wave of the arm in the direction of the Reservations, "these hair-raising Indians! Bless me, and you live so close to them!"

The crisp-faced, gray-headed little lawyer smiled in a sharp, angular manner in Ma Sampson's direction. The farmwife, arrayed in her best mission-going clothes, was ensconced in her husband's large parlor chair, which was sizes too big for her, and smiled back at him through her glasses.

Mr. Charles Irvine, the junior partner of the firm of solicitors, Rodgers, Son, and Irvine, of London, had made his final statement with regard to Rosebud, and had now given himself up to leisure.

There had been no difficulty. Seth's letter had stated all the facts of which he had command. It had been handed on to these solicitors. And what he had told them had been sufficient to bring one of the partners out to investigate. Nor had it taken this practical student of human nature long to realize the honesty of these folk, just as it had needed but one glance of comparison between Rosebud and the portrait of Marjorie Raynor, taken a few weeks before her disappearance, and which he had brought with him, to do the rest. The likeness was magical. The girl had scarcely changed at all, and it was difficult to believe that six years had elapsed since the taking of that portrait. After a long discussion with Seth the lawyer made his final statement to the assembled family.

"You quite understand that this case must go through the courts," he said gravely. "There is considerable property involved. For you, young lady, a long and tedious process. However, the matter will be easier than if there were others fighting for the estate. There are no others, because the will is entirely in your favor, in case of your mother's death. You have some cousins, and an aunt or two, all prepared to welcome you cordially; they are in no way your opponents; they will be useful in the matter of identification. The

124

only other relative is this lost uncle. In taking you back to England I assume sole responsibility. I am convinced myself, therefore I unhesitatingly undertake to escort you, and, if you care to accept our hospitality, will hand you over to the charge of Mrs. Irvine and my daughters. And should the case go against you, a contingency which I do not anticipate for one moment, I will see that you return to your happy home here in perfect safety. I hope I state my case clearly, Mr. Sampson, and you, Mr. Seth. I," and the little man tapped the bosom of his shirt, "will personally guarantee Miss—er—Marjorie Raynor's safety and comfort."

Mr. Irvine beamed in his angular fashion upon Rosebud, in a way that emphatically said, "There, by that I acknowledge your identity."

But this man who felt sure, that, at much discomfort to himself, he was bringing joy into a poor household, was grievously disappointed, for one and all received his assurances as though each were a matter for grief. Seth remained silent, and Rube had no comment to offer. Rosebud forgot even to thank him.

Ma alone rose to the occasion, and she only by a great effort. But when the rest had, on various pretexts, drifted out of the parlor, she managed to give the man of law a better understanding of things. She gave him an insight into their home-life, and hinted at the grief this parting would be to them all, even to Rosebud. And he, keen man of business that he was, encouraged her to talk until she had told him all, even down to the previous night's work on the banks of the White River. Like many women who trust rather to the heart than to the head, Ma had thus done for Rosebud what no purely business procedure could have done. She had enlisted this cool-headed but kindly lawyer's sympathies. And that goes far when a verdict has to be obtained.

In response to the lawyer's horrified realization of the dangerous adjacency of the Reservations, Ma laughed in her gentle, assured manner.

"Maybe it seems queer to you, Mr. Irvine, but it isn't to us. We are used to it. As my Rube always says, says he, 'When our time comes ther' ain't no kickin' goin' to be done. Meanwhiles we'll keep a smart eye, an' ther's allus someun lookin' on to see fair play.'"

The old woman's reply gave this man, who had never before visited any place wilder than a European capital, food for reflection. This was his first glimpse of pioneer life, and he warmed toward the spirit, the fortitude which actuated these people. But he made a mental resolve that the sooner Miss Raynor was removed from the danger zone the better.

There was little work done on the farm that day. When Seth had finished with the lawyer he abruptly took himself away and spent most of the day among the troops. For one thing, he could not stay in the home which was so soon to lose Rosebud. It was one matter for him to carry out the duty he conceived to be his, and another to stand by and receive in silence the self-inflicted chastisement it brought with it. So, with that quiet spirit of activity which was his by nature, and which served him well now, he took his share in the work of the troops, for which his knowledge and experience so fitted him. The most experienced officers were ready to listen to him, for Seth was as well known in those disturbed regions as any of the more popular scouts who have found their names heading columns in the American daily press.

After supper he and Rube devoted themselves to the chores of the farm, and it was while he was occupied in the barn, and Rube was attending to the milch cows in another building, that he received an unexpected visit. He was working slowly, his wounded shoulder handicapping him sorely, for he found difficulty in bedding down the horses with only one available hand. Hearing a light footstep coming down the passage between the double row of stalls, he purposely continued his work.

Rosebud, for it was she, paused at the foot of the stall in which he was working. He glanced round and greeted her casually. The girl stood there a second, then she turned away, and, procuring a fork, proceeded to bed down the stall next to him.

Seth protested at once. Rosebud had never been allowed to do anything like this. His objection came almost roughly, but the girl ignored it and went on working.

"Say, gal, quit right there," he said, in an authoritative manner.

Rosebud laughed. But the old spirit was no longer the same. The light-hearted mirth had gone. Indeed, Rosebud was a child no longer. She was a woman, and it would have surprised these folk to know how serious-minded the last two days had made her.

"Even a prisoner going to be hanged is allowed to amuse himself as he pleases during his last hours, Seth," she responded, pitching out the bedding from under the manger with wonderful dexterity.

Seth flushed, and his eyes were anxious. No physical danger could have brought such an expression to them. It was almost as if he doubted whether what he had done was right. It was the doubt which at times assails the strongest, the most decided. He seemed to be seeking a suitable response, but his habit of silence handicapped him. At last he said—

"But he's goin' to be hanged."

"And so am I." Rosebud fired her retort with all the force of her suppressed passion. Then she laughed again in that hollow fashion, and the straw flew from her fork. "At least I am going out of the world—my world, the world I love, the only world I know. And for what?"

Seth labored steadily. His tongue was terribly slow.

"Ther's your friends, and—the dollars."

"Friends—dollars?" she replied scornfully, while the horse she was bedding moved fearfully away from her fork. "You are always thinking of my dollars. What do I want with dollars? And I am not going to friends. I have no father and mother but Pa and Ma. I have no friends but those who have cared for me these last six years. Why has this little man come out here to disturb me? Because he knows that if the dollars are mine he will make money out of me. He knows that, and for a consideration he will be my friend. Oh, I hate him and the dollars!"

The tide of the girl's passion overwhelmed Seth, and he hardly knew what to say. He passed into another stall and Rosebud did the same. The man was beginning to realize the unsuspected depths of this girl's character, and that, perhaps, after all, there might have been another mode of treatment than his line of duty as he had conceived it. He found an answer at last.

"Say, if I'd located this thing and had done nothin' — —" he began. And she caught him up at once.

"I'd have thanked you," she said.

But Seth saw the unreasonableness of her reply.

"Now, Rosebud," he said gently, "you're talkin' foolish. An' you know it. What I did was only right by you. I'd 'a' been a skunk to have acted different. I lit on the trail o' your folk, don't matter how, an' I had to see you righted, come what might. Now it's done. An' I don't see wher' the hangin' comes in. Guess you ken come an' see Ma later, when things get quiet agin. I don't take it she hates you a heap."

He spoke almost cheerfully, trying hard to disguise what he really felt. He knew that with this girl's going all the light would pass out of his life. He dared not speak in any other way or his resolve would melt before the tide of feeling which he was struggling to repress. He would have given something to find excuse to leave the barn, but he made no effort to do so.

When Rosebud answered him her manner had changed. Seth thought that it was due to the reasonableness of his own arguments, but then his knowledge of women was trifling. The girl had read something underlying the man's words which he had not intended to be there, and had no knowledge of having expressed. Where a woman's affections are concerned a man is a simple study, especially if he permits himself to enter into debate. Seth's strength at all times lay in his silence. He was too honest for his speech not to betray him.

"Yes, I know, Seth, you are right and I am wrong," she said, and her tone was half laughing and half crying, and wholly penitent. "That's just it, I am always wrong. I have done nothing but bring you trouble. I am no help to you at all. Even this fresh trouble with the Indians is my doing. And none of you ever blame me. And—and I don't want to go away. Oh, Seth, you don't know how I want to stay! And you're packing me off like a naughty child. I am not even asked if I want to go." She finished up with that quick change to resentment so characteristic of her.

The touch of resentment saved Seth. He found it possible to answer her, which he did with an assumption of calmness he in no way felt. It was a pathetic little face that looked up into his. The girl's anger had brought a flush to her cheeks, but her beautiful eyes were as tearful as an April sky.

"Guess we've all got to do a heap o' things we don't like, Rosie; a mighty big heap. An' seems to me the less we like 'em the more sure it is they're right for us to do. Some folks calls it 'duty.'"

"And you think it's my duty to go?"

Seth nodded.

"My duty, the same as it was your duty always to help me out when I got into some scrape?"

Without a thought Seth nodded again, and was at once answered by that hollow little laugh which he found so jarring.

"I hate duty! But, since I have had your splendid example before me for six years, it has forced on me the necessity of trying to be like you." The girl's sarcasm was harsh, but Seth ignored it.

As she went on her mood changed again. "I was thinking while that old man was talking so much," she said slowly, "how I shall miss Pa, and Ma, and old General. And I can't bear the idea of leaving even the horses and cattle, and the grain fields. I don't know whatever the little papooses at the Mission will do without me. I wonder if all the people who do their duty feel like that about things? They can't really, or they wouldn't want to do it, and would just be natural and—and human sometimes. Think of it, Seth, I'm going to leave all this beautiful sunshine for the fog of London just for the sake of duty. I begin to feel quite good. Then, you see, when I'm rich I shall have so much to do with my money—so many duties—that I shall have no time to think of White River Farm at all. And if I do happen to squeeze in a thought, perhaps just before I go to sleep at night, it'll be such a comfort to think everybody here is doing their duty. You see nothing else matters, does it?"

Seth took refuge in silence. The girl's words pained him, but he knew that it was only her grief at leaving, and he told himself that her bitterness would soon pass. The pleasure of traveling, of seeing new places, the excitement of her new position would change all that. Receiving no reply Rosebud went on, and her bitterness merged into an assumed brightness which quite deceived her companion.

"Yes," she continued, "after all it won't be so dreadful, will it? I can buy lots of nice things, and I shall have servants. And I can go all over the world. No more washing up. And there'll be parties and dances. And Mr. Irvine said something about estates. I suppose I'll have a country house—like people in books. Yes, and I'll marry some one with a title, and wear diamonds. Do you think somebody with a title would marry me, Seth?"

"Maybe, if you asked him."

"Oh!"

"Wal, you see it's only fine ladies gits asked by fellers as has titles."

The dense Seth felt easier in his mind at the girl's tone, and in his clumsy fashion was trying to join in the spirit of the thing.

"Thank you, I'll not ask any one to marry me."

Seth realized his mistake.

"Course not. I was jest foolin'."

"I know." Rosebud was smiling, and a dash of mischief was in her eyes as she went on—

"It would be awful if a girl had to ask some one to marry her, wouldn't it?"

"Sure."

Seth moved out into the passage; the last horse was bedded down, and they stood together leaning on their forks.

"The man would be a silly, wouldn't he?"

"A reg'lar hobo."

"What's a 'hobo,' Seth?"

"Why, jest a feller who ain't got no 'savee.'"

"'Savee' means 'sense,' doesn't it?" Rosebud's eyes were innocently inquiring, and they gazed blandly up into the man's face.

"Wal, not exac'ly. It's when a feller don't git a notion right, an' musses things up some." They were walking toward the barn door now. Seth was about to go up to the loft to throw down hay. "Same as when I got seein' after the Injuns when I ought to've stayed right here an' seen you didn't go sneakin' off by y'self down by the river," he added slyly, with one of his rare smiles.

The girl laughed and clapped her hands.

"Oh, Seth!" she cried, as she moved out to return to the house, "then you're a regular 'hobo.' What a joke!"

And she ran off, leaving the man mystified.

Rosebud and the lawyer left the following morning. Never had such good fortune caused so much grief. It was a tearful parting; Ma and Rosebud wept copiously, and Rube, too, was visibly affected. Seth avoided everybody as much as possible. He drove the conveyance into Beacon Crossing, but, as they were using the lawyer's hired "democrat," he occupied the driving-seat with the man who had brought the lawyer out to the farm. Thus it was he spoke little to Rosebud on the journey.

Later, at the depot, he found many things to occupy him and only time to say "good-bye" at the last moment, with the lawyer looking on.

The girl was on the platform at the end of the sleeping-car when Seth stepped up to make his farewell.

"Good-bye, little Rosebud," he said, in his quiet, slow manner. His eyes were wonderfully soft. "Maybe you'll write some?"

The girl nodded. Her violet eyes were suspiciously bright as she looked frankly up into his face.

"I hope we shall both be happy. We've done our duty, haven't we?" she asked, with a wistful little smile.

"Sure," replied Seth, with an ineffective attempt at lightness.

The girl still held his hand and almost imperceptibly drew nearer to him. Her face was lifted to him in a manner that few would have mistaken. But Seth gently withdrew his hand, and, as the train began to move, climbed down and dropped upon the low platform.

Rosebud turned away with a laugh, though her eyes filled with tears. She waved a handkerchief, and Seth's tall, slim figure was the last she beheld of Beacon Crossing. And when the train was sufficiently far away she kissed her hand in the direction of the solitary figure still doing sentry at the extremity of the platform. Then she went into the car and gave full vent to the tears she had struggled so long to repress.

CHAPTER XIX

SETH PLAYS A STRONG HAND

It would seem that the Agent's prompt action in summoning the aid of the troops had averted disaster. No trouble followed immediately on Seth's drastic treatment of Little Black Fox, and the majority of the settlers put this result down to the fact of the overawing effect of the cavalry. One or two held different opinions, and amongst these were the men of White River Farm. They were inclined to the belief that the wounding of the chief was the sole reason that the people remained quiet. Anyway, not a shot was fired, much to the satisfaction of the entire white population, and, after two weeks had passed, by slow degrees, a large proportion of the troops were withdrawn.

Then followed a government inquiry, at which Seth was the principal witness. It was a mere formality by which the affair was relegated to the history of the State. The government knew better than to punish the chief. After all, Little Black Fox was a king of his race, and, however much it might desire to be rid of the turbulent Sioux, it would be a dangerous thing to act with a high hand.

But the matter served as an excuse for one of those mistakes which so often have a far-reaching effect. There was an old fort close by the Pine Ridge Reservation, one of those ancient structures erected by old-time traders. It had long been untenanted, and had fallen into decay. The authorities decided to make it habitable, and turn it into a small military post, garrisoning it with a detachment of about one hundred cavalry.

It was a mistake. And every white man of experience in the district knew that it was so. Even the Agents of the two Reservations sounded a warning note. It is fatal to attempt to bluff the Indian. Bluff and back the bluff. But a handful of cavalry is no backing to any bluff. The older settlers shook their heads; the more timorous dared to hope; even old Roiheim, who would make profit by the adjacency of soldiers, would willingly have foregone the extra trade.

Rube and Seth offered no comment outside their own house; but their opinion was worth considering.

"It won't hurt a heap this side of Christmas," Rube said, on learning the decision.

And Seth pointed his remark.

"No, not now, I guess. Mebbe spring 'll see things."

These two had struck at the heart of the thing. It was late summer, and history has long since proved that Indians never go out on the war-path with winter coming on. Besides, Little Black Fox was not likely to be well of his wound for months.

So the farmers went about their work again. Rube and Seth took in their crops, and devoted spare time to building operations. And the district of White River continued its unobtrusive prosperity.

The loss of Rosebud was no small matter to Ma Sampson's little household. But these folk were far too well inured to the hard life of the plains to voice their troubles. They sometimes spoke of her over their meals, but for the most part bore her silently in their thoughts. And the place she occupied with them was surely one that anybody might envy.

For Seth all the brightness of the last six years had gone out of his life, and he fell back on the almost stern devotion, which had always been his, toward the old people who had raised him. That, and the looking forward to the girl's letters from England practically made up his life. He never permitted himself the faintest hope that he would see her again. He had no thought of marriage with her. If nothing else prevented, her fortune was an impassable barrier. Besides he knew that she would be restored to that life—"high-life," was his word—to which she properly belonged. He never thought or hinted to himself that she would forget them, for he had no bitterness, and was much too loyal to think of her otherwise than as the most true-hearted girl. He simply believed he understood social distinctions thoroughly.

But if he were slow in matters of love, it was his only sloth. In action he was swift and thorough, and his perception in all matters pertaining to the plainsman's life was phenomenal.

It was this disposition for swift action which sent him one day, after the troops had withdrawn to their new post, and the plains had returned to their usual pastoral aspect, in search of Nevil Steyne. And it was significant that he knew just when and where to find his man.

He rode into a clearing in the woods down by the river. The spot was about a mile below the wagon bridge, where the pines grew black and ragged—a touch of the primordial in the midst of a younger growth. It was noon; a time when the plainsman knew he would find the wood-cutter at leisure, taking his midday meal, or lazing over a pipe. Nor were his calculations far out.

Nevil was stretched full length beside the smouldering embers on which his coffee billytin was steaming out fragrant odors that blended pleasantly with the resinous fragrance of these ancient woods.

He looked up at the sound of horse's hoofs, and there could be no doubt about the unfriendliness of his expression when he recognized his visitor. He dropped back again into his lounging attitude at once, and his action was itself one of studied discourtesy.

Seth did not appear to notice anything. He surveyed the clearing with a certain appreciation. The vast timbers he beheld seemed of much more consequence to him than the man who lived by their destruction. However, he rode straight over to the fire and dismounted.

"Howdy?" he said, while he loosened the cinches of his saddle.

"What's brought you around?" asked Nevil, ungraciously enough.

Seth turned toward the trees about him.

"Pretty tidy patch," he observed. "We're wantin' big timbers up at the farm. Mebbe you'd notion a contrac'?"

Nevil had noted the loosening of the cinches. He laughed shortly.

"I'm not taking contracts, thanks. But I'll sell you wood which I cut at my pleasure."

"Cord-wood?" Seth shook his head. "Guess we want timbers. Kind o' buildin' a corral around the farm."

"Making a fort of it?"

Nevil's blue eyes followed the upward curling wreath of smoke which dawdled on the still air above the fire.

"Yup."

"Fancy the Injuns are on the racket?"

"Wal, 'tain't what they're doin' now. But ther' ain't no tellin', an' we're slack since the harvest. I 'lows the notion's tol'ble. Mebbe they'll be quiet some—now Rosebud's gone."

There was a quiet emphasis on Seth's final speculation.

"I heard she'd gone away for a bit."

Nevil looked searchingly at this man whom he hated above all men.

"Gone for good," Seth said, with an admirable air of indifference.

"How?"

Nevil suddenly sat up. Seth noted the fact without even glancing in his direction.

"Wal, y' see she's got folks in England. And ther' is a heap o' dollars; an almighty heap. I reckon she'd be a millionairess in this country. Guess it takes a mighty heap o' bills to reckon a million in your country."

This expansiveness was so unusual in the man of the plains that Nevil understood at once he had come purposely to speak of Rosebud. He wondered why. This was the first he had heard of Rosebud's good fortune, and he wished to know more. The matter had been kept from everybody. Even Wanaha had been kept in ignorance of it.

Seth seated himself on a fallen tree-trunk, and now looked squarely into the wood-cutter's thin, mean face.

"Y' see it's kind o' curious. I got that gal from the Injuns more'n six years back, as you'll likely remember. Her folks, her father an' her ma, was killed south o' the Reservations. Guess they were kind o' big folk in your country. An' ther' was a feller come along awhiles back all the way from England to find her. He was a swell law feller; he'd hit her trail, an' when he comes along he said as she owned 'states in your country, a whole heap. Guess she's to be treated like a queen. Dollars? Gee! She ken buy most everything. I 'lows they ken do it slick in your country."

Seth paused to light his pipe. His manner was exquisitely simple. The narration of the story of the girl's good fortune appeared to give him the keenest pleasure. Nevil removed his pipe from his lips and sat chewing the end of his ragged moustache. There was an ugly look in his eyes as he contemplated the ashes of his fire. He might have been staring at the ashes of his own fortunes. However, he contrived a faint smile when he spoke.

"Then I s'pose you've found out her real name?"

"Sure. Marjorie Raynor. Her father was Colonel Landor Raynor."

"Ah."

"An' ther' ain't no question o' the dollars. She hain't no near folk 'cep' an uncle, Stephen Raynor, an' he don't figger anyways, 'cause the dollars are left to her by will. He only comes in, the lawyer feller says, if the gal was to die, or—or get killed."

Seth had become quite reflective; he seemed to find a curious pleasure in thus discussing the girl he loved with a man he at no time had any use for.

Nevil stared uneasily. A quick, furtive glance at Seth, who at that moment seemed to be watching his horse, gave an inkling of his passing thought. If a look could kill Seth would certainly have been a dead man.

"So the whole thing's a dead cinch for her?"

"Yup. Now."

Nevil gave a short laugh.

"You mean—that matter with Little Black Fox. But she brought it on herself. She encouraged him."

Seth was round on him in a twinkling.

"Maybe he was encouraged — but not by her."

"Who then?"

There was unmistakable derision in the wood-cutter's tone. Seth shrugged. A shadowy smile played round his lips, but his eyes were quite serious.

"That's it," he said, relapsing into his reflective manner, "the whole thing's mighty curious. Them law fellers in your country are smartish. They've located a deal. Don't jest know how. They figger that uncle feller is around either this State or Minnesota — likely this one, seein' the Colonel was comin' this aways when he got killed. We got yarnin', an' he was sayin' he thought o' huntin' out this uncle. I guessed ther' wa'an't much need, an' it might set him wantin' the dollars. The law feller said he wouldn't get 'em anyhow — 'cep' the gal was dead. We kind o' left it at that. Y' see the whole thing for the uncle hung around that gal — bein' dead."

"And you think he might have had something — — " Nevil's words came slowly, like a man who realizes the danger of saying too much.

"Wal, it don't seem possible, I guess. Them two was killed by the Injuns, sure. An' she — I guess she ain't never seen him."

A slight sigh escaped Nevil.

"That's so," he said deliberately.

"Howsum, I guess I'm goin' to look around for this feller. Y' see Rosebud's li'ble to like him. Mebbe he ain't well heeled for dollars, an' she's that tender-hearted she might — I've got his pictur'. Mebbe I'll show it around — eh, what's up?" Seth inquired in his blandest tone.

Nevil suddenly sat up and there was a desperate look in his eyes. But he controlled himself, and, with an effort, spoke indifferently.

"Nothing. I want another pipe."

"Ah." Seth fumbled through his pockets, talking the while. "The pictur' was took when he was most a boy. His hair was thick an' he hadn't no moustache nor nothin', which kind o' makes things hard. As I was sayin', I'm goin' to show it around some, an' maybe some

138

one 'll rec'nize the feller. That's why I got yarnin' to you. Mebbe you ken locate him."

As he said the last word he drew a photograph from his pocket and thrust it into Nevil's hand.

The wood-cutter took it with a great assumption of indifference, and found himself looking down on a result of early photographic art. It was the picture of a very young man with an overshot mouth and a thin, narrow face. But, as Seth had said, he wore no moustache, and his hair was still thick.

Nevil looked long at that picture, and once or twice he licked his lips as though they were very dry. All the time Seth's steady eyes were upon his face, and the shadow of a smile was still about his lips.

At last Nevil looked up and Seth's eyes held his. For a moment the two men sat thus. Then the wood-cutter handed back the photograph and shifted his gaze.

"I've never seen the original of that about these parts," he said a little hoarsely.

"I didn't figger you had," Seth replied, rising and proceeding to tighten up the cinches of his saddle preparatory to departing. "The lawyer feller gave me that. Y' see it's an old pictur'. 'Tain't as fancy as they do 'em now. Mebbe I'll find him later on."

He had swung into his saddle. Nevil had also risen as though to proceed with his work.

"It might be a good thing for him, since Rosebud is so well disposed," Nevil laughed; he had almost recovered himself.

"That's so," observed Seth. "Or a mighty bad thing. Y' can't never tell how dollars 'll fix a man. Dollars has a heap to answer for."

And with this vague remark the plainsman rode slowly away.

CHAPTER XX

SETH PAYS

As the weeks crept by and the torrid heat toned down to the delightful temperature of the Indian summer, news began to reach White River Farm from England. After the first excitement of her arrival had worn off, Rosebud settled down to a regular correspondence.

Even her return to the scenes of her childhood in no way aided her memory. It was all new to her. As her letters often said, though she knew she was grown up, yet, as far as memory served her, she was still only six years old. Servants who had nursed her as a baby, who had cared for her as a child of ten, aunts who had lavished childish presents upon her, cousins who had played with her, they were all strangers, every one.

So she turned with her confidences to those she knew;—those old people on the prairie of Dakota, and that man who had been everything to her. To these she wrote by every mail, giving details of the progress of affairs, telling them of her new life, of her pleasures, her little worries, never forgetting that Ma and Pa were still her mother and father.

Thus they learned that the lawyer's prophecies had been fulfilled. Rosebud was in truth her father's heiress. The courts were satisfied, and she was burdened with heritage under certain conditions of the will. These conditions she did not state, probably a girlish oversight in the rush of events so swiftly passing round her.

The winter stole upon the plains; that hard, relentless winter which knows no yielding till spring drives it forth. First the fierce black frosts, then the snow, and later the shrieking blizzard, battling, tearing for possession of the field, carrying death in its breath for belated man and beast, and sweeping the snow into small mountains about the lonely prairie dwellings as though, in its bitter fury at the presence of man, it would bury them out of sight where its blast proved powerless to destroy them. Christmas and New Year were past, that time of peace and festivity which is kept up wherever man sojourns, be it in city or on the plains.

Through these dark months Seth and Rube worked steadily on building their stockade, hauling the logs, cutting, splitting, joining. The weather made no difference to them. The fiercest storm disturbed them no further than to cause them to set a life-line from house to barn, or to their work, wherever that might be. No blizzard could drive them within doors when work was to be done. This was the life they knew, they had always lived, and they accepted it uncomplainingly, just as they accepted the fruits of the earth in their season.

No warning sound came from the Indians. The settlers forgot the recent episode, forgot the past, which is the way of human nature, and lived in the present only, and looked forward happily to the future.

Seth and Rube minded their own affairs. They were never the ones to croak. But their vigilance never relaxed. Seth resumed his visits to the Reservation as unconcernedly as though no trouble had ever occurred. He went on with his Sunday work at the Mission, never altering his tactics by one iota. And in his silent way he learned all that interested him.

He learned of Little Black Fox's protracted recovery, his lately developed moroseness. He knew whenever a council of chiefs took place, and much of what passed on these occasions. The presence of Nevil Steyne at such meetings was a matter which never failed to interest him. He was rarely seen in the company of the Agent, yet a quiet understanding existed between them, and he frequently possessed news which only Parker could have imparted.

So it was clearly shown that whatever the general opinion of the settlers, Seth, and doubtless Rube also, had their own ideas on the calm of those winter months, and lost no opportunity of verifying them.

New Year found the ponderous stockade round the farm only a little more than half finished in spite of the greatest efforts. Rube had hoped for better results, but the logs had been slow in forthcoming. The few Indians who would work in the winter had been scarcer this year, and, in spite of the Agent, whose duty it was to encourage his charges in accepting and carrying out remunerative labor, the work had been very slow.

At Rube's suggestion it was finally decided to seek white labor in Beacon Crossing. It was more expensive, but it was more reliable. When once the new project had been put into full working order it was decided to abandon the Indian labor altogether.

With this object in view Seth went across to the Reservation to consult Parker. He was met by the Agent's sister. Her brother was out, but she expected him home to dinner, which would be in the course of half an hour.

"He went off with Jim Crow," the amiable spinster told her visitor. "Went off this morning early. He said he was going over to the Pine Ridge Agency. But he took Jim Crow with him, and hadn't any idea of going until the scout came."

Seth ensconced himself in an armchair and propped his feet up on the steel bars of a huge wood stove.

"Ah," he said easily. "Guess there's a deal for him to do, come winter. With your permission I'll wait."

Miss Parker was all cordiality. No man, in her somewhat elderly eyes, was more welcome than Seth. The Agent's sister had once been heard to say, if there was a man to be compared with her brother in the whole country it was Seth. She only wondered he'd escaped being married out of hand by one of the town girls, as she characterized the women of Beacon Crossing. But then she was far more prejudiced in favor of Seth than her own sex.

"He'll be glad, Seth," she said at once; "James is always partial to a chat with you. You just make yourself comfortable right there. I've got a boil of beef and dumplings on, which I know you like. You'll stay and have food?"

"I take that real friendly," said Seth, smiling up into the plain, honest face before him. "Guess I'll have a pipe and a warm while you're fixin' things."

Somehow Miss Parker found herself retiring to her kitchen again before she had intended it.

During the next half hour the hostess found various excuses for invading the parlor where Seth was engaged in his promised occupation. She generally had some cheery, inconsequent remark to pass. Seth gave her little encouragement, but he was always polite. At last the dinner was served, and, sharp to time, Jimmy Parker returned. He came by himself, and blustered into the warm room bringing with him that brisk atmosphere of the outside cold which, in winter, always makes the inside of a house on the prairie strike one as a perfect haven of comfort. He greeted Seth cordially as he shook the frost from his fur-coat collar, and gently released his moustache from its coating of ice.

Seth deferred his business until after dinner. He never liked talking business before womenfolk. And Miss Parker, like most of her sex in the district, was likely to exaggerate the importance of any chance hint about the Indians dropped in her presence. So the boil of silverside and dumplings was discussed to the accompaniment of a casual conversation which was chiefly carried on by the Agent's sister. At length the two men found themselves alone, and their understanding of each other was exampled by the prompt inquiry of Parker.

"Well?" he questioned. Seth settled himself in his chair and, from force of habit, spread his hands out to the fire.

"We're finishing our job with white labor," he said. Then as an afterthought, "Y' see we want to git things fixed 'fore spring opens."

The Agent nodded.

"Just so," he said.

The beads on his moccasins had much interest for Seth at the moment.

"I'd never gamble a pile on Injuns' labor," he remarked indifferently. Parker laughed.

"No. It would be a dead loss—just now."

Seth looked round inquiringly.

"I was wondering when you would give them up," the Agent went on. "I've had a great deal of difficulty keeping them at it. And we're liable, I think, to have more."

The last was said very gravely.

"Kind o' how we've figgered right along?" Seth asked.

"Yes."

The two men relapsed into silence for a while, and smoked on. At last Seth spoke with the air of a man who has just finished reviewing matters of importance in his mind.

"We've taken in the well in fixin' that corral."

"Good. We've got no well here."

"No."

"I was over at Pine Ridge to-day."

"That's what your sister said."

"I went for two reasons. Jim Crow has smelt out preparations for Sun-dances. We can't locate where they are going to be held, or when. I went over to consult Jackson, and also to see how he's getting on over there. He's having the same trouble getting the Indians to look at any work. Little Black Fox is about again. Also he sees a heap too much of that white familiar of his, Nevil Steyne. By Jove, I wish we could fix something on that man and get the government to deport him. He's got a great sway over the chief. What the devil is his object?" Jimmy Parker's face flushed under his exasperation.

"I'd give a heap to git a cinch on him," Seth replied thoughtfully. "He's smart. His tracks are covered every time. Howsum, if things git doin' this spring, I've a notion we'll run him down mebbe— later."

The Agent was all interest.

"Have you discovered anything?"

"Wal—nothin' that counts your way. It's jest personal, 'tween him an' me."

The other laughed cheerfully.

"Couldn't be better," he exclaimed. "I'd sooner it depended on you than on the government."

Seth let the tribute pass.

"We must locate them Sun-dances," he said.

"Yes. We've got troops enough to stop them."

"Troops?—pshaw!"

Seth rose. Parker understood his last remark. The presence of troops had long since been discussed between them. The visitor moved toward the door, and the Agent went to his desk. At the door Seth turned as some thought occurred to him.

"Guess I'd not report anything yet. Not till the Sun-dances are located. I'll git around some." He slipped into his fur coat and turned up the storm collar.

Parker nodded.

"Keep a smart eye for yourself, Seth," he said. "Little Black Fox isn't likely to forget. Especially with Steyne around."

Seth smiled faintly.

"And Steyne 'll kind o' remember, sure." He passed out and left his sturdy friend wondering.

"I'd give something to know," that individual said to himself, when the sound of horse's hoofs had died out. "Seth's dead against Steyne, and I'd like to bet it's over Rosebud."

The object of the Agent's thoughts passed unconcernedly on his way. He branched off the ford trail intending to make for the bridge, below which his men were cutting the timbers for the corral. His way was remote from the chief encampment, and not a single Indian showed himself.

The skeleton woods that lined the trail gave a desolate air to the bleak, white prospect. The whole of that northern world offered little promise to the traveler, little inducement to leave the warmth of house or tepee.

As the horseman neared the bridge he paused to listen. Something of his attitude communicated itself to his horse. The animal's ears were laid back, and it seemed to be listening to some sound behind it. Whatever had attracted master and horse must have been very faint.

A moment later Seth let the horse walk on and the animal appeared content. But if the animal were so, its master was not. He turned several times as he approached the bridge, and scanned the crowding branches on each side of the snow-covered trail behind him.

Seth knew that he was followed. More, he knew that the watcher was clumsy, and had not the stealth of the Indian. At the bridge he faced about and sat waiting. The gravity of his face was relieved by a slight smile.

Suddenly the crack of a rifle rang out. The horseman's smile died abruptly. His horse reared, pawing the air, and he saw blood on the beast's shoulder. He saw that the flesh had been ripped by a glancing bullet, and the course of the wound showed him whence the shot had come.

He looked for the man who had fired, and, as he did so, another shot rang out. He reeled forward in his saddle, but straightened up almost at once, and his right hand flew to his revolver, while he tried to swing his horse about. But somehow he had lost power, and the horse was in a frenzy of terror. The next moment the beast was racing across the bridge in the direction of home.

The journey was made at a great pace. Seth was sitting bolt upright. His face was ashen, and his eyelids drooped in spite of his best efforts.

Rube was in the region of the kitchen door as he galloped up, and he called out a greeting.

The rider began to reply. But, at that moment, the horse propped and halted, and the reply was never finished. Seth rolled out of the saddle and fell to the ground like a log.

CHAPTER XXI

TWO HEADS IN CONSPIRACY

Seth was badly hit; so badly that it was impossible to say how long he might be confined to a sick-room. His left shoulder-blade had been broken by the bullet, which, striking under the arm, had glanced round his ribs, and made its way dangerously adjacent to the spine. Its path was marked by a shocking furrow of lacerated flesh. Though neither gave expression to the thought, both Ma and Rube marveled at the escape he had had, and even the doctor from Beacon Crossing, accustomed as he was to such matters, found food for grave reflection on the ways of Providence.

When the patient recovered consciousness he maintained an impenetrable silence on the subject of the attack made upon him. Parker and Hargreaves protested. The military authorities demanded explanation in vain. To all but the Agent Seth vouchsafed the curtest of replies, and to him he made only a slight concession.

"Guess this is my racket," he said, with just a touch of invalid peevishness. "Mebbe I'll see it thro' my own way—later."

Ma and Rube refrained from question. It was theirs to help, and they knew that if there was anything which Seth had to tell he would tell it in his own time.

But time passed on, and no explanation was forthcoming. Taking their meals together in the kitchen, or passing quiet evenings in the parlor while their patient slept up-stairs, Ma and Rube frequently discussed the matter, but their speculations led them nowhere. Still, as the sick man slowly progressed toward recovery, they were satisfied. It was all they asked.

Rube accepted the burden of the work thus thrust upon him in cheerful silence. There was something horse-like in his willingness for work. He just put forth a double exertion without one single thought of self.

Every week the English mail brought Ma a letter from Rosebud, and ever since Seth had taken up his abode in the sick-room the opening and reading of these long, girlish epistles had become a function reserved for his entertainment. It was a brief ray of sunshine in the gray monotony of his long imprisonment. On these occasions, generally Tuesdays, the entire evening would be spent with the invalid.

They were happy, single-hearted little gatherings. Ma was seated at the bedside in a great armchair before a table on which the letter was spread out. An additional lamp was requisitioned for the occasion, and her glasses were polished until they shone and gleamed in the yellow light. Seth was propped up, and Rube, large, silent, like a great reflective St. Bernard dog, reclined ponderously at the foot of the wooden bedstead. The reading proceeded with much halting and many corrections and rereadings, but with never an interruption from the attentive audience.

The men listened to the frivolous, inconsequent gossip of the girl, now thousands of miles away from them, with a seriousness, a delighted happiness that nothing else in their lives could have afforded them. Comment came afterward, and usually from Ma, the two men merely punctuating her remarks with affirmative or negative monosyllables.

It was on the receipt of one of these letters that Ma saw her way to a small scheme which had been slowly revolving itself in her brain ever since Seth was wounded. Seth had been in the habit of enclosing occasional short notes under cover of the old woman's more bulky and labored replies to the girl. Since his misadventure these, of course, had been discontinued, with the result that now, at last, Rosebud was asking for an explanation.

In reading the letter aloud Ma avoided that portion of it which referred to the matter. Her reason was obviously to keep her own plans from her boy's knowledge, but so clumsily did she skip to another part of the letter, that, all unconscious of it, she drew from her audience a sharp look of inquiry.

Nothing was said at the time, but the following day, at supper, when Ma and Rube were alone, the man, who had taken the whole day to consider the matter, spoke of it in the blunt fashion habitual to him.

"Guess ther' was suthin' in that letter you didn't read, Ma?" he said without preamble.

Ma looked up. Her bright eyes peered keenly through her spectacles into her husband's massive face.

"An' if ther' was?" she said interrogatively.

The old man shrugged.

"Guess I was wonderin'," he said, plying his knife and fork with some show of indifference.

A silence followed. Ma helped herself to more tea and refilled her husband's mug.

"Guess we'll have to tell the child," she said presently.

"Seems like."

A longer silence followed.

"She was jest askin' why Seth didn't write."

"I kind o' figgered suthin' o' that natur'. You'd best tell her."

Rube rested the ends of his knife and fork on the extremities of his plate and took a noisy draught from his huge mug of tea. A quiet smile lurked in the old woman's eyes.

"Rosebud's mighty impulsive," she observed slowly.

"Ef you mean she kind o' jumps at things, I take it that's how."

The old woman nodded, and a reflection of her smile twinkled in her husband's eyes as he gazed over at the little figure opposite him.

"Wal," said Rube, expansively, "it ain't fer me to tell you, Ma, but we've got our dooty. Guess I ain't a heap at writin' fancy notions, but mebbe I ken help some. Y' see it's you an' me. I 'lows Seth would hate to worrit Rosie wi' things, but as I said we've got our dooty, an' it seems— —"

"Dooty?" Ma chuckled. "Say, Rube, we'll write to the girl, you an' me. An' we don't need to ask no by-your-leave of nobody. Not even Seth."

"Not even Seth."

The two conspirators eyed one another slyly, smiled with a quaint knowingness, and resumed their supper in silence.

A common thought, a common hope, held them. Neither would have spoken it openly, even though no one was there to overhear. Each felt that they were somehow taking advantage of Seth and, perhaps, not doing quite the right thing by Rosebud; but after all they were old, simple people who loved these two, and had never quite given up the hope of seeing them ultimately brought together.

The meal was finished, and half an hour later they were further working out their mild conspiracy in the parlor. Ma was the scribe, and was seated at the table surrounded by all the appurtenances of her business. Rube, in a great mental effort, was clouding the atmosphere with the reeking fumes of his pipe. The letter was a delicate matter, and its responsibility sat heavily on this man of the plains. Ma was less embarrassed; her woman's instinct helped her. Besides, since Rosebud had been away she had almost become used to writing letters.

"Say, Rube," she said, looking up after heading her note-paper, "how d' you think it'll fix her when she hears?"

Rube gazed at the twinkling eyes raised to his; he gave a chuckling grunt, and his words came with elephantine meaning.

"She'll be all of a muss-up at it."

Ma's smile broadened.

"What's makin' you laff, Ma?" the old man asked.

"Jest nuthin'. I was figgerin' if the gal could—if we could git her reply before spring opens."

"Seems likely—if the boat don't sink."

Ma put the end of her pen in her mouth and eyed her man. Rube scratched his head and smoked hard. Neither spoke. At last the woman jerked out an impatient inquiry.

"Well?" she exclaimed.

Rube removed his pipe from his lips with great deliberation and eased himself in his chair.

"You've located the name of the farm on top, an' the State, an' the date?" he inquired, by way of gaining time.

"Guess I ain't daft, Rube."

"No." The man spoke as though his answer were the result of deliberate thought. Then he cleared his throat, took a long final pull at his pipe, removed it from his mouth, held it poised in the manner of one who has something of importance to say, and sat bolt upright. "Then I guess we ken git right on." And having thus clearly marked their course he sat back and complacently surveyed his wife.

But the brilliancy of his suggestion was lost on Ma, and she urged him further.

"Well?"

"Wal—I'd jest say, 'Honored Lady,'" he suggested doubtfully.

"Mussy on the man, we're writin' to Rosebud!" exclaimed the old woman.

"Sure." Rube nodded patronizingly, but he seemed a little uncomfortable under his wife's stare of amazement. "But," he added, in a tone meant to clinch the argument, "she ain't 'Rosebud' no longer."

"Rubbish an' stuff! She's 'Rosebud'—jest 'Rosebud.' An' 'dearest Rosebud' at that, an' so I've got it," Ma said, hurriedly writing the words as she spoke. "Now," she went on, looking up, "you can git on wi' the notions to foller."

Again Rube cleared his throat. Ma watched him, chewing the end of her penholder the while. The man knocked his pipe out and slowly began to refill it. He looked out the window into the blackness of the winter night. His vast face was heavy with thought, and his shaggy gray brows were closely knit. As she watched, the old woman's bright eyes smiled. Her thoughts had gone back to their courting days. She thought of the two or three letters Rube had contrived to send her, which were still up-stairs in an old trunk containing her few treasures. She remembered that these letters had, in each case, begun with "Honored Lady." She wondered where he had obtained the notion which still remained with him after all these years.

Feeling the silence becoming irksome Rube moved uneasily.

"Y' see it's kind o' del'cate. Don't need handlin' rough," he said. "Seems you'd best go on like this. Mebbe you ken jest pop it down rough-like an' fix it after. 'Which it's my painful dooty an' pleasure— —'"

"La, but you always was neat at fixin' words, Rube," Ma murmured, while she proceeded to write. "How's this?" she went on presently, reading what she had just written. "I'm sorry to have to tell you as Seth's got hurt pretty bad. He's mighty sick, an' liable to be abed come spring. Pore feller, he's patient as he always is, but he's all mussed-up an' broken shocking; shot in the side an' got bones smashed up. Howsum, he's goin' on all right, an' we hope for the best."

"I 'lows that's neat," Rube said, lighting his pipe. "'Tain't jest what I'd fancy. Sounds kind o' familiar. An' I guess it's li'ble to scare her some."

"Well?"

"Wal, I tho't we'd put it easy-like."

Ma looked a little scornful. Rube was certainly lacking in duplicity.

"Say, Rube, you ain't a bit smarter than when you courted me. I jest want that gal to think it's mighty bad."

"Eh?" Rube stared.

Ma was getting impatient.

"I guess you never could see a mile from your own nose, Rube; you're that dull an' slow wher' gals is concerned. I'll write this letter in my own way. You'd best go an' yarn with Seth. An' you needn't say nuthin' o' this to him. We'll git a quick answer from Rosebud, or I'm ter'ble slow 'bout some things, like you."

The cloud of responsibility suddenly lifted from the farmer's heavy features. He smiled his relief at his partner in conspiracy. He knew that in such a matter as the letter he was as much out of place as one of his own steers would be. Ma, he was convinced, was one of the cleverest of her sex, and if Seth and Rosebud were ever to be brought together again she would do it. So he rose, and, moving round to the back of his wife's chair, laid his great hand tenderly on her soft, gray hair.

"You git right to it, Ma," he said. "We ain't got no chick of our own. Ther's jest Seth to foller us, an' if you ken help him out in this thing, same as you once helped me out, you're doin' a real fine thing. The boy ain't happy wi'out Rosebud, an' ain't never like to be. You fix it, an' I'll buy you a noo buggy. Guess I'll go to Seth."

Ma looked up at the gigantic man, and the tender look she gave him belied the practical brusqueness of her words.

"Don't you git talkin' foolish. Ther' was a time when I'd 'a' liked you to talk foolish, but you couldn't do it then, you were that slow. Git right along. I'll fix this letter, an' read it to you when it's done."

Rube passed out of the room, gurgling a deep-throated chuckle, while his wife went steadily on with the all-important matter in hand.

CHAPTER XXII

ROSEBUD'S ANSWER

It was a dazzling morning nearly five weeks after the dispatching of Ma Sampson's letter to Rosebud. The heralds of spring, the warm, southern breezes, which brought trailing flights of geese and wild duck winging northward, and turned the pallor of the snow to a dirty drab hue, like a soiled white dress, had already swept across the plains. The sunlight was fiercely blinding. Even the plainsman is wary at this time of the year, for the perils of snow-blindness are as real to him as to the "tenderfoot."

There had been no reply from Rosebud. Two more letters from her reached the farm, but they had been written before the letter, which Rube helped to compose, had been received. Since then no word had come from the girl. Ma was satisfied, and accepted her silence with equanimity, but for appearances' sake assumed an attitude of complaint. Rube said nothing; he had no subtlety in these matters. Seth was quite in the dark. He never complained, but he was distressed at this sudden and unaccountable desertion.

Seth's wound and broken shoulder had healed. He had been up a week, but this was his first day out of the house. Now he stood staring out with shaded eyes in the direction of the Reservations. During the past week he had received visits from many of the neighboring settlers. Parker, particularly, had been his frequent companion. He had learned all that it was possible for him to learn by hearsay of the things which most interested him; but, even so, he felt that he had much time to make up, much to learn that could come only from his own observation.

Now, on this his first day out in the open, he found himself feeling very weak, a thin, pale shadow of his former self. Curiously enough he had little inclination for anything. He simply stood gazing upon the scene before him, drinking in deep draughts of the pure, bracing, spring air. Though his thoughts should have been with those matters which concerned the welfare of the homestead, they were thousands of miles away, somewhere in a London of his own imagination, among people he had never seen, looking on at a life and pleasures of which he had no knowledge of, and through it all he was struggling to understand how it was Rosebud had come to forget them all so utterly, and so suddenly.

He tried to make allowances, to point out to himself the obligations of the girl's new life. He excused her at every point; yet, when it was all done, when he had proved to himself the utter impossibility of her keeping up a weekly correspondence, he was   dissatisfied, disappointed. There was something behind it all, some reason which he could not fathom.

In the midst of these reflections he was joined by Rube. The old man was smoking his after-breakfast pipe.

"She's openin'," he said, indicating the brown patches of earth already showing through the snow. Seth nodded.

They were standing just outside the great stockade which had been completed during Seth's long illness. There were only the gates waiting to be hung upon their vast iron hinges.

After the old man's opening remark a long silence fell. Seth's thoughts ran on unchecked in spite of the other's presence. Rube smoked and watched the lean figure beside him out of the corners of his eyes. He was speculating, too, but his thought was of their own immediate surroundings. Now that Seth was about again he felt that it would be good to talk with him. He knew there was much to consider. Though perhaps he lacked something of the younger man's keen Indian knowledge he lacked nothing in experience, and experience told him that the winter, after what had gone before, had been, but for the one significant incident of Seth's wound, very, very quiet—too quiet.

"Say, boy," the old man went on, some minutes later, "guess you ain't yarned a heap 'bout your shootin' racket?"

Seth was suddenly brought back to his surroundings. His eyes thoughtfully settled on the distant line of woodland that marked the river and the Reservation. He answered readily enough.

"That shootin' don't affect nothin'—nothin' but me," he said with meaning.

"I thought Little— —"

Seth shook his head. He took Rube's meaning at once.

"That's to come, I guess," he said gravely.

Rube suddenly looked away down the trail in the direction of Beacon Crossing. His quick ears had caught an unusual sound. It was a "Coo-ee," but so thin and faint that it came to him like the cry of some small bird. Seth heard it, too, and he turned and gazed over the rotting sleigh track which spring was fast rendering impassable. There was nothing in sight. Just the gray expanse of melting snow, dismal, uninteresting even in the flooding sunlight.

Rube turned back to the gateway of the stockade. His pipe was finished and he had work to do. Seth was evidently in no mood for talk.

"I'd git around and breathe good air fer awhiles," he said kindly, "y' ain't goin' to git strong of a sudden, Seth."

"Guess I'll ride this afternoon. Hello!"

The cry reached them again, louder, still high-pitched and shrill, but nearer. Away down the trail a figure in black furs was moving toward them.

Both men watched the object with the keenest interest. It was a mere speck on the gray horizon, but it was plainly human, and evidently wishful to draw their attention.

"Some'un wantin' us?" said Rube in a puzzled tone.

"Seems." Seth was intent upon the figure.

Another "Coo-ee" rang out, and Rube responded with his deep guttural voice. And, in answer, the bundle of furs raised two arms and waved them beckoningly.

Rube moved along the trail. Without knowing quite why, but roused to a certain curiosity, he was going to meet the newcomer. Seth followed him.

Seth's gait was slower than the older man's, and he soon dropped behind. Suddenly he saw Rube stop and turn, beckoning him on. When he came up the old man pointed down the road.

"It's a woman," he said, and there was a curious look in his eyes.

The muffled figure was more than a hundred and fifty yards away, but still laboriously stumbling along the snow-bound trail toward them.

Before Seth could find a reply another "Coo-ee" reached them, followed quickly by some words that were blurred by the distance. Seth started. The voice had a curiously familiar sound. He glanced at Rube, and the old man's face wore a look of grinning incredulity.

"Sounds like— —" Seth began to speak but broke off.

"Gee! Come on!" cried Rube, in a boisterous tone. "It's Rosebud!"

The two men hastened forward. Rube's announcement seemed incredible. How could it be Rosebud—and on foot? The surface of the trail gave way under their feet at almost every step. But they were undeterred. Slush or ice, deep snow or floundering in water holes, it made no difference. It was a race for that muffled figure, and Rube was an easy winner. When Seth came up he found the bundle of furs in the bear-like embrace of the older man. It was Rosebud!

Questions raced through Seth's brain as he looked on, panting with the exertion his enfeebled frame had been put to. How? Why? What was the meaning of it all? But his questions remained unspoken. Nor was he left in doubt long. Rosebud laughing, her wonderful eyes dancing with an inexpressible delight, released herself and turned to Seth. Immediately her face fell as she looked on the shadow of a man standing before her.

"Why, Seth," she cried, in a tone of great pity and alarm that deceived even Rube, "what's the matter that you look so ill?" She turned swiftly and flashed a meaning look into Rube's eyes. "What is it? Quick! Oh, you two sillies, tell me! Seth, you've been ill, and you never told me!"

Slow of wit, utterly devoid of subterfuge as Rube was, for once he grasped the situation.

"Why, gal, it's jest nothin'. Seth's been mighty sick, but he's right enough now, ain't you, Seth, boy?"

"Sure."

Seth had nothing to add, but he held out his hand, and the girl seized it in both of hers, while her eyes darkened to an expression which these men failed to interpret, but which Ma Sampson could have read aright. Seth cleared his throat, and his dark eyes gazed beyond the girl and down the trail.

"How'd you come, Rosie?" he asked practically. "You ain't traipsed from Beacon?"

Suddenly the girl's laugh rang out. It was the old irresponsible laugh that had always been the joy of these men's hearts, and it brought a responsive smile to their faces now.

"Oh, I forgot," she cried. "The delight of seeing you two dears put it out of my silly head. Why, we drove out from Beacon, and the wagon's stuck in a hollow away back, and my cousin, I call her 'aunt,' and her maid, and all the luggage are mired on the road, calling down I don't know what terrible curses upon the country and its people, and our teamster in particular. So I just left them to it and came right on to get help. Auntie was horrified at my going, you know. Said I'd get rheumatic fever and pneumonia, and threatened to take me back home if I went, and I told her she couldn't unless I got help to move the wagon, and so here I am."

Rube's great face had never ceased to beam, and now, as the girl paused for breath, he turned for home.

"Guess I'll jest get the team out. Gee!" And he went off at a great gait.

Seth looked gravely at the girl's laughing face.

"Guess you'd best come on home. Mebbe your feet *are* wet."

Thus, after months of parting, despite the changed conditions of the girl's life, the old order was resumed. Rosebud accepted Seth's domination as though it was his perfect right. Without one word or thought of protest she walked at his side. In silence he helped her over the broken trail to the home she had so long known and still claimed. Once only was that silence broken. It was when the girl beheld the fortified appearance of the farm. She put her question in a low, slightly awed tone.

"What's all this for, Seth?" she asked. She knew, but she felt that she must ask.

"Them logs?" The man responded indifferently.

"Yes, that stockade."

"Oh, jest nothin'. Y' see we need a bit o' fence-like."

Rosebud looked at him from out of the corners of her eyes as she trudged at his side.

"I'm glad I came, Seth. I'm just in time. Poor auntie!"

The next moment her arms were around Ma Sampson's neck, hugging the old woman, who had heard of the girl's arrival from Rube and had come out to meet her.

"La sakes, come right in at once, Rosie, gal!" she exclaimed, when she was permitted a chance of speech. And laughing and chattering in the very wildest delight, Rosebud led the way and romped into the house.

In the dear familiar kitchen, after the girl had gazed at the various simple furnishings she had so long known and loved, she poured out her tale, the reason of her coming, with a blissful disregard for truth. Ma took her cue and listened to the wonderful fabrication the girl piled up for her astonished ears, and more particularly Seth's. Apparently the one thing that had not entered into her madcap considerations was Seth's illness.

Just as her story came to an end, and the sound of wheels outside warned them of the arrival of the wagon, Rosebud turned upon Seth with something of her old wilful impetuosity.

"And now, Seth," she said, her eyes dancing with audacity and mischief, "you're a sick man and all that, so there's every excuse for you, but you haven't said you're glad to see me."

Seth smiled thoughtfully as he gazed on the fair, trim-figured woman challenging him. He noted with a man's pleasure the perfectly fitting tailor-made traveling costume, the beautifully arranged hair, the delightful Parisian hat. He looked into the animated face, the only thing about her that seemed to be as of old.

Though he saw that her outward appearance was changed, even improved, he knew that that was all. It was the same Rosebud, the same old spirit, honest, fearless, warm-hearted, loving, that looked out of her wondrous eyes, and he felt his pulses stir and something like a lump rose in his throat as he answered her.

"Wal, little gal, I guess you don't need me to tell you. Pleased! that don't cut no meanin'. Yet I'm kind o' sorry too. Y' see ther's things——"

Ma interrupted him.

"He's right, Rosebud dear, it's a bad time."

The girl's reply came with a laugh full of careless mischief and confidence.

"Poor auntie!" Then she became suddenly serious. "They're outside," she went on. "Let us go and bring her in."

A moment later Ma found herself greeting Rosebud's second cousin and chaperone. Mrs. Rickards was an elderly lady, stout, florid, and fashionably dressed, who had never been further afield in her life than the Europe of society.

Her greeting was an effort. She was struggling to conceal a natural anger and resentment against the inconvenience of their journey from Beacon Crossing, and the final undignified catastrophe of the wagon sticking fast in the slush and mud on the trail, and against Rosebud in particular, under a polite attempt at cordiality. She would probably have succeeded in recovering her natural good-humored composure but for the girl herself, who, in the midst of the good creature's expostulations, put the final touch to her mischief. Mrs. Rickards had turned solicitously upon her charge with an admonitory finger raised in her direction.

"And as for Rosie,—she insists on being called Rosebud still, Mrs. Sampson—after her tramp through all that dreadful snow and slush she must be utterly done up," she said kindly.

"Done up, auntie? Tired?" the girl said, with a little scornful laugh. "Don't you believe it. Why the fun's only just beginning, isn't it, Seth? Do you know, auntie dear, the Indians are getting troublesome; they're going out on the war-path. Aren't they, Seth? And we're just in time to get scalped."

But Seth had no responsive smile for the girl's sally. His face was grave enough as he turned to the horrified woman.

"Ma'am," he said, in that slow drawling fashion which gave so much gravity and dignity to his speech, "I'll take it kindly if you won't gamble a heap on this little gal's nonsense. I've known her some few years, an' I guess she's nigh the worst savage in these parts—which, I guess, says a deal."

Seth's rebuke lost nothing of its sharpness by reason of the gentle manner in which it was spoken. Rosebud felt its full force keenly. She flushed to the roots of her hair and her eyes were bright with resentment. She pouted her displeasure and, without a word, abruptly left the room.

Ma and Mrs. Rickards—the latter's composure quite restored by Seth's reassurance—looked after her. Both smiled.

Seth remained grave. The girl's mischief had brought home to him the full responsibility which devolved upon Rube and himself.

Truly it was the old Rosebud who had returned to White River Farm.

CHAPTER XXIII

LOVE'S PROGRESS

It was the night of Rosebud's arrival. Seth and Rube were just leaving the barn. The long day's work was done. Seth had been out all the afternoon riding. Although his ride was nominally in pursuit of health and strength, he had by no means been idle. Now he was bodily weary, and at the door of the barn he sat down on the corn-bin. Rube, pausing to prepare his pipe, saw, by the flickering light of the stable lantern, that his companion's face was ghastly pale.

"Feelin' kind o' mean?" he suggested with gruff sympathy.

"Meaner'n a yaller dawg."

There was anxiety in the older man's deep-set eyes as he noted the flicker of a smile which accompanied the reply.

"There ain't nothin' fresh?" Rube pursued, as the other remained silent.

"Wal, no, 'cep' Rosebud's got back."

"How?"

Seth shrugged.

"Guess it means a heap," he said, and paused. Then a faint flush slowly spread over his thin, drawn face. "Nothin' could 'a' happened along now wuss than Rosie's gettin' around," he went on with intense feeling. "Can't you see, Rube?" He reached out and laid an emphatic hand on his companion's arm. "Can't you see what's goin' to come? Ther's trouble comin' sure. Trouble for us all. Trouble for that gal. The news is around the Reservation now. It'll reach Black Fox 'fore to-morrow mornin', an' then— —Pshaw! Rube, I love that gal. She's more to me than even you an' Ma; she's more to me than life. I can't never marry her, seein' how things are, but that don't cut no figger. But I'm goin' to see after her whatever happens. Ther' ain't no help comin'. Them few soldier-fellers don't amount to a heap o' beans. The Injuns 'll chaw 'em up if they notion it. An' I'm like a dead man, Rube—jest a hulk. God, Rube, if harm comes to that pore gal— —Pshaw!"

Seth's outburst was so unusual that Rube stared in silent amazement. It seemed as if his bodily weakness had utterly broken down the stern self-repression usually his. It was as though with the weakening of muscle had come a collapse of his wonderful self-reliance, and against his will he was driven to seek support.

Rube removed his pipe from his mouth. His slow moving brain was hard at work. His sympathy was not easy for him to express.

"Guess it ain't easy, Seth, boy," he said judicially, at last. "Them things never come easy if a man's a man. I've felt the same in the old days, 'fore Ma an' me got hitched. Y' see the Injuns wus wuss them days—a sight. Guess I jest sat tight."

Though so gently spoken, the old man's words had instant effect. Already Seth was ashamed of his weakness. He knew, no one better, the strenuous life of single-hearted courage this old man had lived.

"I'm kind o' sorry I spoke, Rube. But I ain't jest thinkin' o' myself."

"I know, boy. You're jest worritin' 'cause you're sick. I know you. You an' me are goin' to set tight. Your eye 'll be on the gal; guess I'll figger on Ma. These sort o' troubles jest come and go. I've seen 'em before. So've you. It's the gal that makes the diff'rence fer you. Say, lad," Rube laid a kindly hand on the sick man's drooping shoulders, and his manner became lighter, and there was a twinkle in his deep-set eyes, "when I'd located that I wanted Ma fer wife I jest up an' sez so. I 'lows the job wa'n't easy. I'd a heap sooner 'a' let daylight into the carkises of a dozen Injuns. Y' see wimmin's li'ble to fool you some. When they knows you're fixed on 'em they jest makes you hate yourself fer a foolhead. It's in the natur' of 'em. They're most like young fillies 'fore they're broke—I sez it wi'out disrespec'. Y' see a wummin ain't got a roarin' time of it in this world. An' jest about when a man gets fixed on 'em is their real fancy time, an' they ain't slow to take all ther' is comin'. An' I sez they're dead right. An' jest when you're bustin' to tell 'em how you're feelin'—an' ain't got the savee—they're jest bustin' to hear that same. An' that's how I got figgerin' after awhiles, an' so I ups an' has it out squar'. Y' see," he finished, with an air of pride which brought a smile to Seth's face, "I kind o' swep' Ma off her feet."

The younger man had no reply to make. His mind went back to Ma's version of Rube's courtship. Rube, thoroughly enjoying his task of rousing the other's drooping spirits, went on, carried away by his own enthusiasm.

"Say, why has Rosie come back, boy, I'd like to know."

"She said as she couldn't endure a city no longer. She wanted the plains, the Injuns, Ma, you, an' the farm."

"Pshaw—boy! Plains! Farm! Injuns! Ha, ha! Say, Seth, you ain't smart, not wuth a cent. She come back 'cos she's jest bustin' to hear what you darsen't tell her. She's come back 'cos she's a wummin, an' couldn't stay away when you wus sick an' wounded to death. I know. I ain't bin married fer five an' twenty year an' more wi'out gittin' to the bottom o' female natur'—I——"

"But she didn't know I was sick, Rube."

"Eh?"

Rube stood aghast at what he had said. Seth's remark had, in his own way of thinking, "struck him all of a heap." He realized in a flash where his blundering had led him. He had run past himself in his enthusiasm, and given Ma's little scheme away, and, for the moment, the enormity of his offence robbed him of the power of speech. However, he pulled himself together with an effort.

"Guess I wus chawin' more'n I could swaller," he said ruefully. "Ma allus did say my head wus mostly mutton, an' I kind o' figger she has a power o' wisdom. An' it wus a dead secret—'tween her an' me. Say, Seth, boy, you won't give me away? Y' see Ma's mighty easy, but she's got a way wi' her, Ma has."

The old man's distress was painfully comical. The perspiration stood out on his rugged forehead in large beads, and his kindly eyes were full of a great trouble. Seth's next remark came in the form of an uncompromising question.

"Then Ma wrote an' told her?"

"Why, yes, if it comes to that I guess she must have."

Seth rose wearily from his seat, and ranged his lean figure beside the old man's bulk. "All right, dad," he said, in his quiet, sober way. "I'm glad you've told me. But it don't alter nothin', I guess. Meanwhile I'll git round, an' quit whinin'."

The arrival of Rosebud's cousin and her maid somewhat disorganized the Sampsons' simple household. Rosebud's love of mischief was traceable in this incongruous descent upon the farm. Her own coming was a matter which no obstacle would have stayed. Ma's letter had nearly broken her heart, and her anxiety was absolutely pitiable until the actual start had been made.

That Seth was ill—wounded—and she had not known from the first, had distracted her, and her mind was made up before she had finished reading the letter. Her obligations to her new life were set aside without a second thought. What if there were invitations to social functions accepted? What if her cousin's household were thrown into confusion by her going? These things were nothing to her; Seth might be dying, and her heart ached, and something very like terror urged her to hasten.

She had long since learned that Seth, and Seth alone, was all her world. Then the old mischievous leaning possessed her, and she resolved, willy-nilly, that Mrs. Rickards, whose love she had long since won, as she won everybody's with whom she came into contact, should accompany her.

This old lady, used only to the very acme of comfort, had welcomed the idea of visiting Rosebud's home in the wilds. Moreover, until the final stage of the journey, she thoroughly enjoyed herself. It was not until traveling from Beacon Crossing, and the camping out at the half-way house, that the roughness of the country was brought home to her. Then came the final miring of the wagon, and she reviled the whole proceeding.

But the ultimate arrival at the farm, and the meeting with its homely folk, soon restored her equanimity. She at once warmed to Ma, whose gentle practical disposition displayed such a wealth of true womanliness as to be quite irresistible, and, in the confidence of her bedchamber, which she shared with Rosebud, she imparted her favorable impressions. She assured the girl she no longer wondered that she, Rosebud, with everything that money could purchase, still longed to return to the shelter of the love which these rough frontier-folk so surely lavished upon her.

"But, my dear," she added, as a warning proviso, and with a touch of worldliness which her own life in England had made almost part of her nature, "though Mrs. Sampson is so deliciously simple and good, and Mr. Sampson is such an exquisite rough diamond, this Seth, whose trouble has brought us out here, with such undignified haste, is not the man to make the fuss about that you have been doing all the journey. He's a fine man, or will be when he recovers from his illness, I have no doubt; but, after all, I feel it my duty by your dead father to warn you that I think you are much too concerned about him for a girl in your position."

"What on earth do you mean, auntie?" Rosebud exclaimed, pausing in the process of brushing out her obstinately curling hair. "What position have I but that which these dear people have helped me to—that Seth, himself, has made for me? I owe all I have, or am at this moment, to Seth. He saved me from a fate too terrible to contemplate. He has saved my life, not once, but half a dozen times; he found me my father's fortune, or the fortune which father has left for me when I marry. You are more unkind than ever I thought you could be. You wait, auntie, you may yet learn to—to appreciate Seth as I do. You see I know—you don't. You're good, and wise, and all that; but you don't know—Seth."

"And it's very evident that you think you do, dear," Mrs. Rickards said, wearily rolling over and snuggling down amidst the snowy sheets of the soft feather-bed.

"There is no question of thinking," Rosebud smiled mischievously into the looking-glass in the direction of her relative. "And if Seth were to ask me I would marry him to-morrow—there. Yes, and I'd make him get a special license to avoid unnecessary delay."

Of a sudden Mrs. Rickards started up in bed. For one moment she severely eyed the girl's laughing face. Then her anger died out, and she dropped back on the pillow.

"For the moment I thought you meant it," she said.

"And so I do," was the girl's swift retort. "But there," as a horrified exclamation came from the bed, "he won't ask me, auntie," the girl went on, with a dash of angry impatience in her voice, "so you needn't worry. Seth has a sense of honor which I call quixotic, and one that might reasonably shame the impecunious fortune-hunters I've met since I have lived in England. No, I'm afraid if I were to marry Seth it wouldn't be his doing."

"This Seth said you were a savage—and he's right."

With this parting shot Mrs. Rickards turned over, and, a moment later, was comfortably asleep, as her heavy breathing indicated. Rosebud remained a long time at the dressing-table, but her hair didn't trouble her. Her head was bowed on her arms, and she was quietly weeping. Nor could she have explained her tears. They were the result of a blending of both joy and sorrow. Joy at returning to the farm and at finding Seth on the highroad to recovery; and sorrow—who shall attempt to probe the depths of this maiden's heart?

The day following Rosebud's return was a momentous one. True to her impulsive character the girl, unknown to anybody, saddled her own mare and rode off on a visit to Wanaha. Seth was away from the farm, or he would probably have stopped her. Rube knew nothing of her going, and Ma had her time too much occupied with Mrs. Rickards and her maid to attend to anything but her household duties. So Rosebud was left to her own devices, which, as might have been expected, led her to do the one thing least desirable.

Wanaha was overjoyed at the girl's return. The good Indian woman had experienced a very real sense of loss, when, without even a farewell, Rosebud suddenly departed from their midst. Added to this Wanaha had had a pretty bad time with her husband after the affair in the river woods. Abnormally shrewd where all others were concerned, she was utterly blind in her husband's favor. His temper suddenly soured with Rosebud's going, and the loyal wife suffered in consequence. Yet she failed to appreciate the significance of the change.

There was no suspicion in her mind of the manner in which she had foiled his plans, or even of the nature of them. The attempt to kidnap the white girl she put down to the enterprise of her brother's fierce, lawless nature, and as having nothing whatever to do with her husband. In fact she still believed it was of that very danger which Nevil had wanted to warn Rosebud.

Now, when the girl suddenly burst in upon her, Wanaha was overjoyed, for she thought she had surely left the prairie world forever. They spent the best part of the morning together. Then Nevil came in for his dinner. When he beheld the girl, fair and deliciously fresh in her old prairie habit, sitting on the bed in the hut, a wave of devilish joy swept over him. He already knew that she had returned to the farm—how, it would have been impossible to say—but that she should still come to his shack seemed incredible.

Evidently Seth had held his tongue. Though he wondered a little uneasily at the reason, he was quick to see his advantage and the possibilities opening before him. He had passed from the stage when he was content to avail himself of chance opportunities. Now he would seek them—he would make opportunities.

"And so you have come back to us again," he said, after greeting the girl, while Wanaha smiled with her deep black eyes upon them from the table beyond the stove.

"Couldn't stay away," the girl responded lightly. "The prairie's in my bones."

Rosebud had never liked Nevil. To her there was something fish-like in those pale eyes and overshot jaw, but just now everybody connected with the old life was welcome. They chatted for a while, and presently, as Wanaha began to put the food on the table, the girl rose to depart.

"It's time I was getting home," she said reluctantly. "I'm not sure that they know where I am, so I mustn't stay away too long—after the scrape I got into months ago. I should like to go across to the Reservation, but I've already promised not to go there alone. Seth warned me against it, and after what has passed I know he's right. But I would like to see Miss Parker, and dear old Mr. Hargreaves. However, I must wait."

Nevil crossed over to the table. He looked serious, but his blue eyes shone.

"Seth's quite right. You mustn't go alone. Little Black Fox is about again, you know. And — and the people are very restless just now."

"That's what he said. And I nearly frightened auntie to death telling her she'd get scalped, and nonsense like that."

Nevil laughed in response.

"If you'd like to go — —" he began doubtfully.

"It doesn't matter."

"I only meant I've got to go across directly after dinner. I could accompany you. No one will interfere with you while I am there."

Nevil turned to his food with apparent indifference. Wanaha stood patiently by. Rosebud was tempted. She wanted to see the Reservation again with that strange longing which all people of impulse have for revisiting the scenes of old associations. Always she was possessed by that curious fascination for the Indian country which was something stronger than mere association, something that had to do with the long illness she had passed through nearly seven years ago.

Nevil waited. He knew by the delay of her answer that she would accept his invitation, and he wanted her to go over to the Reservation.

"Are you sure I shan't be in the way? Sure I'm not troubling you?"

Nevil smiled.

"By no means. Just let me have my dinner, and I'll be ready. I've half a dozen cords of wood to haul into Beacon, and I have to go and borrow ponies for the work. The roads are so bad just now that my own ponies couldn't do it by themselves."

Rosebud's scruples thus being quieted she returned to her seat on the bed, and they talked on while the man ate his dinner. She watched the almost slavish devotion of Wanaha with interest and sympathy, but her feelings were all for the tall, beautiful woman. For the man she had no respect. She tolerated him because of her friend only.

An hour later they were on the Reservation. And they had come by way of the ford. Rosebud was all interest, and everything else was forgotten, even her dislike of Nevil, as they made their way past Little Black Fox's house, and through the encampment of which it was the centre. She was still more delighted when her companion paused and spoke to some of the Indians idling about there. She was free to watch the squaws, and the papooses she loved so well. The little savages were running wild about the tepees, dodging amongst the trailers and poles, or frolicking with the half-starved currish camp dogs. The air was busy with shrieks of delight, and frequently through it all could be detected the note of small ferocity, native to these little red-skinned creatures.

It was all so familiar to her, so homely, so different from that other life she had just left. The past few months were utterly forgotten; she was back in her old world again. Back in the only world she really knew and loved.

It came as no sort of surprise to her, when, in the midst of this scene, the great chief himself appeared. He came alone, without ceremony or attendants. He stood in the midst of the clearing—tall, commanding, and as handsome as ever. His dusky face was wreathed in a proud, half disdainful smile. He did not attempt to draw near, and, except for a haughty inclination of the head, made no sign.

Rosebud had no suspicion. She had no thought of the man with her. She was far too interested in all she saw to wonder how the chief came to be in the midst of the clearing just as she was passing through it.

On the far side of the camp a path led to the Agency. Its course was tortuous, winding in the shape of the letter S. It was at the second curve that an unexpected, and to Nevil, at least, unwelcome meeting occurred.

Seth, mounted on his own tough broncho, was standing close against the backing of brush which lined the way. He had every appearance of having been awaiting their coming. Nevil's furtive eyes turned hither and thither with the quick glance of a man who prefers a safe retreat to a bold encounter.

Rosebud looked serious, and thought of the scolding that might be forthcoming. Then she laughed and urged her horse quickly forward.

"Why, Seth——" she cried. But she broke off abruptly. The rest of what she was about to say died out of her mind. Seth was not even looking at her. His eyes were on Nevil Steyne in a hard, cold stare. Physically weak as he was there could be no mistaking the utter hatred conveyed in that look.

Rosebud had drawn up beside him. For once she was at a loss, helpless. Nevil was some ten yards in rear of her. There was a moment's silence after the girl's greeting, then Seth said quite sharply—

"You stay right here."

He urged his horse forward and went to meet Nevil. The girl was very anxious, hardly knowing why. She heard Seth's voice low but commanding. His words were lost upon her, but their effect was plain enough. Nevil first smiled contemptuously, then he paled and finally turned his horse about, and slowly returned the way he had come.

Then, and not until then, Rosebud observed that Seth was grasping the butt of his revolver.

CHAPTER XXIV

ROSEBUD'S FORTUNE

Something of the old spirit seemed to have gone out of Rosebud when Seth rode back to her. A strange fascination held her; and now, as he came up, she had no thought of questioning him, no desire. She was ready to obey. She watched the emaciated figure as it drew near with eyes that told a story which only he could have misinterpreted. She was ready for a scolding, a scolding which she felt she merited. But Seth made no attempt to blame her. And this very fact made her wish that he would.

"Say, Rosie, gal, I guess we'll be gettin' back," he said, in a manner which suggested that they had been out together merely, and that it was time for returning.

"Yes, Seth."

There was unusual humility in the reply. It may have been that the girl remembered that scene in the woods so many months ago. Perhaps the scene she had just witnessed had told her something that no explanations could have made so clear. Seth was always the dominating factor in their intercourse, but this outward submission was quite foreign to the girl.

They rode off together, the man's horse leading slightly. Neither spoke for a while, but Rosebud noticed that almost imperceptibly they had branched off and were heading for the bridge by unfrequented by-paths which frequently demanded their riding in Indian-file.

Seth displayed no haste and no inclination to talk, and the silence soon began to jar on the girl. It was one thing for her to give ready obedience, but to be led like some culprit marching to execution was something which roused her out of her docility. At the first opportunity she ranged her horse alongside her companion's and asserted her presence.

"I want you to answer me a question, Seth," she said quietly. "How did you get wounded?"

The man's face never relaxed a muscle, but there was a dryness in the tone of his reply.

"Guess some bussock of a feller got monkeyin' with a gun an' didn't know a heap."

Rosebud favored him with a little knowing smile. They were still amidst the broken woodlands, and she was quick to observe her companion's swift-moving eyes as they flashed this way and that in their ceaseless watchfulness.

"I'm not to be cheated. Some one shot at you who meant—business."

"Guess I ain't aware jest how he figgered, Rosie." A smile accompanied Seth's words this time.

"Well, who did it?"

"I never seen him; so I can't rightly say."

"But you guess?"

"I ain't good at guessin'."

The girl laughed.

"Very well, I won't bother you."

Then after a little silence the man spoke again.

"Those letters of yours was mortal fine," he said. "Seems to me I could most find my way around London, with its stores an' nigglin' trails. It's a tol'ble city. A mighty good eddication, travelin'."

"I suppose it is." Rosebud seemed to have lost her desire for conversation.

"Makes you think some," Seth went on, heedless of the girl's abstraction. "Makes you feel as the sun don't jest rise and set on your own p'tickler patch o' ploughin'. Makes you feel you're kind o' like a grain o' wheat at seedin' time. I allow a man don't amount to a heap noways."

Rosebud turned on him with a bright smile in her wonderful eyes.

"That depends, Seth. I should say a man is as he chooses to make himself. I met a lot of men in England; some of them were much better than others. Some were extremely nice."

"Ah." Seth turned his earnest eyes on the girl's face. He lost the significance of the mischievous down-turning of the corners of her mouth. "I guess them gilt-edge folk are a dandy lot. Y' see them 'lords' an' such, they've got to be pretty nigh the mark."

"Why, yes, I suppose they have."

There was another brief pause while the man's eyes glanced keenly about.

"Maybe you mixed a deal with them sort o' folk," he went on presently.

"Oh, yes." The violet eyes were again alight.

"Pretty tidy sort o' fellers, eh?"

"Rather. I liked one or two very much—very much indeed. There was Bob—Bob Vinceps, you know—he was a splendid fellow. He was awfully nice to me. Took auntie and me everywhere. I wonder how he's getting on. I must see if there's a letter from him at Beacon. He asked me if he might write. And wasn't it nice of him, Seth? He came all the way from London to Liverpool to see me, I mean us, off. It's a long way—a dreadful long way."

"Ah, mebbe when I go into Beacon Crossing I'll fetch that letter out for you, Rosie."

But Seth's simple-heartedness—Rosebud called it "stupidity,"—was too much. The girl's smile vanished in a second and she answered sharply.

"Thanks, I'll get my own letters." Then she went on demurely. "You see if there happened to be a letter from Bob I shouldn't like auntie to see it. She is very—very—well, she mightn't like it."

"How?"

Seth looked squarely into the face beside him.

"She thinks—well, you see, she says I'm very young, and—and——"

"Ah, I tho't mebbe ther's suthin' agin him. You see, Rosie, ther' mustn't be anythin' agin the man you marry. He's got to be a jo-dandy clear thro'. I— —"

"But I'm not going to marry Lord Vinceps, you silly, at least—I don't think so. Besides," as an afterthought, "it's nothing to you who I marry."

"Wal, no. Mebbe that's so, only ef you'd get hitched, as the sayin' is, to some mule-headed son of a gun that wa'n't squar' by you, I'd git around an' drop him in his tracks, ef I had to cross the water to do it."

Rosebud listened with a queer stirring at her heart, yet she could not repress the impatience she felt at the calm matter-of-fact manner in which the threat was made. The one redeeming point about it was that she knew one of Seth's quiet assurances to be far more certain, far more deadly, than anybody's else wildest spoken threats. However, she laughed as she answered him.

"Well, you won't have to cross the ocean to find the man I marry. I'm not going to England again, except, perhaps, on a business visit. I intend to stay here, unless Pa and Ma turn me out."

Seth caught his breath. For a second his whole face lit up.

"Say, I didn't jest take you right," he said. "You're goin' to stay right here?"

Rosebud gave a joyous little nod. She had stirred Seth out of his usual calm. There was no mistaking the light in his hollow eyes. He made no movement, he spoke as quietly as ever, but the girl saw something in his eyes that set her heart beating like a steam hammer. The next moment she was chilled as though she had received a cold douche.

"Wal, I'm sorry," he went on imperturbably. "Real sorry. Which I mean lookin' at it reas'nable. 'Tain't right. You belong ther'. Ther's your folk an' your property, an' the dollars. You jest ought to fix up wi' some high soundin' feller— —"

"Seth, mind your own business!"

Rosebud's exasperation broke all bounds. If a look could have withered him Seth would have shriveled to bare bones. The next moment the girl's lips trembled and two big tears rolled slowly down her cheeks. She urged her horse ahead of her companion and kept that lead until they had crossed the bridge. Seth's eyes, busy in every other direction, had failed to witness her distress, just as he failed to take any heed of her words.

"You see, Rosie, ther's a heap o' trouble comin' along here," he said presently, when he had drawn level.

"Yes," the girl replied, without turning her head; "and I'm going to stay for it. Auntie can go back when she likes, but this is my home, and—Seth, why do you always want to be rid of me?"

Seth remained silent for a moment. Then he spoke in a voice that was a little unsteady.

"I don't want to be rid of you, Rosie. No; I'm jest thinkin' of you," he added.

The old impulsive Rosebud was uppermost in an instant. She turned on him, and reached out a hand which he took in both of his.

"Seth, you are a dear, and I'm sorry for being so rude to you. It's always been like this, hasn't it? You've always thought of me, for me. I wish, sometimes, you wouldn't think—for me."

She withdrew her hand, and, touching her horse with her heel, galloped on toward the farm, leaving Seth to come on behind. She gave him no chance of overtaking her this time.

Supper-time brought a lively scene with it. Rosebud, for some unexplained reason, was in a more than usually contradictory mood. Mrs. Rickards had thoroughly enjoyed her day in spite of the sloppy condition of everything outside the house. She was a woman who took a deep interest in life. She was worldly and practical in all matters which she considered to be the business of a woman's life, but her mental vision was not bounded by such a horizon.

Everything interested her, provided her personal comfort was not too much disturbed. The farm was strange, new, and as such was welcome, but Ma Sampson was a study which fascinated her. She was in the best of spirits when the little family gathered for the evening meal. This had been much elaborated by Ma in her visitors' honor.

At this repast came her first real chance of observing Seth. She studied him for some time in silence while the others talked. Then she joined in the conversation herself, and quickly contrived to twist it into the direction she required.

They were laughing over Rosebud's attempt to scare her cousin with her threat of the Indians.

"You see, auntie," the girl said roguishly, "you are a 'tenderfoot.' It is always the privilege of 'old hands' to ridicule newcomers. In your world there is little for you to learn. In ours you must be duly initiated."

"In my world?" Mrs. Rickards smiled and raised her eyebrows. She had a pleasant smile which lit up her round fat face till she looked the picture of hearty good-nature. And she was on the whole decidedly good-natured. Only her good-nature never ran away with her. "My dear, why not your world also? This is not your world any longer."

Ma smiled down upon the teapot, while the men waited expectantly. With all their simplicity, these people understood Rosebud as far as it was possible to understand her. Without appearing too keen, each watched the violet eyes as they opened wide and wondering by upon the cousin.

"Why, auntie! I—I don't understand."

"You belong to the same world as I do. Dakota no longer claims you."

"You mean—England." Rosebud laughed; and at least three people understood that laugh.

Mrs. Rickards turned to Ma.

"You know, Mrs. Sampson, Rosebud has never yet regarded her position seriously. She is curiously situated—but pleasantly, if she will only enter into the spirit of her father's will. Has she told you about it?"

Ma shook her head. The men went on with their meal in silence. At this point the subject of her aunt's talk broke in.

"Go on, auntie, you tell the story. You are the prosecution, I am the defendant, and these are the judges. I'll have my say last, so fire ahead." There was a look of determination in the girl's eyes as she laughingly challenged her aunt.

Mrs. Rickards smiled indulgently.

"Very well, my dear; but for goodness' sake don't be so slangy. Now Mrs. Sampson and—gentlemen of the jury. Is that right, Rosie?" The girl nodded, and her aunt went on. "You must quite understand I am entirely disinterested in Rosie's affairs. My only interest is that I have found it possible to—er—tolerate this madcap, and she has found it possible to put up with me; in fact I am her nominal guardian—by mutual choice."

"You've hit it dead centre, auntie," interrupted the girl mischievously.

"Don't interrupt or—I'll clear the court. Well, the child comes to me fresh from the prairie. She is good as good can be; but she is quite helpless in her new life. And more than this she is burdened—I say it advisedly—with great wealth under, what I consider, an extraordinary will. How the colonel came to make such a will I cannot understand. The only thing I can think of is that when that will was made he feared there might be some person or persons, possibly relatives, into whose hands she might fall, when she was young, and who might misuse her fortune. This is surmise. Anyway, after providing for her mother he leaves everything to Rosebud. But the legacy is not to take effect until the day she marries.

"Further, the property left to her mother devolved upon her at her mother's death. This, of course, she has already inherited; the rest still remains in trust. Now, of course, as the child's social mother, it is my first duty to watch the men with whom she comes into contact. I have given her every opportunity to meet the most eligible bachelors. Men of title and wealth. Men who cannot possibly be charged with fortune-hunting. What is the result? She sends them all to the right-about. She is positively rude to them—little barbarian.

And the others—the undesirables—well, she just encourages them outrageously."

"Oh, auntie!"

"Wait a minute. The prosecution has not done yet. Now, Mrs. Sampson, I ask you, what am I to do? The truth is she can marry whom she pleases. I have no power over her. I feel sure she will throw herself away on some dreadful, undesirable fortune-hunter. She is in such a position that no poor man can ask her to marry him without becoming a fortune-hunter. Why, out of all the people she has met since she has been with me, who do you think she encourages? Quite the worst man I know. Lord Vinceps. He's a peer, I know; but he's poor, and up to his neck in debts. She is a great trial."

She smiled fondly at the girl whose shortcomings were causing her so much anxiety. But there was no answering smile to meet hers. Rosebud's face was serious for once, and her beautiful eyes quite cold. Mrs. Rickards had addressed herself to Ma, but the girl knew well enough, and resented the fact, that her words were meant for another. Rube and Seth still remained silent. But the impeachment was not allowed to pass unchallenged. Rosebud was up in arms at once.

"About Lord Vinceps, auntie; you know that is all nonsense. I don't care if I never see him again. I understood him within five minutes of our meeting. And that understanding would never permit me to think twice about him. He is a cheerful companion; but—no, auntie, count him out. As for the others—no, thanks. The man I marry will have to be a man, some one who, when I do wrong, can figuratively take me across his knee. The man I marry must be my master, auntie. Don't be shocked. I mean it. And I haven't met such a man under your roof. You see all my ideas are savage, barbarous."

The girl paused. Ma's smile had broadened. Rosebud had not changed. Rube listened in open-mouthed astonishment. He was out of his depth, but enjoying himself. Seth alone gave no sign of approval or otherwise.

"Now, look here, auntie," Rosebud had gathered herself together for a final blow. One little hand was clenched, and it rested on the edge of the table ready to emphasize her words. "I do regard my position seriously. But I have to live my life myself, and will not be trammeled by any conventions of your social world. I'll marry whom I please, because I want to, and not because the world says I ought to do so. Rest assured, I won't marry any fortune-hunter. The man I marry I shall be able to love, honor, and obey, or I'll not marry at all."

The girl suddenly rose from her seat. Her color heightened. There was something in her manner that kept her aunt's eyes fixed upon her in wondering anticipation. She watched her move round the table and lean over and kiss Ma on the crown of the head, and then pass on to Rube, round whose neck she gently placed her arms. Thus she stood for a second looking smilingly over the great rough head across at Ma, who, like the others, was wondering what was coming.

"Furthermore I am not going back to England any more unless I am turned out of here. You won't turn me out, Pa, will you?" She bent down and softly rubbed her cheek against Rube's bristling face.

There was a dead silence. Then Mrs. Rickards broke in weakly.

"But—but your—property?"

"I arranged that with Mr. Irvine before I came out. It's no use, auntie, I am quite determined. That is—you won't—you won't turn me out, Pa, will you? I'll be so good. I'll never do anything wrong, and I'll—I'll even hoe potatoes if any one wants me to."

The girl's laughing eyes shot a mischievous glance in Seth's direction. Rube raised one great hand and drew her face to his and kissed her.

"Guess this is your home if you've a notion to it, Rosie, gal. Guess Ma wants you, jest as we all do."

Ma nodded and beamed through her glasses. Seth smiled in his slow fashion.

"An' I guess I ain't bustin' fer you to hoe p'taters neither," he said.

For a moment Mrs. Rickards looked about her helplessly; she hardly knew what to say. Then, at last, she, too, joined in the spirit which pervaded the party.

"Well, you are the strangest creature—but there, I said you were a little savage, and so did Mr. Seth."

CHAPTER XXV

IN WHICH THE UNDERCURRENT BELIES THE SUPERFICIAL
CALM

THE snow is gone, and the earth is passing through a process of
airing. The sun licks up the moisture like some creature possessed of
an unquenchable thirst. Wherever it is sufficiently dry the settlers are
already at work seeding. Some are even breaking virgin soil, or
turning over old ploughing. There is an atmosphere of leisurely
industry about the plains. Even in these unsettled regions work goes
forward with precision. The farmer's life is one of routine with
which he permits nothing to interfere. He lives by the fruits of the
earth which ripen in due season. If fortune favors him he reaps the
harvest. Whatever his lot he must accept it. The elements rule his life.
The Indians may or may not disorganize the process.

The folk on White River Farm are in no way behind their neighbors.
Seth's returning strength permits him to take his share in the work,
and thus Rube finds his burden lightened. But only partially, for Seth
has much else to do, or seems to have, for he has many comings and
goings which take up time.

Mrs. Rickards is still staying on at the farm. She thoroughly enjoys
this new, simple life. Besides, in the brief fortnight which has
elapsed since her coming, she has learnt something of the true worth,
the wonderful kindliness and honesty of these frontier-folk.

Even Seth, whom at first she was less certain about, she has learned
to look upon with favor. His silent, direct fashion of going through
his daily life has given her an inkling of qualities, which, if not
altogether companionable, show a manliness she has not always
been accustomed to.

Her change of opinion found vent one night at bedtime. Rosebud
listened to the worldly-wise woman's remarks with a glow of
pleasure and pride.

"Seth is a queer fellow, Rosie, so darkly reticent and all that," she
said, with a thoughtful smile. "Do you know I sometimes think if I

were in great danger—personal danger, you know—he's the sort of man I'd like to have about. He gives me the impression of a great reserve of strength. He is what one might—well, what you would call a 'man.'"

Rosebud added her word without the least hesitation.

"He's more than that, auntie; he's the bravest and best man in the world."

"Just so, my dear; and in consequence you don't want to return to England," Mrs. Rickards said slyly.

Rosebud encountered the glance which accompanied the words. She shook her head with a little despairing gesture.

"But he loves me only as a sort of daughter."

"Does he, my dear?"

Mrs. Rickards' tone was quite incredulous; she was at home in matters of love and marriage.

The object of all this thought went about blissfully unconscious of the heart stirrings he was causing. Every moment of his life was full—full to the brim and even overflowing. There was not a settler in the district whom he had not visited during the fortnight. And his business was with the men alone.

The result of his visits would have been visible to the eye of only the most experienced. Work went on the same as before, but there were many half hours which might have been spent in well-earned idleness now devoted by the men to a quiet, undemonstrative overhauling of their armory.

As it was at these outlying farms so it was at White River. In the short twilight of evening Rube and Seth would wander round their buildings and the stockade, noting this defect, suggesting this alteration, or that repair. All their ideas were based on the single thought of emergency. Large supplies of cord-wood were brought in and stacked on the inner side of the stockade, thus adding to its powers of resistance. Every now and then Ma would receive casually dropped hints on the subject of her storeroom. A large supply of ammunition arrived from Beacon Crossing. Many cases of tinned provisions came along, and Ma, wondering, took them in without question or comment at the time. Later in the day when she happened to find Seth alone she told him of them, adopting a casual tone, the tone which these people invariably assumed when the signs of the times wore their most significant aspect.

"There was a heap of canned truck come from the Crossing, Seth," she said. "I laid it down in the cellars. Maybe you sent it along?"

And Seth replied —

"Why, yes, Ma. I figgered we'd like a change from fresh meat. You see I happened along to Beacon Crossing, an' I guessed I'd save a journey later."

"I see."

Ma's bright old eyes read all there was underlying her boy's words, and she, like the rest, continued steadily on with her work.

So the days crept slowly by. Now the snow and ice were gone, and the tawny hue of the prairie was tinged with that perfect emerald of budding spring. The woodlands of the river and the Reservation had lost their barren blackness. The earth was opening its eyes and stretching itself after its months of heavy slumber. Life was in the very air of the plains. The whole world seemed to be bursting with renewed life.

Seth was now restored to something like his old self. His vigor was a thing to marvel at. His regular day's work was only a tithe of what he did. That which went on after the rest of the household had retired to rest was known to only two others. Rube possessed the younger man's confidence, and Jimmy Parker was in constant communication with him. Seth and the latter worked hand in hand for the common welfare, but they were silent. Each knew the character of the dangers which ever surrounded them. Each knew that an absolute silence and apparent indifference were the only means of learning the plans, the meaning of the furtive unrest of the warlike Sioux. All that they learned was carefully stored and docketed for future reference.

Parker's responsibility was official. Seth's was voluntary and humanitarian. Now he had a double incentive. Rosebud was in danger. He knew that he alone stood between her and the treacherous machinations of Nevil Steyne, and the lawless passion of an unscrupulous savage. He dared not spare himself. He must know of every movement on the Reservation. He quite understood the men he was dealing with. He knew the motive of each. All he hoped was that he might prove himself just a shade cleverer, a shade quicker in emergency when the time came for him to act.

It was impossible, however, that Seth should leave the house night after night and no member of the household be the wiser. Oddly enough it was Mrs. Rickards' maid who discovered his movements. She, with a discretion which a confidential servant may always be expected to possess, whispered her discovery to her mistress, and her mistress was not slow in drawing Rosebud's attention. As they were retiring one night she told the girl of her maid's discovery.

"Janet tells me that Mr. Seth goes out every night and doesn't return till two or three in the morning, Rosie," she said abruptly, as she was preparing for bed. "You know the girl sleeps over the kitchen, and some nights ago she saw him ride off from the barn in the moonlight. Last night she was awake when he got back. It was daylight. I wonder where he goes?"

Rosebud responded in a matter-of-fact tone, but with a quick look at her friend.

"I wonder."

Mrs. Rickards wondered and speculated on, but Rosebud's manner gave her no encouragement, and she was fain to let the matter drop. There was no malice in her remarks, but a very profound curiosity.

Her announcement had its effect.

The next night Rosebud did not go to bed after retiring to their room. She made no explanation, merely telling her aunt that she was not going to bed yet. And Mrs. Rickards nodded a comprehensive smile at her.

The girl waited a reasonable time till she thought the others were asleep, then she crept softly down-stairs. She went into the kitchen, but it was dark and empty. The parlor was also in darkness, except for the moonlight pouring in through the window. But as she stood in the doorway, peering closely into the remoter corners, she felt a cool draught playing upon her face. Then she saw that the door opening on the verandah was open.

She walked across the room, and, looking out on the moonlit scene, was promptly greeted by a low growl from General. The next moment she stepped out, and beheld Seth's tall figure leaning against one of the great gate-posts of the stockade, while General came over to her and rubbed his keen nose against her skirts.

Just for a moment she hesitated. It suddenly occurred to her that her action might be construed into spying, and she was possessed by a sense of shame at the bare thought. She knew that she was not spying in the baser sense of the word. She had no doubts of Seth. Instinct told her why he was out. She had come to find out the facts, but not by spying. She meant to question him.

She felt her heart thumping in her chest as she stepped quickly across the verandah. She was nervous, and a strange feeling of shyness made her long to turn back before the man became aware of her presence. But she controlled the impulse, and, though feeling herself flush in the cool air of the night, walked bravely on.

She believed she was unobserved. Her slippers gave out no sound, but as she came within a few yards of the still figure, the man's voice greeted her.

"Thought you was abed, Rosie."

The girl started at the sound. Seth had not moved, had not even turned his head. Then she answered.

"How did you know I was here?" she said quickly.

"Guess I heard General talkin' to you."

She was at his side now.

"But you never looked round?"

"Ef it was Rube, I'd have heard his feet. Ma ain't wanderin' around o' nights. An' I guess your auntie ain't bustin' fer a moonlight ramble. It didn't need a heap o' figgerin'."

Rosebud had no answer ready. The argument was so simple.

A brief silence fell, while both looked out across the moonlit plains at the dark line of distant woods. There was a slight glow in the sky in two different directions. One was away over the Pine Ridge Reservation, the other was nearer at hand, but on the far side of the Rosebud Reservation. The girl saw these things and they held her silent. Her breathing came quickly. There was a sensation of excitement running through her body. She knew these lights were what Seth was staring at.

The man stirred at last.

"Guess you'd best git back to bed, Rosie," he said. "I'm goin' to saddle up my plug. I'm goin' to ride some."

"Where are you going?" The girl's question came with a little nervous energy.

The man turned upon her gravely.

"I'm meetin' Parker to-night," he said briefly.

"What for?" The violet eyes held the other's with their steady gaze. The pretty, irregular face was set and determined.

Seth moved. Then he turned away to glance at the lurid reflection in the sky. Presently his eyes came back to her face.

"It's them," he said, indicating the reflected fires.

"And what are they?" Rosebud's voice was quietly commanding. The irresponsible girl had gone from the woman talking now.

"Sun-dances. They're doin' it at night to cover their tracks. The Injuns are gettin' wise."

"You mean?"

There was no avoiding the sharp, direct questioning.

"We're goin' to git it, and when it comes it'll be—sudden. Sudden an' bad. It's both Reservations. All of 'em."

Rosebud was silent. Her wide open eyes were on the lights, but her thoughts were on other things,—so many other things, that her head whirled. At last she spoke again, in a tense, nervous manner.

"Tell me about it. Tell me all."

Seth shook his head.

"Ther' ain't a deal."

"Tell me."

"See you, Rosie, ef I go out o' here presently, will you jest close these gates an' fix 'em? An' will you be up to open 'em for me?"

"Yes. But tell me."

Seth gazed at the horizon again.

"As I said, ther' ain't much," he began presently. "This has been goin' on fer days. Ther's Injuns out most every night, an' they are lyin' this side o' the fort. They're all about it, an' them soldier-fellers ain't wise to it. What's more we darsen't to put 'em wise. They're li'ble to butt right in, an' then ther' won't be any stoppin' them pesky redskins. Y' see ther's only a handful at the fort, an' the Injuns could eat 'em."

"Yes, you always said it was a mistake to bluff with soldiers so near the Reservation. I suppose the Indians resent their presence. Is that it?"

"Mebbe."

"There's another reason?"

"Can't rightly say."

Rosebud knew that the man was prevaricating.

She stood lost in thought for some moments. And as she thought a sudden light came to her. She drew closer to her companion and laid one hand on his arm.

"I think I see, Seth," she said, and then became silent.

The man moved, and his action was almost a rebuff. That touch had stirred him. The gentle pressure of her hand sent the blood coursing through his veins, and he restrained the hot, passionate words that sprang to his lips only with a great effort. The girl accepted his movement as a rebuff and shrank away. But she spoke vehemently.

"If I'd only thought—oh, if I'd only thought! I should have known. All that has gone before should have told me. It is my coming back that has precipitated matters." Her voice had sunk to a low tone of humility and self-accusation. "And, Seth, now I understand why you were shot. It was Little Black Fox. And I, fool that I was, dared to show myself on the Reservation. And he saw me. I might have known, I might have known."

There was a piteous ring in her low tones. Seth stirred again, but she went on desperately.

"Yes, I see it all. A descent will be made upon us, upon this farm. You will be done to death for me. Ma and Pa, and auntie and — and you."

She paused, but went on again at once.

"Yes, and I see further now. I see what you have already grasped. They have these scouts out around the fort to watch. When it comes they mean to cut the soldiers off. There will be no help for us. Only — only this stockade. Oh, Seth, how can you forgive me! You and Pa have foreseen all this trouble. And you have prepared for it all you can. Is there no help? Can I do nothing to atone for what I have done? You stand there without a word of blame for me. You never blame me — any of you. I wish I were dead! Seth, why don't you kill me?"

But as the girl's hysterical outburst reached its culminating point, Seth regained perfect mastery of himself. He noted the rush of tears which followed her words with a pang of infinite pity, but he told himself that he dare not attempt to comfort her. Instead, his calm voice, with its wonderful power of reassurance, fell upon the stillness of the night.

"Little gal, things are jest as they must be. The blame is on me fer not bein' quicker an' handier wi' my gun when I had the chance. But, howsum, Parker's a hefty man. He ken think an' act quick. We're ready, far as we ken be."

Rosebud dried her tears. Never in her life had Seth appeared to her as he appeared now. The steady, unruffled purpose of the man exalted him in her eyes to an impossible position. Somehow the feelings he roused in her lifted her out of her womanly weakness. She, too, was capable of great, unswerving devotion, but she did not realize it. She only felt that she, too, must bear her part in whatever fortune had in store for them. She would range herself beside this man and share in his success or failure. If it were to be failure she was ready to die at his side. If it were success—a great exultation swept over her at the thought. She went no further. Success at his side would be worth—everything.

"Tell me what I can do—anything!" she cried. Her tone was low, but it rang with a note the man had never heard in it before. There was a joy in it that startled him. "Seth, I believe—I know—I want to—to fight. My blood is running like fire. Tell me what I am to do."

It was a few moments before Seth answered her. He was thinking hard. He knew she could do much. But he was debating with himself. A great pride was his as he contemplated the small face with its wonderful eyes out of which looked such steadfast courage. He, too, thrilled at the thought of fighting at her side, but he tried to tell himself that he had no right to ask anything of her. Perhaps Rosebud saw the drift of his thoughts in his face, for she gave him no chance of denial.

"Yes, the gates. That's all right. I understand. Now, what else? Can't I reconnoitre, or—or something in the meantime?"

Her enthusiasm carried the day.

"No, I guess not. But——"

"Yes, yes——"

"See, Rosie, we want time. I kind o' think it's to-morrow. Parker thinks so too. So does Hargreaves. We may be wrong. But—see right here, I'm due back here by two o'clock sure. If I'm not here by ten minutes after ther's this you ken do. Go straight back o' the barn 'bout a hundred paces; on the hill are two bunches of stuff piled up, one's wood, t'other's dried grass an' stuff. You go right out an' kindle 'em both. They're signals to the settlers around. Guess ther's eyes watchin' for 'em at every farm. When you see 'em burnin' steady, git right back and rouse Rube an' Ma. I'll git back later—sure. An' ther'll be others with me."

"Yes. Anything more?"

"Nope. I 'lows I'll saddle up."

They walked back to the barn in silence. Seth saddled his horse and brought him out. Together they walked to the gate of the stockade. They still remained silent. At the gate the man mounted. Rosebud, very frail looking in the moonlight, stood beside him smoothing the horse's silky neck. Her face was anxious but determined. Suddenly she looked up. Her great eyes were full of appeal. There was no wavering in her gaze, nothing but sincerity and appeal.

"Seth, dear," she said in a steady voice, "be careful of yourself—for my sake." Then, lowering her gaze, and turning to the distant reflection of the fires, "Remember, we all depend on you."

"I'll remember, Rosie, gal," the man replied, with a tender inflection he could not altogether repress. "So long."

The horse moved away with General at its heels.

For a long time Rosebud stood where the parting had left her. Now that Seth had gone she was a prey to every womanly anxiety. And her anxiety was solely for him. None of those peacefully slumbering in the house entered into her thoughts. Her care was for this one man; his image filled her heart. At that moment hers was the selfishness of a maiden's first great love. Even in her anxiety her thoughts were not unhappy ones.

At last she moved away, and with the action came a desire to do. Unknown to her the spirit of her dead father and mother roused within her. She was a woman, gentle, loving, but strong with an invincible courage which had been handed down to her from those two brave souls of whom she had no recollection. Time would prove if the tragedy of the parents should fall upon the child.

Quietly she stole up-stairs to her bedroom. Her cousin was still sleeping. She opened a chest of drawers and drew out an old leather belt filled with ammunition, and bearing two holsters containing a pair of revolvers. These had been a present from Seth in the old days. She loaded both weapons, and then secured them about her waist. Then she closed the drawer, and crept noiselessly down-stairs again.

She made her way out into the moonlight. Passing out of the stockade she located the exact position of the beacon-fires. The forethought in their arrangement pleased her. She understood that the wood-fire was for night, and the grass and dung for day. The smoke of the latter would be easily detected in the brightest sunlight. She came back and barred the gates, and sat out on the verandah with a small metal clock beside her. Thus her vigil began.

The time crept by. Twelve, one, two o'clock. Seth had not returned. She gave him the exact ten minutes' grace. Then, her face pale and a little drawn by the unaccustomed strain, she went out and lit the beacons. She obeyed implicitly. There was no haste, no fear. Her heart was thumping hard in her bosom as she came and went, but it was not with fear.

Finally she roused Rube and Ma. Returning to the verandah she was in time to answer a sharp summons at the gates. To her dismay she discovered that Seth had not returned. The Agent and Mr. Hargreaves had brought their womenfolk. The minister greeted the girl with a quiet announcement which lost nothing of its significance by the easy manner in which it was made.

"They're out, Rosie," he said. And a moment later the gates were closed behind the party.

CHAPTER XXVI

THE SUN-DANCE

The pale moon shone down upon a strange scene.

Four great fires marked the limits of a wide clearing. And these were set with consummate accuracy at the cardinal points. Superstition demanded this setting.

The ruddy glow threw into uncertain relief the faces and unkempt figures of a vast concourse of men and women gathered, in one great circle, within the boundary limits of the fires. On the faces of all was an expression of fierce revelry. A dark setting completed the picture. Beyond the fires all was shadow, profound, ghostly. The woods in all directions closed in that weird concourse of beings, and even the devilish light of the fires could not relieve the savagery of the scene.

Like the hub of a gigantic wheel, in the midst of the circle stood a cluster of leafless trees, mighty patriarchs, gnarled and twisted, with great overhanging limbs as stout and rugged as only hoary age can make them.

The clearing inside the human circle was empty for a time, but the crowd without was momentarily increasing, augmented by an incessant stream of dusky, silent figures pouring from the adjacent forest depths. As the minutes wore on the human tide slackened; it became broken, finally it ceased altogether. Men, women and children, all the able-bodied inhabitants of the Rosebud Reservation had foregathered, and the significance of the gathering could not be mistaken.

Now a distant murmur comes from out of the blackness of the woods. At first it is low, faint, and without character. But it grows, it gains in power till its raucous din breaks upon the waiting multitude, and immediately a responsive murmur rises from ten thousand voices. Those who hear know the meaning of the discordant noise. The "med'cine" men of the tribe are approaching, chanting airs which accord with their "med'cine," and serve at the same time to herald the coming of the great Sioux chief, Little Black Fox.

Nearer and nearer, louder and louder. All eyes are upon the black fringe of the forest where the trees no longer have power to obstruct the moonlight. And of a sudden a number of writhing, twisting figures come dancing into view.

They draw nearer to the expectant throng. Necks are craned, eyes are straining to watch the antics so significant to these creatures of superstition. For have not these strange beings power to invoke the spirits, to drive away evil influence from the path of him whose approach they herald?

They reach the clearing; they leap within the human circle. Their painted faces are distorted with the effort of their wild exertions; their befeathered heads are rendered still more hideous by the lurid blending of conflicting lights. Thirty creatures, hardly recognizable as human beings, dance to the accompaniment of a strange crooning of the women onlookers; to the beating of sad-toned drums, and the harsh scraping of stringed instruments. But the dance is marked by a distinct time. It has unmistakable features and figures, and it proceeds to its natural finish which leaves the dancers prostrate upon the ground, with their faces pressed hard into the dusty earth. It is a wild scene.

But the Sun-dance has only begun. There is much to follow.

Now a single figure moves out of the crowd, and takes its position in the arena. It is the young chief. His attitude is one of sublime dignity. His erect figure and haughty carriage bear the indelible stamp of his illustrious forbears. Silently he raises one hand, and a deathly hush falls upon his people.

And Little Black Fox speaks.

Tall, handsome, lithe, a frame of great bone and smooth sinewy muscle, he is an imposing figure. He wears no blanket, just the buckskin, beaded as becomes his high rank.

He harangues mightily, now working himself into an almost uncontrolled fury, again letting his voice die down to that plaintive, musical note which alone belongs to the Sioux tongue. And his speech is of war—wild, fierce, unreasonable war, such as his people love. He is thrilling with the untamed spirit of his ancestors, and every word he utters carries a ready conviction to the untutored souls to whom it is addressed.

He sweeps on in a torrential flow of passion, and those who listen are roused at once to a savage enthusiasm. There are no interruptions. The oration is received in complete silence. These are Indians taken into their sovereign's council; they are there to hear while the young brave pronounces, with all the fire of his ardent, aboriginal nature, the doom of their white masters.

The wise men of the council are grouped together and sit aloof. They sit like mummies, smoking, and with every appearance of indifference. But their ears are wide open. One alone displays interest, and it is noticeable that he is different from all the rest of the aged group. He is younger. He has blue eyes and fair hair, and his skin is pale. Yet he, too, is blanketed like his companions. He listens acutely to the end of the speech. Then he silently moves away, and, unheeded, becomes lost in the adjacent woods.

As the chieftain's last words die away the men of "med'cine" rise from their groveling attitude and a fresh dance begins. But this time it is not confined to the clearing. It is one which launches them into the midst of the audience. Hither and thither they caper, and from their tracks emerge a number of very young men. It might be that this is the "Dance of Selection," for it undoubtedly has the result of bringing forth a number of striplings from the ranks of the onlookers.

The dancers have made the complete circuit, and about one hundred young men, little more than boys, join in the great Sun-dance.

Now ensues one of the most terrible scenes of human barbarity conceivable. In the course of the dance the "med'cine" men seize upon each of the willing victims in turn. On the breast of each boy incisions are made with long, keen knives; two parallel incisions on each side of the chest. The flesh between each two of these is then literally torn from the underlying tissues, and a rough stick is thrust through the gaping wounds. So the would-be brave is spitted.

Now a rawhide rope is attached to the centre of the stick, the end of it is thrown over the gnarled limb of one of the trees in the centre of the clearing, and the youth is lifted from the ground and remains suspended, the whole weight of his body borne by the two straps of bloody flesh cut from his chest.

The dance proceeds until each youth is spitted and suspended from the central cluster of trees, then, with one accord, the men of the audience break from their places and join in the war-dance. They dance about the victims with a fierce glee like hundreds of fiends; they beat them, they slash them with knives, they thrust lighted brands upon the fresh young flesh till it blisters and throws out nauseous odors. Their acts are acts of diabolical torture, inconceivably savage. But the worst agony is endured in desperate silence by each victim. That is, by all but one.

Out of all the number hanging like dead men upon the trees only one youth finds the torture unendurable.

He cries aloud for mercy, and his shrieks rise high above the pandemonium going on about him.

Instantly he is cut down, the stick is removed from his body, and he is driven from the ceremony by the waiting squaws, amidst a storm of feminine vituperation. He is the only one whose heart is faint. He will never be permitted to fight. He must live with the squaws all his days. He is considered a squaw-man, the greatest indignity that can be put upon him.

Thus are the braves made.

While the Sun-dance was still at its height two men who had taken no part in it, except that of secret spectators, moved quickly and silently away through the forest. Their gait was almost a flight, but not of fear.

Ten minutes of half running and half walking brought them to a spot where two horses were tethered under the guardianship of the fierce General. Here they mounted, and, without a word, proceeded with all speed in the direction of the Agency.

At the door they halted, and Seth spoke for the first time since leaving the Sun-dance. Parker had already dismounted, but the other remained in his saddle.

"Say, you'll move right off," he said quickly, "an' git Hargreaves an' his wimminfolk clear, too. Guess you'll make the farm 'fore me, sure. Take the bridge for it. Rosebud 'll let you in. Guess you'll find plenty o' company 'fore daylight. Rosie 'll see to the signals."

"Yes," Parker nodded. "They're moving to-night. This is a carefully planned surprise."

Seth glanced at the eastern sky.

"Four hours to daylight," he mused. Then: "Yes, guess there's more'n Black Fox's hand in this. So long."

He rode off with his faithful dog at his heels, making for the ford, and watchful of every shadow as he went. His night's work was yet only half done.

Crossing the river he climbed the opposite bank and rode out upon the prairie. Making a wide detour he came to within a hundred yards of the front of Nevil Steyne's hut. Here he halted and dismounted. Crouching upon the ground he scanned the sky-line carefully in every direction. At last he seemed satisfied, and, flinging his bridle reins to the dog, who promptly took them in his powerful jaws and quietly sat down in front of the horse's head, moved cautiously forward.

In a few moments he came upon two horses standing asleep, tethered by long ropes to picket-pins. One of these he released and led back to his own. Then he remounted and rode on. Again he circled wide of his destination, and this time struck into the woods that lined the river. His way now lay down the black aisles of tree trunks which he pursued until he came to a spot he was evidently in search of. Then he again dismounted, and, entrusting the two horses to the dog's care, moved forward on foot.

With unerring judgment he broke cover directly in rear of Nevil's log hut. There was neither window nor door on this side, a fact which he was evidently aware of, for, without hesitation, but with movements as silent as any Indian, he crept round to the front, and sidled to the window. Here there was a light shining dully, but no means of obtaining a view of the interior. He moved on, and, crouching at the doorway, listened intently. A few seconds satisfied him. Wanaha was inside; she was awake, for he heard her moving about. He knew at once that Nevil was out.

With a satisfied sigh he moved away. This time he walked eastward toward the bridge, keeping close in the shadow of the woods. A couple of hundred yards from the hut he stopped and took up a position just within the shelter of the undergrowth, whence he had a perfect view of the open plain in front, and yet was sufficiently sheltered by the echoing woods to hear the least movement of any one passing that way. And so he waited.

Nor did he wait long. Eyes and ears trained to this sort of work were kept ever on the alert. But it was his ears which told him at last of some one approaching. Some one was moving through the woods. The sound was faint and distant, but he heard it. There was no mistake. And he knew it was Nevil Steyne returning home.

Clearing the brush he made his way into the midst of the aisles of leafless tree-trunks. Pausing in the shadow of one of the forest giants he waited. The footsteps came nearer. He shifted his position again; for his ears told him that he was not yet on the track which Nevil would take.

At last, however, he came to a stand, and did not move again. Guided by a wonderful hearing, he knew that he was in a direct line between the man approaching and his home.

He leant against a tree, his eyes and ears straining. Some few yards away there was a shaft of moonlight stretching right across the path which Nevil must take, and on this path Seth kept his eyes.

The man came on all unconscious of who and what was awaiting him. He had no thought of his presence at the Sun-dance having been detected. His thoughts were on what the morrow was to bring forth; on what it would mean to him when Rosebud was removed from his path. She alone stood between him and that which he had schemed for ever since the arrival of the memorable letter from his brother. He was in a mood of intense satisfaction. He knew that at last he was to realize his desires, that at last he was to pay off a long score which he owed Seth of White River Farm.

He stepped into the moonlit patch. The sudden flash of light made him pause. It startled him. He looked beyond apprehensively, then he looked up, and the great moon above reassured him. He moved on. The next moment he stopped dead. He could proceed no further. A ring of metal was pressing against his forehead, and Seth was behind it, and his smooth, even voice, coldly compelling, held him.

"Say, I've been lookin' fer you," it said. "You're comin' right up to the farm. The Injuns are out. Savee? Jest fer once you're goin' to work on our side. Say, you're goin' to fight 'em—with us."

There was a deathly silence. Neither moved. The gun was pressing the man's forehead still. Nevil stood like one paralyzed.

"Wal?" questioned the cold voice, proceeding from Seth's shadowy figure.

And Nevil was driven to speech.

"I'm not a fighting man. I——"

But his denial was cut short.

"You've jest got ten seconds to make up your mind. You're goin' to fight—for us, or——"

Seth had in no way raised his tones from the cold level of his manner at the beginning. His victim had only a shadowy impression of him. He saw only a hazy outline in the blackness of the forest; and he needed no further sight to convince him. There was sufficient in the tone, and in the pressure of the gun at his head. He knew the rest. Here was a sudden collapse of all his schemes. There could be no resistance. Seth had the drop on him.

"I'll go," he said sullenly.

CHAPTER XXVII

IN DESPERATE PLIGHT

At daylight the truth was known. The greatest Indian rising of two decades had begun.

The Bad-Lands had entered upon a period of slaughter, of wanton massacre, which was to form one of the bloodiest pages in the history of Indian warfare.

The first to realize the full terror of the situation were the troops in the small trader's fort overlooking the Reservations. They awoke to find themselves hemmed in by a vast army of red-skinned warriors, entirely cut off from the outside world. The climax of their discovery was reached when an attempt was made to dispatch a telegraphic message to headquarters. The wire was cut.

The next to grasp the situation were the citizens of Beacon Crossing. The railroad track was destroyed, and all telegraphic communication was cut off. A horde of warriors from Pine Ridge Reservation, some thousands strong, threatened the township from the east, thus cutting them off from the settlers on the plains.

The full knowledge of these things came in driblets to the refugees gathering at White River Farm, filtering through piece by piece as each party came in. But as yet not an Indian had shown himself in the vicinity of the farm. Already twelve families had sought the shelter of Rube's stockade. And all was in readiness for the siege.

The morning passed, and still two families lying farther out than all the others had not yet arrived. It was an anxious waiting.

It was three o'clock in the afternoon when at last one of the missing parties appeared on the horizon. It was at once seen that the two vehicles were being driven at a desperate pace. They were approaching from the north, and even at that distance the lookout could see the drivers flogging their horses into a furious gallop.

Seth passed the order to stand by. The defenders responded, and the stockade immediately bristled with rifles.

The wagons came on. Then suddenly a small party of Indians appeared over the horizon, racing in hot pursuit. But evidently the view of the farm altered their plans, for they reined in, halted, and, a moment later, wheeling about, vanished whence they came.

Seth, watching from the top of the stockade, realized something of the significance of their movements. And far graver fears than the manœuvre seemed to warrant assailed him.

The late arrivals brought further bad tidings. The Indians on the Cheyenne River Reservation were out, and working in concert with the others. It is a bad business when Indian tribes band together against a common foe. There was consternation among the women when they heard the news. The men smiled grimly, but there was no lightness in their hearts.

The time of waiting dragged wearily. Every one within the stockade felt the suspense to be far worse than the fiercest fighting. The intangible threat of this unnatural calm was dreadful. Still, the respite was not without its uses. Defences were strengthened with earthworks hastily thrown up on the inside of the stockade, and the upper rooms of the house were made ready for a selected firing party, whilst the women made every preparation for the comfort of their men.

Nevil Steyne moved about bearing his share in the labors. He was morosely silent, and his presence caused much speculation amongst those who knew nothing of what had happened on the previous night. Seth's replies when questioned on the subject were evasive. Rube and Parker were no wiser than the rest, except that Seth had told them that Nevil was his prisoner, and must on no account be allowed to escape.

The gray spring twilight had settled over the plains. Still the last family, Joe Smith and his belongings, had not come in. Seth intended to give them their chance up to the very last, before he finally closed the gates. As the sun dropped he dispatched four mounted men to act as vedettes. They took up their positions a mile out from the farm, with orders to fire two shots in quick succession on sight of any Indians, and then to ride in with all speed.

After delivering his instructions he took up his position upon the stockade and watched them go. He was very anxious for the safety of Joe Smith; his place was nearly ten miles out, and away to the northeast. He knew that if the northern Indians were out it was quite possible that the old man had been cut off.

Now, as the day drew to a close, something of the gloomy prospect before them all seemed to have entered his soul. He was no alarmist, but he knew only too well the meaning of a big general Indian rising. The horrors he had witnessed in his early days were strong upon him, and the presence of all these white women under his charge weighed sorely. Nor did he glean much satisfaction from the thought that, at least, should disaster fall upon them he still had power to punish the man whom he knew to be the author of all this trouble. It would be poor consolation.

The darkness was growing. Now the reflection of Indian fires could be seen in almost every direction. There seemed to be a perfect ring of them, in the distance, around the farm.

He was disturbed in his gloomy reverie by the sound of some one scrambling up the newly-made earthworks to his side. It was Rosebud.

She took her seat at his side in silence. She was clad in her old prairie riding-habit of canvas, strong and rough, and eminently suited to the present condition of things. They had hardly met since the first alarm, so busy had everybody been. But now that all was ready the final lull before the breaking of the storm had provided even the busiest with leisure. The girl's first words came abruptly, and displayed her wonderful faith in the man to whom they all looked for help and protection.

"Shall we pull through, Seth?" she asked.

"Can't say, Rosie."

The man's reply was spoken slowly.

"Poor auntie!" Rosebud went on. "I can't help thinking of her. I wish I'd never said anything about 'scalping' to her. But she's very good and brave. She hasn't complained, and she's worked as hard as anybody. Do you know, I believe, now she's got over the first shock of it, she rather enjoys it. What do you think she said to me half an hour ago? She said, with such a smile, 'When I get home I shall have something to tell them. I'm keeping a diary.' Like a fool I said, 'You aren't home yet, auntie.' I said it without thinking. What do you suppose she replied?"

"Can't guess."

"Oh, I'll get home all right. Mr. Seth 'll see to that."

But Seth was impervious to the compliment. The girl smilingly watched his sombre face out of the corners of her eyes. There was no responsive smile.

"It's jest them things make it hard," he said, with something very like a sigh.

Rosebud's face had become serious. Her thoughts were hard at work.

"Is it as bad as that?" she asked presently.

"'Tain't no use lookin' at it easy. We're facin' the music—hard—this time. But we ain't done yet. Not by a sight. It's kind o' lucky we've laid in a big store of ammunition an' things."

It was dark by now, except for the glow of Indian fires, which gave a weird light on all sides.

Rosebud drew closer to the man's side. Her action passed unnoticed. His eyes were intent upon the dark horizon. He was watching, watching, with every faculty alert. He was listening, his ears ready to catch the faintest sound.

"It would be all right if only they could have sent word to the headquarters of the troops, I s'pose," the girl said thoughtfully. "Just fancy the Indians cutting the telegraph wires and destroying the railway."

"Yup. Guess they've had all winter to get things settled," Seth responded indifferently, while he turned a keen ear to windward.

"What are you listening for?" asked Rosebud, quickly.

"General's out scoutin'."

"Good old General!"

"Yes, he'll locate the Injuns when they git around."

But just then Rosebud was thinking of other things.

"Why can't you find some one who will try to get through to the troops? I mean the headquarters?"

Seth shook his head.

"Can't spare a single man," he said conclusively. "I 'lows no white folk 'ud get through anyways. An' we ain't got an Injun, an' if we had I wouldn't trust him no more'n I'd trust a 'rattler.' No, Rosie, gal, we've got to fight this out on our own. An' make no sort o' mistake we're goin' to fight good an' hard. I've figgered to hold this place fer two weeks an' more. That's how I've figgered."

It was the final repetition which filled Rosebud with misgivings. She realized the man's doubt. Suddenly she slipped a hand through his arm, and it gently closed over one of his. Her soft eyes were raised to his face as she put another question in a low tone.

"And if we go under, Seth?"

The man moved uneasily, but the little hand retained its hold of his.

"What then?"

Seth cleared his throat, but remained silent.

"What then?" the girl persisted.

"Don't ask me."

"I've thought once or twice of my poor father and mother," Rosebud said presently. "I was wondering what happened to them at—at the end."

Seth eyed the girl for a second. His face was troubled.

"I've a notion he was killed by the Injuns," he said.

"And mother?"

"Can't jest say. I don't fancy, though, he let the brutes worrit her any."

There was another pause. With an involuntary movement Rosebud's hand tightened trustfully upon his.

"I think father was right—to do that," she said simply.

The man nodded.

The next moment he was kneeling, his body bending forward, and his eyes straining in the direction of the horizon.

"What is it?" the girl asked.

"Ther's something movin'."

But Rosebud could hear nothing. Still she was content to accept his assurance.

"It's wheels," he said after a few moments.

"Is it Joe Smith's outfit?"

"Yup."

They both listened. The girl could now hear the faintest possible rattle of wheels. Suddenly she turned upon him. Her breath was coming quickly. She was smiling, and her eyes were soft under cover of the dim starlight.

"Seth, I want you to let me do something. In the old days you used to be my dear old 'daddy.' You used to scold me when I did wrong. You used to get angry with me, and I used to get more angry with you. Since I've grown up, of course, things have changed, haven't they?"

"Yes." The man looked into her face wonderingly.

"Well, daddy dear," the girl laughed nervously. "Maybe when the trouble begins I shan't see much of you. You'll be busy, and so will I. It's peace now, and I just want you to fall back into the old way. I want you for my 'daddy'—my dear, dear old 'daddy'—just for these few minutes. I want to be the silly scatterbrain I used to be."

"I ain't a heap at guessin', Rosie," Seth said doubtfully, but smiling tenderly at the upturned face.

"No, you never were." Rosebud gave a queer little laugh. "Well, I just want you to let me ride out and meet dear old Mrs. Smith. You know what a nervous old dear she is. I just thought if I rode out it might brighten her up. You see, she'd think the danger less, if a woman came to meet her."

"Wal, I won't say you no, gal," Seth replied gravely. "Guess it ain't right. But ther' ain't a heap of danger. Y' see in them old days I most gener'ly let you do as you notioned," he finished up with a shadowy smile.

"Dear old daddy!" Rosebud squeezed his arm with both her hands.

"Ther' be off, an' git your plug saddled, or mebbe I'll change my mind." The man could stand the temptation no longer. He gently released himself, and the girl moved as though to descend. But she altered her mind. Fortunately neither could see the other's face distinctly.

"Seth," she said, with forced brightness, "in the old days when I asked your permission for anything and you gave it to me you—you didn't let me go like that. It was customary for me to show my gratitude—like—like this."

She suddenly leant forward and imprinted a swift kiss on the man's thin cheek. And before he could reply, or even move, she had clambered down from the wall and made off. Nor was it until he heard her horse galloping out of the stockade, which occurred suspiciously soon after her leaving him, that he became aware that his cheek was wet with tears that had not been of his shedding.

CHAPTER XXVIII

A LAST ADVENTURE

It was not without a guilty feeling that Rosebud rode out of the stockade. She knew that she was deceiving Seth. She knew that she had lied to him deliberately. Worse, she had played upon his feelings with intent to deceive him. But her motive was good, and she tried to draw consolation from the knowledge.

Her argument was worthy of her. It was impulsive, and would not stand the test of logical inspection. She had thought long before putting her plan into execution; at least, long for her. She told herself that no deceit was unpardonable which had an honest, sound motive. In fact it was not deceit at all, only subterfuge.

Her argument was something after this fashion. She had been the chief source of trouble. Therefore she owed something to the general welfare. Seth was harassed with his responsibilities, and the chances were terribly against him and those under his charge. There was something she could do, something which might turn the tide in their favor, might save the situation. What if to carry it out she must act a lie? Who would blame her if she were successful? If it failed it would not matter to her who blamed.

She was a child no longer, but a strong woman whose devotion to those she loved rose boundless over every other feeling. It was this very devotion that urged her and shut out every scruple, every qualm of conscience, at the manner in which she had gained her ends.

Thus she passed out into the dark, starlit world, with its strange glare of fire.

Once clear of the farm she heaved a deep sigh. The tension had relaxed now that she felt herself to be doing at last. Cooped within the stockade, her plans still waiting to be set in motion, she had felt nigh to choking with nervousness. Her anxiety to be gone had been overwhelming. Perhaps none knew better than she what the task of cajoling Seth meant, for he was not an easy man when duty was uppermost in his mind. But that was all done with now; she was out at last.

The freedom of her horse's gait felt good under her. There was confidence, exhilaration to be drawn from each springing stride. And, too, there was a new and delightful sense of responsibility in the heavy lolling of the revolver holsters upon her hips. But above all there was the supreme feeling that she was endeavoring to help those she had left behind.

Her tears had dried before she mounted to the back of the animal to which she was now pinning her faith. The parting kiss she had imprinted upon the man's thin cheek had inspired her. Life meant nothing to her without him. Her fortune was nothing to her, no one was anything to her compared with him. He stood out over everything else in her thoughts.

She heard the rumbling of the wheels of Joe Smith's wagons, but gave no heed to them. Instead, she rode straight on to the south, purposely avoiding the newcomers she was ostensibly going to meet. In a few minutes she drew rein at Wanaha's log hut.

She was not without some doubts when she saw that the place was in darkness. But her apprehensions were quickly dissipated. Her first summons brought the squaw to the door, where her tall, dark figure stood out in the gentle starlight.

As was her custom Rosebud handed the woman the reins to hook upon the wall. She was constrained to do without her usual greeting, for she knew that, here too, she must deceive to gain her ends. It would be madness to tell the half-tamed savage her real intentions. Wanaha's love for her was great, but well she knew that blood is thicker than water, and a savage's blood more particularly so than anybody's else.

Once inside the hut Wanaha was the first to speak.

"You come? On this night?" she questioned, choosing her English words with her usual care.

The girl permitted no unnecessary delay in plunging into the object of her visit.

"Yes, yes, my Wana," she replied, drawing the tall woman to her, so that, in the dim starlight, they sat together on the edge of the bed. Her action was one of tender affection. Wanaha submitted, well pleased that her white friend had allowed nothing of the doings of her people to come between them. "Yes, I come to you for help. I come to you because I want to remove the cause of all the trouble between your people and mine. Do you know the source of the trouble? I'll tell you. I am!"

Rosebud looked fixedly in the great dark eyes, so soft yet so radiant in the starlight.

"I know. It is—my brother. He want you. He fight for you. Kill, slay. It matter not so he have you."

The woman nodded gravely. The girl's heart bounded, for she saw that her task was to be an easy one.

"Yes, so it is. I have thought much about this thing. I should never have come back to the farm. It was bad."

Again Wanaha nodded.

"And that is why I come to you. I love my friends. There is some one I love, like you love your Nevil, and I want to save him. They will all be killed if I stay, for your brother is mighty—a great warrior. So I am going away."

Rosebud's allusion to the squaw's love for her husband was tactful. She was completely won. The girl, who was clasping one of Wanaha's hands, felt a warm, responsive pressure of sympathy, and she knew.

"Yes, now I want you to help me," she hurried on. "To go as I am now, a white girl in white girl's clothing, would be madness. I know your people. I should never escape their all-seeing eyes. I must go like one of your people."

"You would be—a squaw?" A wonderful smile was in the great black eyes as Wanaha put the question.

"Yes."

"Yes, I see. Wana sees." A rising excitement seemed to stir the squaw. She came closer to her white friend and spoke quickly, stumbling over her English in a manner she would never have permitted in cooler moments. "An' in these way you mak' yourself go. You fly, you run; so my brother, the great chief, no more you find. Yes? Then him say, 'him gone.' We no more use him fight. We go by tepee quick. An' there is great peace. Is that how?"

"That is it," cried Rosebud, in her eagerness flinging her arms about the squaw's neck. "We must be quick. Seth will miss me from the farm, and then there'll be a to-do, and he will come hunting for me. Lend me your clothes, a blanket, and an Indian saddle. Quick, my Wana! you'll help me, won't you? Oh, make haste and say, and set my doubts at rest!"

The tide of the girl's appeal had its effect. The squaw rose swiftly, silently. She moved off and presently came back with a bundle of beaded buckskin clothing.

"You wear these, they my own. I get him for you. See. You put on, I go get saddle. The blanket here. So. Nevil, my Nevil, from home. Wana not know where. But maybe he come quick an' find you an' then——"

Wana did not finish expressing her fears. She seemed suddenly to remember of whom she was speaking, and that there was disloyalty in what she was saying.

But Rosebud was paying little heed. She was already changing her clothes. She knew the value of time just then, and she had been forced to waste much already. While she was completing the transformation, the squaw went out and changed her saddle and bridle for an Indian blanket and surcingle with stirrups attached to it, and a plaited, gaudy rope bridle and spade bit.

When she came back the white girl had completed her toilet, even to the moccasins and buckskin chapps. Even the undemonstrative Wanaha exclaimed at the metamorphosis.

She saw before her in the dim starlight the most delightful picture of a squaw. Rosebud's wealth of golden hair was hidden beneath the folds of the colored blanket, and only her fair white face with its dazzling eyes, bright now with excitement, shone out and destroyed the illusion.

"You are much beautiful," the Indian declared in amazement. Then she stood gazing until Rosebud's practical voice roused her.

"Food, my Wana."

"I give bread and meat. It in bags on the horse. So. Now you go?"

"Yes, dear Wana. I must go."

Rosebud reached her arms up to the tall woman's neck, and drawing her dark face down to her own, kissed her. Though she loved this dark princess she knew that her kiss was the kiss of Judas. Then she passed out, and, mounting her horse, rode away.

Within five minutes of her going, and while Wanaha was still standing in the doorway looking after her, a party of warriors, headed by Little Black Fox himself, rode up to the house. The chief had come in search of Nevil Steyne. He angrily demanded the white man's whereabouts of the woman who was his sister.

The ensuing scene was one of ferocious rage on the part of the headstrong man, and fear, hidden under an exterior of calm debate, on the part of Wanaha. She knew her brother, and in her mind tried to account for her husband's absence. After the warriors had departed she passed a night of gloomy foreboding.

All unconscious of her narrow escape, Rosebud headed away to the northeast. She had no elaborate scheme of route. With the instinct of her prairie training she knew her direction. She would make her destination as the crow flies, chancing everything, every danger, so that she could make the best time; no personal considerations entered into her calculations.

She could see the reflections of the camp-fires in the sky in every direction, but, with a reckless courage, she cared nothing for this. A more calculating mind might well have shrunk from the dangers they suggested. To her they meant no more than obstacles which must be confronted and overcome. She knew nothing of strategy in warfare; of cover there was none in the direction she was taking.

Like the line of great soldiers from whom she was descended she understood riding straight only. Let the fences and pitfalls come, let them be what they might, she would not swerve. Whatever the emergency, she was prepared to confront it, and, like a thorough sportswoman but a bad general, to take her chance, relying only on her good horse and the darkness, and the proverbial luck of the reckless.

Though this was her general idea she did all she could to help. A featherweight, she still strove to ride lighter. Then she had her firearms, and she steeled her heart to their use. After all she came from splendid fighting stock.

She allowed herself no thought of failure. She must not fail, she told herself. They were waiting for help in the stockade behind her; patient, strong, a man of lion heart, who knew defeat only when the last shot was fired, the last blow struck, and he was left helpless to defend himself and those others, he was waiting. Her thoughts inspired her with the courage of a brave woman whose lover is in grave peril, than which there is no greater courage in the world.

Now the moment of her peril drew near. Every raking stride of her willing horse cut the brief seconds shorter and shorter. The lurid reflections of the camp-fires in the sky had given place to the starlike glow of the fires themselves, and every yard of the distance covered showed them larger and plainer against the sky-line.

She was riding straight for the middle course of the black space dividing two of the fires ahead. There was little to choose in any direction, so complete was the circle around the farm, but she had been quick to see that that little lay here.

She measured the distance she had to go with her eye. It was not far, and instinctively she reined her horse up to give him breathing for the great effort to come; an effort which she knew was to be very real indeed. Approaching steadily she made her preparations. Freeing her right arm from her blanket she drew one of her revolvers and saw that it was fully loaded. Then she closely scrutinized the fires. She could make out the general outline of two vast camps away to the right and left of her. The fires were in the midst, and right to the limits of the lurid light, she could see the dim outlines of innumerable tepees, and crowds of moving figures. It was a sight to put fear into the heart of a daring man, then how much more so into the heart of a frail woman?

The black stretch before her seemed devoid of tepees, but she was not sure. Of one thing she felt convinced, even if the camps were confined to the fires there was no likelihood of these wide intervals being left unguarded.

Her horse refreshed, she put him into a strong gallop, and in a few minutes had entered the danger zone. Almost on the instant her surmise proved correct. The air directly ahead of her split with a fierce yell. She knew it. It was the Sioux war-cry. The supreme moment had come. It must be now or never. Clinching her moccasined heels into her horse's barrel she sent him racing headlong. And as he rushed forward she gripped her revolver ready for immediate use.

An Indian mounted on a pony suddenly loomed ahead of her. Such was her pace that he seemed to rush out of the darkness upon her. Yet his pony had not moved. There was a clatter of speeding hoofs on either side, and she knew that the alarm had been taken up, and the bloodthirsty warriors from the camps were in pursuit.

The man ahead appeared only for an instant. Her revolver was covering him, the terrific speed of her horse helped her aim. She saw the sights of her weapon; she saw the man. The hammer fell. There was a cry, and the biting report of the revolver died away in the darkness. She had passed the spot where the man had been. Horse and rider had vanished. She had no thought for anything now. She was conscious of only one thing, the din of pursuit.

Thrusting the revolver back into its holster she offered up a silent prayer to heaven. Then she leaned over her horse's neck to relieve him of her weight, and, with the yelling horde hard upon her heels, gave herself up to the race.

CHAPTER XXIX

HARD PRESSED

During those first terrible days of the Indian outbreak the horrors that befell could only be guessed at. The government, the people living without the danger zone, gradually learned the full details, but those most concerned only knew what was happening in their immediate neighborhood. Every one, even those who had made a life-study of their red-skinned neighbors, were taken unawares. The methods of the untried chieftain had proved themselves absolutely Napoleonic.

There could be no doubt that the whole campaign was the result of long and secret preparation. But it had been put into execution at the psychological moment, which was its warrant of success. That this moment had been unpremeditated, and that something very like chance alone had precipitated matters, afforded neither hope nor consolation.

And this chance. A frail white woman; Rosebud's return to the farm—her visit in Nevil Steyne's company to the Reservation. For a few moments the wild, haughty chieftain had stood observing her as she rode through the encampment; and in those few moments the mischief was done.

The old trading fort offered little resistance to the Indian attack, and the handful of troops within it very little more. Being soldiers they were treated to the Indians' first attention. An overwhelming horde of picked warriors was sent to deal with them, and, by the end of the second day, the massacre and sacking of the post were accomplished.

In this way a large reinforcement was added to the party threatening Beacon Crossing. Intoxicated with their first success the whole army rushed upon the unfortunate township. And all the more fierce was the onslaught for the reason that the attack was made up of rival tribes.

The Rosebuds had wiped out the troops, and, in consequence, the men of Pine Ridge, fired by jealousy, advanced like a raging torrent mad with the desire for slaughter. Utterly unprepared for such rapid movements, the men at the Crossing, unorganized, hardly realizing what had happened, fell easy victims.

The township, like the fort, was wiped from the fair face of the budding prairie-land. The horrors of the massacre were too terrible to be dealt with here. Every man, woman, and child now living in the country has heard the tales of that awful week. Few people escaped, and those only by taking to the Black Hills, where they suffered untold privations from want and exposure.

Having thus disposed of the two principal centres from which interference might spring, the Indians proceeded to devote themselves to the individual settlers upon the prairie. Not a farm escaped their attention. North and south, east and west, for miles and miles the red tide swept over the face of the plains, burning, sacking, murdering.

A track of blood was left behind them wherever they went. Charred monuments marked the tombs of hardy settlers caught in the red flood; where peace and prosperity had so recently reigned, now were only ruin and devastation.

With each succeeding day the horror grew. The northern Indians threw in their lot with their warlike Sioux brothers, and all the smaller and more distant tribes, numerically too weak for initiative, hastened to the bloody field of battle. The rebellion grew; it spread over the country like a running sore. The Bad Lands were maintaining their title.

At first the news that filtered through to the outside world was meagre, and devoid of reliable detail. Thus it happened that only a few troops were hurried to the scene of action. It was not until these, like the handful at the fort, had served to swell the roll of massacre, and the fact became known that the northern posts, where large forces were always kept in readiness, were cut off from all communications, that the world learned the full horror that had befallen the Indian territory of Dakota.

Through these days the one place to hold out against the fierce onslaught of an overwhelming foe was the fortified farm of White River. But it was in a desperate plight.

So far only the foresight of the defenders had saved them. The vast strength of the stockade and the inner earthworks, hurriedly thrown up at the last moment, and the unswerving devotion of the little band of settlers within its shelter, had formed a combination of stout resistance. But as the time passed, and each day brought with it its tally of casualties, the position became more and more desperate.

With each attack the fortifications suffered. Twice the ramparts were breached, and only nightfall had saved the situation. At long range fighting the white defenders had the best of it, but hand to hand the issue was reversed. Each day saw one or two of the white men laid low, and the burden of the rest proportionately increased. Thus, out of a total of thirty available men and youths, at the end of six days the force was reduced by nearly a third.

But worst of all was the strain. Every man within the stockade, and for that matter, most of the women, too, knew that the pressure could not endure much longer without disastrous results. Ammunition was plentiful, provisions also, and the well supplied all the water necessary. It was none of these; it was the nerve strain, the lack of proper rest and sleep. The men only snatched odd half hours in the daytime. At night every eye and ear had to be alert.

Seth and Parker headed everything. In the councils they were the leaders, just as they were in the fighting. And on them devolved the full control of affairs, from the distribution of rations, in which Ma Sampson and Miss Parker were their lieutenants, to the regulations for the sanitation of the fort.

All the time Nevil Steyne was never lost sight of. He was driven to fight beside his leader with Rube close behind him ready for any treachery. He knew that Seth knew him, knew his secret, knew his relations with the Indians, and he quite understood that his only hope lay in implicit obedience, and a watchful eye for escape. His nature was such that he had no qualms of conscience in regard to opposing his red-skinned friends. That part he accepted philosophically. He had so long played a game of self-seeking treachery that his present condition came quite easily to him.

For Seth, who shall say what that dreadful period of suspense must have been? He went about his work with his usual quiet, thoughtful face, a perfect mask for that which lay behind it. There was no change of manner or expression. Success or disaster could not alter his stern, unyielding ways. He fought with the abandon and desperation of any Indian warrior when it came to close quarters, returning to his quiet, alert manner of command the moment the fighting was over. He was uncomplaining, always reassuring those about him, and carrying in his quiet personality something that fired his companions to exertions which no words of encouragement could have done.

Yet he was passing through an agony of heart and mind such as few men are submitted to. Rosebud had gone, vanished, and no one could answer the question that was forever in his mind. He had looked for her return when Joe Smith's party came in, only to be confounded by the fact that she had not even been seen by them. That night he had risked everything for her. He scouted till dawn, visiting Wanaha's hut, but only to find it deserted. Finally he returned to the farm, a broken-hearted man, bitter with the reflection that he alone was to blame for what had happened.

The girl's loss cast a terrible gloom over the whole fort. It was only her sense of responsibility which saved Ma from breaking down altogether. Rube said not a word, but, like Seth, he perhaps suffered the more.

It was on the seventh day that a curious change came over the situation. At first it was greeted with delight, but after the novelty had passed, a grave suspicion grew in the minds of the worn and weary defenders. There was not a shot fired. The enemy had withdrawn to their distant camps, and a heavy peace prevailed. But the move was so unaccountable that all sought the reason of it.

Counsel was taken by the heads of the defence, and the feeling of uneasiness grew. The more experienced conceived it to be the herald of a final, overwhelming onslaught. The younger preferred optimistic views, which they found unconvincing. However, every one took care that advantage was taken of the respite.

Seth had his supper in one of the upper rooms in company with Parker and Nevil Steyne. He sat at the open window watching, watching with eyes straining and nerves painfully alert. Others might rest, he could not, dared not.

The sun dipped below the horizon. The brief spring twilight changed from gold to gray. A footstep sounded outside the door of the room where the three men were sitting. A moment later Mrs. Rickards came in. Rosebud's cousin had changed considerably in those seven days. Her ample proportions were shrunken. Her face was less round, but had gained in character. The education of a lifetime had been crowded into the past week for her. And it had roused a spirit within her bosom, the presence of which she had not even suspected.

"Rube wants you, Seth," she announced. "He's on the north side of the stockade. It's something particular, I think," she added. "That's why he asked me to tell you."

With a few words of thanks, Seth accompanied her from the room and moved down-stairs. It was on their way down that Mrs. Rickards laid a hand, already work-worn, upon the man's arm.

"They're advancing again. Seth, shall we get out of this trouble?"

The question was asked without any expression of fear, and the man knew that the woman wanted a plain, truthful answer.

"It don't seem like it," he answered quietly.

"Yet, I kind o' notion we shall." Then after a pause he asked, "What's your work now?"

"The wounded."

"Ah! Did you ever fire a gun, ma'am?"

"No."

"Have you a notion to try?"

"If necessary."

"Mebbe it's going to be."

"You can count on me."

Wondering at the change in this Englishwoman, her companion left her to join Rube.

He found the whole garrison agog with excitement and alarm. There was a large gathering at the north side of the stockade, behind the barn and outbuildings. Even in the swift falling darkness it was evident that a big move was going on in the distant Indian camps. Nor did it take long to convince everybody that the move was in the nature of an advance.

After a long and earnest scrutiny through a pair of old field-glasses, Seth, followed by Rube, made a round of the fortifications. The movement was going on in every direction, and he knew that by morning, at any rate, they would have to confront a grand assault. He had completed the round, and was in the midst of discussing the necessary preparations with Rube, still examining the outlook through the glasses, when suddenly he broke off with a sharp ejaculation. The next moment he turned to the old man below him.

"Take these glasses, Rube," he said rapidly, "an' stay right here. Guess I'm goin' to drop over. I'll be back in awhiles. There's somethin' movin' among the grass within gunshot."

With a cheery "aye," Rube clambered to the top of the stockade as the younger man disappeared on the other side.

Seth landed on his hands and knees and moved out in that manner. Whatever his quarry the plainsman's movements would have been difficult of detection, for he crept along toward his goal with that rapid, serpentine movement so essentially Indian.

Rube watched him until darkness hid him from view. Then, stooping low, and scanning the sky-line a few minutes later, he distinctly made out the silhouette of two men standing talking together.

Seth found himself confronting an Indian. The man was plastered with war-paint, and his befeathered head was an imposing sight. But, even in the darkness, he recognized the broad face and slit-like eyes of the scout, Jim Crow. He was fully armed, but the white man's gun held him covered. In response to the summons of the threatening weapon, the man laid his arms upon the ground. Then he stood erect, and, grinning in his habitual manner, he waved an arm in the direction of the moving Indians.

"Wal?" inquired Seth, coldly.

"I, Jim Crow, come. I know heap. Fi' dollar an' I say."

Seth thought rapidly. And the result was another sharp inquiry.

"What is it?"

"Fi' dollar?"

"If it's worth it, sure, yes."

"It heap worth," replied the scout readily.

Seth's comment was short.

"You're a durned scoundrel anyway."

But Jim Crow was quite unabashed.

"See, it this," he said, and for the moment his face had ceased to grin. "I see much. I learn much. See." He waved an arm, comprehensively taking in the whole countryside. "White men all dead—all kill. Beacon—it gone. Fort—it gone. Farm—all gone. So. Miles an' miles. They all kill. Soldiers, come by south. They, too, all kill. Indian man everywhere. So. To-morrow they eat up dis farm. So. They kill all."

"Wal?" Seth seemed quite unconcerned by the man's graphic picture.

At once Jim Crow assumed a look of cunning. His eyes became narrower slits than ever.

"So. It dis way," he said, holding up a hand and indicating each finger as he proceeded to make his points. "Black Fox—him angry. Much. Big soldier men come from north. They fight—very fierce, an' tousands of 'em. They drive Indian back, back. Indian man everywhere kill. So. They come. Chief him much angry. Him say, 'They come. But I kill all white men first.' So to-morrow he burn the farm right up, an' kill everybody much dead."

"And the soldiers are near?"

The white man's words were coldly inquiring, but inwardly it was very different. A mighty hope was surging through him. The awful suspense had for the moment dropped from his sickening heart, and he felt like shouting aloud in his joy. The Indian saw nothing of this, however.

"Yes, they near. So. One sun."

Seth heard the news and remained silent. One day off! He could hardly realize it. He turned away and scanned the horizon. Jim Crow grew impatient.

"An' the fi' dollar?"

There was something so unsophisticated in the man's rascality that Seth almost smiled. He turned on him severely, however.

"You've been workin' with your countrymen, murderin' an' lootin', an' now you see the game's up you come around to me, ready to sell 'em same as you'd sell us. Say, you're a durned skunk of an Indian!"

"Jim Crow no Indian. I, Jim Crow, scout," the man retorted.

Seth eyed him.

"I see. You figger to git scoutin' agin when this is through. Say, you're wuss'n I thought. You're wuss'n——"

He broke off, struck with a sudden thought. In a moment he had dropped his tone of severity.

"See, I'm goin' to hand you twenty dollars," he said, holding the other's shifty eyes with his own steady gaze, "if you've a notion to earn 'em an' act squar'. Say, I ken trust you if I pay you. You ain't like the white Injun, Nevil Steyne, who's bin Black Fox's wise man so long. After he'd fixed the mischief he gits around to us an' turns on the Indians. He's fought with us. An' he's goin' to fight with us to-morrow. He's a traitor to the Indians. You belong to the whites, and you come to help us when you can. Now, see here. You're goin' to make north hard as hell 'll let you, savee? An' if the soldiers git here at sundown to-morrow night, I'm goin' to give you twenty dollars, and I'll see you're made head scout agin."

Seth waited for his answer. It came in a great tone of self-confidence.

"I, Jim Crow, make soldiers dis night. So."

"Good. You act squar'. You ain't no traitor to the white man, same as Nevil Steyne's traitor to the Indian, which I guess Black Fox likely knows by this time."

"Yes. Black Fox know."

CHAPTER XXX

THE LAST STAND

Sunrise brought the alarm. The call to arms came in the midst of breakfast. But it came to men who were discussing possibilities with smiling faces, and to women who were no longer held silent by the dread of the last few days. For all had shared in Seth's news. And if ever words were graven on the hearts of human beings, Seth's announcement, "Troops are comin' from the north," would most certainly have been found inscribed on the hearts of the defenders of White River Farm.

The attack began as the sun cleared the horizon, and continued all day. Like the first few raindrops of a storm-shower the enemy's bullets hissed through the air or spattered upon the buildings. Their long-range firing did little harm, for Indians are notoriously bad marksmen.

The sun mounted; the hours crept by. The attack was general, and each minute diminished the enveloping circle. The Indians had learned many lessons during the past six days, and not the least of them the utter folly of recklessness. Now they crawled upon their bellies through the grass, offering the smallest possible target to the keen-eyed garrison. But even so their death-roll was enormous. The plainsmen held them at their mercy, and it was only their vast numbers that gave them headway. Death had no terrors for them. As each man drooped his head upon the earth another was there to take his place; and so the advance was maintained.

Noon drew near; the ever-narrowing circle was close upon the farm.

There was no sound of voices, only the sharp cracking of rifles, or the ping of bullets whistling through the air as the Indians returned the biting fire of their intended victims. It was a life and death struggle against time, and both besieged and besiegers knew it.

Seth watched with quiet eyes but with mind no less anxious that he did not show it. He had no fixed station like the others. He moved here, there, and everywhere watching, watching, and encouraging with a quiet word, or lending his aid with a shot wherever pressure seemed to be greatest.

Noon passed. The whole plain was now alive with the slowly creeping foe stealing upon the doomed fort. The head of the advance was within three hundred yards of the stockade.

Parker was at Seth's side. Both were aiming at a party of young braves, endeavoring to outstrip their fellows by a series of short rushes. For some moments they silently picked them off, like men breaking pipes in a shooting gallery. The last had just fallen.

"It's red-hot this time," observed the Agent, turning his attention in a fresh direction. "We'll be lucky if we hold out until to-night." He was blackened with perspiration and dust. He wore three bandoliers bristling with ammunition over a torn and stained shirt.

"Guess so," Seth replied. "This 'll last another two hours, I'm figgerin', then we'll—git busy."

A fresh rush had started and the two rifles were kept at work. The Indians fell like ninepins, but there were always more to come on.

Hargreaves joined them a moment. He, too, was terribly war-worn. He still wore his clerical stock, but it had lost all semblance to its original shape.

"They're rushing us everywhere, Seth," he said.

Seth replied while he aimed at another daring warrior.

"I know," he said, and fired.

Hargreaves went back to his post. There must be no waste of time. This gentle pastor had little of gentleness about him now. A good Christian in every way, he still had no thought of turning the other cheek when women were in peril.

By three o'clock in the afternoon the rush became general. The defenders had no time even to keep their rifles cool. A steady fire was kept up, and the Indians were picked off like flies. But the gaps were filled by men beyond all description in their recklessness. Nothing could stem the tide. They drew nearer and nearer like the waters of an oncoming sea. The end was looming. It was very near.

Suddenly, in response to an order from Seth, some of the women left the shelter of the house and followed him. A few minutes later the well was working, and a chain of buckets was passing up to the roof of the house. A process of saturation was put into operation. The thatch was soaked until the water ran through the ceilings.

While this was going on a cry came from the northern extremity. The first Indian had reached the stockade and paid the penalty of his temerity.

Now orders, swift and sharp, passed from lip to lip. Seth was everywhere. The battle would be in full swing in a minute.

Suddenly Rube and Nevil appeared from a small outhouse rolling two large barrels. These were stood on end and the heads knocked out of them. The pails used for water were requisitioned; a fresh saturation went forward; this time it was the log stockade, and the saturation was being performed with coal-oil.

The sun was already dropping over the western horizon when a party of the enemy, in face of the fiercest fire, reached the defences. It was the moment Seth had awaited. From the stockade he called out a sharp order to the women in the upper parts of the house, and the loyal creatures, distracted with the nervous tension of inaction, poured out a deadly volley.

The terrible bombardment of short range weapons had instant effect. The enemy fell back under the withering hail. Headed by Seth a dozen men mounted the ramparts, and the next instant the vast corral formed a circle of leaping flame in the faces of the besiegers. The coal-oil had done its work, and the resinous pine logs yielded to the demands of those who needed their service.

The defence was consummate. For the great walls were sufficiently far from the buildings to render life possible within the fiery circle.

Baffled and furious, the Indians fell back before a foe they were powerless to combat. At a respectful distance they watched the conflagration with wonder. The magical abruptness of it filled them for a moment with superstitious awe. But this phase did not last long.

The gates were the weak spot, and they quickly burnt through. In half an hour they crashed from their hinges, and the lynx-eyed foe beheld the breach thus open before them. They charged to the assault, while inside the defenders stood ready for them just beyond the range of the fierce heat.

Now was given an example of that strange, fanatical courage for which the red man is so famous. To pass the breach was like passing through a living furnace, for the fire was raging at its full height upon each side. There was no hesitation, no shrinking.

Those nearest it charged the opening, and as they came were mowed down by the rifles waiting for them. Again and again was the gateway besieged, and the roasting human flesh sent up a nauseous reek upon the smoke-laden air. Nothing could exceed the insensate fearlessness of these benighted creatures, nothing the awful slaughter which the white defenders dealt out.

But the superior intelligence and skill of the white men served them for only a time against the daring horde. Dozens rushed to the sacrifice, but ever there were more behind asking for the death of their comrades. And inch by inch they drove through the opening to within striking distance. They had abandoned their firearms, and, with hatchet and tomahawk, their natural close-quarter weapons, the final struggle began.

All that had gone before was as nothing to the fight that waxed now. The howling mob were within the defences, and there was only one possible outcome. The position was one of those when the true spirit of the frontiersman is at its highest and grandest pitch.

Gradually the riflemen on each flank dropped back before the raging mob.

The rank, of which Rube was the centre, stood. Here was no rifle practice. Revolvers were at work with the rapidity of maxim guns. As they were emptied, they were passed back and reloaded by the women. But even this was inadequate to hold the mob.

Suddenly Rube, prompted by that feeling which is in the heart of every man of mighty muscle, abandoned his revolver, and, clubbing his rifle, reverted to the methods of the old savage. He swung it around his head like a flail, and crashed it amongst those directly in front of him. And his action became an example for the rest. Every rifle was clubbed, and by sheer might, and desperate exertion, the defenders cleared a space before them. The great Rube advanced, his rugged face fiercely alight. He could no longer wait for attack; he went to meet it, his giant form towering amidst the crowd, and the rest following.

The scene was one never to be forgotten. He hewed a road for himself through the living crush, his rifle butt crashing amongst heads recklessly, indiscriminately, but urged with all the might of his giant strength. Seth and the Agent, and Nevil and the minister were his chief supporters. And there was a light in the cleric's eyes, such as had never been seen there before by any of his flock, and a devilish joy in his heart as he felt the concussion of his blows upon heads that crushed beneath them.

Back they drove the howling throng, back toward the fiery gateway. It literally crumpled before their furious attack. But as the warriors fell back the progress of the white men slowed and finally ceased altogether, for the masses beyond were pressing, and so packed were the savages that they could not retreat.

Darkness was settling over the land. The Indians rallied as the first fury of the white men's onslaught spent itself. The red men, stern fighters at all times, were quick to seize upon the advantage. And their counter was no less furious than the defenders' assault had been. Step by step, with hatchets gleaming in the yellow light, they regained their lost ground.

Slowly the white men were beaten back; all but Rube, whose fury was unabated. He had cleared a space for himself, from which the fiercest efforts of the enemy could not dislodge him.

Shouting to those behind to care for the women, Seth sprang to the old man's side, and, setting his back to his, stood to help him. Retreat was cut off, but, all unconcerned for everything, like a maddened bull, Rube sought only to slay, to crush, to add to the tally of the dying and dead.

How the last moments of that terrible final stand were passed, Seth could never have told. His long illness was telling on him. His weakness affected him sorely. All he was aware of were his companion's mighty blows, and the fury that was driving him. That, and the necessity to defend him on his unprotected side. He fought as he could. No skill guided him. Now, at last, he had no cunning, and he was hazily conscious of his ineffectiveness.

Once he was forced to his knees by the blow of a hatchet, which, glancing down his clubbed rifle, took him in the neck with its flat. It was at that moment that his senses became aware of a distant bugle call. He scarcely recognized it, and, certainly, at the moment, it brought him no understanding.

Instinctively he struggled to his feet and fought on. Curiously enough, a moment later, his dulled senses made him aware of a shudder passing over his companion's frame. He knew that Rube staggered, just as he was made aware that he recovered, and, with a sudden access of fury, renewed the fight. He knew that his friend had been badly hit, and was putting forth his last reserve of strength.

In the midst of this last struggle he heard the bugle again, but this time it was louder. Its note rose high above the noise of battle, the roar of the flames. But even so, he did not take its meaning until he heard a mighty cheer go up from his comrades within the defences.

He roused; a great joy thrilled him. His head suddenly became clear, and his weakness passed from him like the lifting of some depressing cloud. He found himself able to put forth a last exertion, and at this juncture he was somehow standing at Rube's side, instead of at his back.

Of one accord, and without a word, they charged the howling mob. They smote with their heavy rifles in every direction, shouting as they went, driving all before them. A mighty triumph was in Seth's heart; he had no room for anything else, no thought for anything else. Even he was blinded to the old man's condition. It was not until he was joined by the rest of the defenders, and the Indians were wildly struggling over one another to escape through the still blazing gateway, and the old man fell like a log at his side in the midst of the pursuit, that he realized what had happened. Rube was bleeding from a gaping wound at the base of his neck.

Just for one instant he saw the gateway fill with uniformed horsemen, then Seth fell on his knees at his foster-father's side.

There was no attempt to pursue the Indians. Weary and exhausted the little garrison gathered mutely round the fallen man. Ma was at Seth's side. She had raised her husband's head, and her old gray eyes were peering tenderly anxious into his. While she was still supporting him, some one pushed a way to her side. One bare white arm was thrust through hers, and a hand was gently laid on the old man's rugged forehead. Ma turned inquiringly upon the intruder, and found herself staring into a pair of tearful, violet eyes.

"Rosebud!" she cried. And instantly the tears slowly rolled down her worn cheeks, the first tears, she had shed during that last terrible week.

CHAPTER XXXI

THE SENTENCE

The relief of the farm was really only the beginning of the campaign. It meant that following on its heels the great northern posts were pouring out their thousands of troops, and that a general advance was in progress. It meant that now, at last, but, alas! too late to avert the awful massacre of the white settlers, the force was adequate to the task of subjugating the savages.

The flying column that had ridden to the rescue was a small band of picked men, with a couple of light machine guns. It was composed of veteran Indian fighters, who, fully understanding the desperate chances of thus cutting themselves off from their supports, and riding into the very jaws of death, were yet ready to do it again and again.

The Indians, believing this initial attack of white troops to be the immediate advance guard of an overwhelming force, withdrew in something very like panic. But with morning light they realized they had been "bluffed" and at once returned to the attack.

For the defenders, however, all real anxiety was past. They knew that a sweeping movement was in progress throughout the whole disturbed area, and it was only a question of days before the Indians would be shepherded back to their Reservations.

The mischief, however, was done, the country was devastated. The prosperous farming region was laid waste, and the labor of years utterly destroyed. Of the survivors of the awful holocaust the majority found themselves utterly ruined; their homes destroyed; their possessions gone. Many were wounded, and all were homeless. Their plight was pitiable.

While others showered their praise and thanks and rough compliments upon the girl who had dared all to bring her friends the help they so sorely needed; while old men and young rivaled each other in their admiration of her reckless courage; while the women sought to minister to her, and wept over her, Seth held aloof, working and organizing for the general comfort and well-being with that everlasting thought for others which was so great a part of his nature.

It was not that he was indifferent; it was not that he had no thanks to tender. His heart was full, full to the brim with pride for this girl he loved. Hers, he felt, had been the great foresight, hers the great courage to carry out their only possible salvation. When his grave eyes had first fallen upon the slight blanketed figure of the little white squaw he recognized indeed the clever head which had done more than trust to rash courage. It would have been impossible for him to love her more.

Nevertheless his was the first greeting when she had been discovered in their midst. His had been the first hand to grip hers. But there was no effusion. Nothing but what, to strange ears, might have sounded cold and wanting.

"Thanks, little Rosie," was all he had said, while his hand held hers. But, at that moment, the girl would rather have foregone life itself than the glance he bestowed upon her out of his grave, dark eyes.

It was many days before any freedom from the fortress farm could be enjoyed. But at last the time came round when the troops began to converge upon the Reservations, and the shepherding process swept the Indians to their homes, a dejected horde, hating but cowed for the moment. As before, as always, their fierce fires of savagery were alight; they were only burning low, for, as every plainsman knows, they are unquenchable.

It was late in the afternoon when the news of their freedom flew through the camp. None but those who have passed through a similar ordeal can realize the unutterable joy and thankfulness that filled each heart. Though possessions had gone and many were absolutely ruined, still liberty was theirs at last. Liberty with its boundless possibilities.

Seth was sitting alone, propped against the charred gate-post of the stockade. He was smoking and resting, and incidentally thinking deeply after a long day's work. There was much to think about. Rube was slowly recovering under the careful hands of his devoted wife. Mrs. Rickards and Rosebud had relieved the farmwife of all her duties that she might be free to lavish her utmost care upon her staunch old friend and husband. The future prospects of the farm were less involved than the affairs of most of the farmers. The setback of the rebellion was tremendous, but years of thrift had left White River Farm independent of a single year's crops. Besides the farmhouse and buildings were intact.

But none of these things was in his mind just now. There was something else which filled his heart with unutterable bitterness, which revealed itself in the hard, thoughtful stare of his dark eyes as he gazed out upon the wide encampment of soldiers spreading itself out in all directions.

Every now and then he shifted his gaze into a certain direction, only to turn away with apparent indifference and let his eyes wander over every chance object that attracted them. Once the Agent came to him and they spoke for some moments in a low tone. Then he was again left to his thoughts. The sun dipped below the horizon, and the twilight waned. He remained at his post. There could be no doubt now that he was waiting with some fixed purpose.

At last he turned decidedly in the direction in which he had been so frequently glancing, and this time his movement was anticipatory. A dark figure was approaching from among the tents. It was the scout, Jim Crow, who came up and squatted at the white man's side. The two talked together for a long time, and at last the Indian rose to depart.

"So," he said, in his pompous fashion, "I do these things. I, Jim Crow. Good."

"You've done good work," Seth responded casually. "And you've been paid for it, I guess. See you do this, sure."

He watched the Indian while he solemnly spat upon the ground.

"I, Jim Crow, have said." And with this vaunting claim to honesty the scout abruptly turned and moved away.

A moment later Seth made his way slowly to a small outhouse. He raised the latch of the door and passed within. There were two occupants. The Indian Agent was sitting at a little table smoking and reading, and Nevil Steyne was lying full length upon some outspread blankets upon the floor. This place was the temporary abode of the three men. The farmhouse had been given up to the women and children.

Seth took a seat. As he came in Parker closed his book and put it away. From his blankets Nevil glanced up quickly, and continued to watch the movements of both with expectant eyes. He was aware that permission had been given for every one to leave the farm. Nor did he delude himself. He knew that he was a prisoner.

Seth placed his chair so that he was in full view of the man on the blankets. And his first words were addressed to him.

"Guess you're goin' to quit this farm," he said, calmly, but in a manner which compelled his prisoner's attention. "I've thought a heap, an' that's how I've got figgerin'. You're goin' to quit this night. That is ef you're so minded."

He paused, but his grave eyes still surveyed the ungainly form, still stared coldly into the lean unshaven face, into the shifty pale eyes. Nevil made no response. He knew instinctively that this was only a prelude to more that was to follow.

Parker watched Seth. In a measure he was mystified, for the plainsman had never given him his full confidence with regard to Nevil. He suspected a lot, but that was all.

"Guess I don't need to tell you a deal about yourself," Seth went on presently. "I'll just mention that Nevil Steyne ain't your real name, an' it wouldn't take me guessin' long to locate the other. That's as mebbe. You're a skunk," he proceeded, without raising his voice. "You're wuss'n a yaller dawg, but even a yaller dawg mostly has an option. That's how it is wi' you, seein' you're o' that breed. I ain't no feelin' o' mercy for you anyways, but I'll give you a chance. Ef you stay right here ther's the courts as 'll hang you sure; ef you quit, ther's the Injuns as you've lived by, an' as you fooled to suit your own dirty schemes. I don't see as ther's a great choice for you. Your game's played, an' you're goin' to cash in, an' it kind o' seems to me you've got to pay anyways. Wal, you'll choose right now."

Nevil had sat up while the other was speaking. He gave no outward sign beyond that one movement. Now he slowly rose to his feet and looked down upon the set face of the arbiter of his fate a little uncertainly. He turned from him to the Agent, who was looking on in no little puzzlement. Then his eyes came back to the relentless face of Seth, and he seemed to be struggling to penetrate the sphinx-like expression he beheld.

He scented danger, he knew there was danger. But even so his mind was made up. He would not face the jury of his white brothers. He believed he understood the Indians, and saw chances in this direction. But there was the wonder why Seth had given him the chance. He had no time to debate the question. His answer was needed.

"I'll go back to the Indians," he said, with a hateful laugh, in which there was no semblance of mirth. "As you suggest, a yellow dog can always run for it."

"Jest so. It ken allus run."

Then the full bitterness of his position swept over the renegade, and a deep rage stirred the hatred he held for this man who had outwitted him at every turn, and now was in a position to pronounce sentence upon him. And his words came low with concentrated fury.

"Yes, blast you, you can sneer! But I tell you you're making a mistake. I can twist the Indians around my finger. Bah, I care nothing for them! I shall get clear and save myself, and, as sure as there's a hell for the damned, you shall pay!"

But the man he addressed remained undisturbed. His manner was imperturbable. He nodded gravely.

"Good," he said. "Now git—git quick!"

And the man who posed as Nevil Steyne passed out of the hut and out of the fort, urged almost to precipitancy by the suggestion of Seth's final command.

After his going silence reigned in the little corn shed. Parker had a hundred questions to ask, but none of them came readily to his lips in face of his companion's silence. In the end it was Seth who spoke first.

"Wal," he said, with a sigh, "that's settled." His words were an expression of relief.

"I don't understand. You've let him go. You've given him a chance to get away in safety after——"

"Yes," responded the other grimly, "a dawg's chance."

The answer silenced all further protest.

"Yes," Seth went on reflectively, "I've done with him, I guess; we all have. Say, he's Rosebud's uncle."

"Ah!" Parker was beginning to understand. But he was not yet satisfied, and his ejaculation was an invitation to the other.

Seth went on as though in soliloquy.

"Yes. He's gone, an' ther' ain't no tellin' where he'll finish. Ther's a hell some'eres. Mebbe he ken twist 'em, the Injuns, around his finger, mebbe he can't. I 'lows he goin' to face 'em. They'll deal out by him as they notion justice, I guess."

"But he may escape them. He's slippery." Parker hated the thought of the man going scot-free.

Seth shook his head.

"No," he said. "He'll face 'em. I've seen to that, I guess. Jim Crow follers him wherever he goes. An' Jim Crow hain't no use for Stephen Raynor."

"What do you think will happen?"

Parker looked up into the taller man's face as they stood in the doorway of the hut.

Seth turned. His shoulders shrugged expressively as he moved out and walked toward the farmhouse.

CHAPTER XXXII

WANAHA THE INDIAN

The moon at its full shone down upon a scene of profound silence. Its silvery rays overpowered the milder starry sheen of the heavens. The woods upon the banks of the White River were tipped with a hard, cold burnish, but their black depths remained unyielding. All was still—so still.

Thousands of Indians are awaiting in silent, stubborn hatred the morrow's sentence of their white shepherds. A deep passion of hatred and revenge lies heavy on their tempestuous hearts; and upon the heart of their warlike chieftain most of all.

The heart that beats within the Indian bosom is invincible. It is beyond the reach of sympathy, as it is beyond the reach of fear. It stands alone in its devotion to warlike brutality. Hatred is its supreme passion, just as fearlessness is its supreme virtue. And hatred and revenge are moving to-night—moving under the calm covering of apparent peace; moving now lest the morrow should put it beyond the power of the red man to mete out the full measure of his lust for native savagery. And so at last there comes a breaking of the perfect peace of night.

A dark figure moves out of the depths of the woods. It moves slowly toward the log hut of Nevil Steyne. It pauses at a distance and surveys the dim outline against the woodland backing.

Another figure moves out from the woods, and a moment later another and yet another; and each figure follows in the track of the foremost, and they stand talking in low murmurs. Thus twenty-five blanketed figures are gathered before the hut of the white renegade. They are Indians, hoary-headed patriarchs of their race, but glowing with the fierce spirit of youth in their sluggish hearts.

Presently they file away one by one, and it becomes apparent that each old man is well armed. They spread out and form themselves into a wide circle, which slowly closes in upon the hut. Then each decrepit figure huddles itself down upon its haunches, like some bald-headed vulture settling with heavily flapping wings upon its prey.

Sleep has not visited the eyes of those within the hut. When things go awry with those who live by double-dealing, sleep does not come easily. Nevil Steyne is awake, and his faithful wife keeps him company.

The interior of the hut is dismantled. Bundles of furnishings lie scattered about on the floor. It is plain that this is to be the last night which these two intend to spend in the log hut which has sheltered them so long.

The squaw is lying fully dressed upon the bed, and the man is sitting beside her smoking. They are talking, discussing eagerly that which has held the man's feverish interest the whole night.

There is no kindness in the man's tone as he speaks to the woman. He is beset with a fear he cannot conceal. It is in his tone, it is in his eyes, it is in his very restlessness.

The woman is calm. She is an Indian, and in her veins runs the blood of generations of great chiefs. Fear has no place in her heart, but her devotion to her man makes her anxious for him. Her slow, labored use of his language is meant to encourage him, but he takes no comfort from it. His utter selfishness, his cowardice, place him beyond mere verbal encouragement.

"It still wants two hours to dawn," Nevil exclaimed, referring to his watch for about the twentieth time in the last hour. "God, how the time hangs!"

The woman's dark eyes were upon his nervous face. She noted the anxious straining of his shifty eyes. Their whites were bloodshot, and his brows were drawn together in the painful concentration of a mind fixed upon one thought.

"It will pass," she said, with all the hopefulness she could express.

"Of course it will. Do you suppose I don't know?" The man spoke with harsh irritation. "You—you don't seem to understand."

"Wanaha understands." The squaw nodded. Then she, too, gave way to a slight irritation. "Why you not sleep, my Nevil? Wanaha watch. It a long journey. Sleep, my husband. You fear foolish. So."

The man turned scornful eyes in her direction, and for a moment did not speak. Then presently he said—

"Sometimes I think it's unnecessary for us to go. I can't make up my mind. I never had such difficulty in seeing clearly before. Your brother was so quiet and calm. He spoke so generously. I told him the whole story. How I was forced by that damned Seth to go into the fort. And how I was forced to fight. Pshaw! what's the use of talking? I've told you all this already. Yet he listened to all I had to say, and as I made each point he nodded in that quiet, assured way of his—you know. I think he understood and was satisfied. I think so—and yet—it's no use, I can't be sure. I wish he'd lost his temper in his usual headstrong way. I understand him when he is like that. But he didn't. He was very calm.

"Do you know, my Wana, it seemed to me that he'd heard my story before, told by some one else, probably told with variations to suit themselves. It seemed to me that—well, he was only listening to me because he had to. I swear I'd give ten years of my life to know what he really thinks. Yes, I think I'm right. Once away from here we are safe. Neither he nor any of the braves can follow us. The soldiers will see that none leave the Reservations. Yes, I'm sure it's best to get away. It can do no harm, and it's best to be sure. Still an hour and three-quarters," he finished up, again referring to his watch.

"Yes, it best so," the woman said in reply. She understood the condition of her husband's mind. She saw clearly that she must humor him.

Whatever her innermost thoughts may have been she made her replies subservient to his humor. She had listened closely to his account of his interview with her brother, and there is little doubt that she had formed her own opinion, and, being of the blood of the chief, she probably understood him better than this white man did. But whatever she really thought no word of it escaped her.

Another silence fell. Again it was the man who broke it.

"That Jim Crow is very active. He comes and goes all day. He interviews Little Black Fox whenever he pleases. He's a two-faced rascal. Do you know, it was he who brought the news of relief to the farm. And what's more, he came in with the soldiers. I always seem to see him about. Once I thought he was watching my movements. I wonder why?"

The man drooped dejectedly as he tried to unravel this fresh tangle. Why was Jim Crow shadowing him? In the interests of the Indians? Again he pulled out his watch. And the woman beside him saw that his hand was shaking as he held it out to the light of the stove.

It was time to hitch up his horses, he said. Yet they were not starting until dawn, and it still wanted a full hour to the time.

Wanaha sat up, and Nevil moved about amongst the litter of their belongings. There was coffee on the stove and food on the table. He helped himself to both, bolting meat and drink in a nervous, hasty manner. Wanaha joined him. She ate sparingly, and then began to gather their goods together.

Nevil turned to her. He was preparing to fetch the horses which were picketed out on the prairie. He was in better mood now. Action restored in him a certain amount of confidence.

"It will be good to get away, my Wana," he said, for a moment laying one hand upon her shoulder.

The woman looked up into his mean face with a world of love in her profound eyes.

"It good to be with you—anywhere, my Nevil," she said, in her quiet way.

The man turned to the door.

He raised the latch and threw it open. He stood speechless. A panic was upon him; he could not move, he could not think. Little Black Fox was standing in the doorway, and, behind him, two of his war-councilors leaning on their long, old-fashioned rifles.

Without a word, the chief, followed by his two attendants, stepped within. The door was closed again. Then Little Black Fox signed to

Wanaha for a light. The squaw took the oil-lamp from a shelf and lit it, and the dull, yellow rays revealed the disorder of the place.

The chief gazed about him. His handsome face was unmoved. Finally he looked into the face of the terror-stricken renegade. Nevil was tall, but he was dwarfed by the magnificent carriage and superb figure of the savage.

It was the chief who was the first to speak. The flowing tongue of the Sioux sounded melodious in the rich tones of the speaker's voice. He spoke without a touch of the fiery eloquence which had been his when he was yet the untried leader of his race. The man seemed to have suddenly matured. He was no longer the headstrong boy that had conceived an overwhelming passion for a white girl, but a warrior of his race, a warrior and a leader.

"My brother would go from his friends? So?" he said in feigned surprise. "And my sister, Wanaha?"

"Wanaha obeys her lord. Whither he goes she goes. It is good."

The squaw was alive to the position, but, unlike her white husband, she rose to the occasion. The haughty manner of the chief was no more haughty than hers. She was blood of this man, and no less royal than he. Her deep eyes were alert and shining now. The savage was dominant in her again. She was, indeed, a princess of her race.

"And whither would they go, this white brother and his squaw?" There was a slight irony in the Indian's voice.

Again the squaw answered.

"We go where white men and Indians live in peace."

"No white man or Indian lives in peace where he goes."

Little Black Fox pointed scornfully at the cowering white man. The squaw had no answer ready. But the renegade himself found his tongue and answered.

"We go until the white man's anger is passed," he said. "Then we return to the great chief's camp."

For a while the young chieftain's eyes seemed to burn into those of the man before him, so intense was the angry fire of his gaze.

"You go," he said at last, "because you fear to stay. It is not the white man you fear, but the Indian you have betrayed. Your tongue lies, your heart lies. You are neither brave nor squaw-man. Your heart is the heart of a snake that is filled with venom. Your brain is like the mire of the muskeg which sucks, sucks its victims down to destruction. Your blood is like the water of a mosquito swamp, poisonous even to the air. I have eyes; I have ears. I learn all these things, and I say nothing. The hunter uses a poisoned weapon. It matters not so that he brings down his quarry. But his weapon is for his quarry, and not for himself. He destroys it when there is danger that he shall get hurt by it. You are a poisoned weapon, and you have sought to hurt me. So."

Wanaha suddenly stepped forward. Her great eyes blazed up into her brother's.

"The great chief wrongs my man. All he has done he was forced to do. His has been the heart to help you. His has been the hand to help you. His has been the brain to plan for you. So. The others come. They take him prisoner. He must fight for them or die."

"Then if he fights he is traitor. So he must die."

Nevil had no word for himself. He was beyond words. Even in his extremity he remembered what Seth had said to him. And he knew now that Seth's knowledge of the Indians was greater, far deeper, than his. This was his "dog's chance," but he had not even the privilege of a run.

The irony of his lot did not strike him. Crimes which he had been guilty of had nothing to do with his present position. Instead, he stood arraigned for a treachery which had not been his, toward the one man to whom he had ever been faithful.

But while his craven heart wilted before his savage judge; while his mind was racked with tortures of suspense, and his scheming brain had lost its power of concentration; while his limbs shook at the presentiment of his doom, his woman stood fearless at his side, ready to serve him to the bitter end, ready to sacrifice herself if need be that his wretched life might be saved.

Now she replied to her brother's charge, with her beautiful head erect and her bosom heaving.

"No man is coward who serves you as he has served you," she cried, her eyes confronting her brother's with all the fearless pride of her race. "The coward is the other. The one who turns upon his friend and helper when misfortune drives."

The words stung as they were meant to sting. And something of the old headstrong passion leapt into the young chief's heart. He pointed at his sister.

"Enough!" he cried; and a movement of the head conveyed a command to his attendants. They stepped forward. But Wanaha was quicker. She met them, and, with upraised hand, waved them back in a manner so imperious that they paused.

"Little Black Fox forgets!" she cried, addressing herself to her brother, and ignoring the war-councilors. "No brave may lay hand upon the daughter of my father. Little Black Fox is chief. My blood is his blood. By the laws of our race his is the hand that must strike. The daughter of Big Wolf awaits. Let my brother strike."

As she finished speaking Wanaha bowed her head in token of submission. But for all his rage the chief was no slayer of his womenfolk. The ready-witted woman understood the lofty Indian spirit of her brother. She saw her advantage and meant to hold it. She did not know what she hoped. She did not pause to think. She had a woman's desire to gain time only. And as she saw her brother draw back she felt that, for the moment at least, she was mistress of the situation.

"So," she went on, raising her head again and proudly confronting the angry-eyed youth, "my brother, even in his wrath, remembers the law of our race. Let him think further, and he will also remember other things. Let him say to himself, 'I may not slay this man while my sister, Wanaha, lives. She alone has power to strike. The council of chiefs may condemn, but she must be the executioner.' So! And my brother will be in the right, for Wanaha is the blood of Big Wolf, and the white man is her husband."

The headstrong chief was baffled. He knew that the woman was right. The laws of the Sioux race were as she had said. And they were so stringent that it would be dangerous to set them aside, even though this man's death had been decided upon by the unanimous vote of the council. He stood irresolute, and Wanaha added triumph to her tone as she went on.

"So, great chief, this man's life is mine. And I, Wanaha, your sister, refuse to take it. For me he is free."

But Wanaha in her womanish enthusiasm had overshot her mark. The laws were strong, but this wild savage's nature was as untamed and fearless as any beast of the field. It was her tone of triumph that undid her.

Little Black Fox suddenly whipped out a long hunting-knife from his belt and flung it upon the table with a great clatter. It lay there, its vicious, gleaming blade shining dully in the yellow lamplight.

"See!" he cried, his voice thick with fury. "Have your rights! I go. With the first streak of dawn I come again. Then I slay! Wanaha shall die by my hand, and then she has no right to the life of the white man!"

The first streak of dawn lit the eastern sky. The horses were grazing, tethered to their picket ropes within view of the log hut down by the river. The wagon stood in its place at the side of the building. There was no firelight to be seen within the building, no lamplight.

The circle of silent squatting figures still held their vigil.

As the daylight grew three figures emerged from the woods and moved silently to the door of the hut. They paused, listening, but no sound came from within. One, much taller than his companions, reached out and raised the latch. The door swung open. He paused again. Then he stepped across the threshold.

The new-born day cast a gray twilight over the interior. The man sniffed, like a beast of prey scenting the trail of blood. And that which came to his nostrils seemed to satisfy him, for he passed within and strode to the bedside. He stood for a few moments gazing down at the figures of a man and a woman locked in each other's arms.

He looked long and earnestly upon the calm features of the faces so closely pressed together. There was no pity, no remorse in his heart, for life and death were matters which touched him not at all. War was as the breath of his nostrils.

Presently he moved away. There was nothing to keep him there. These two had passed together to the shores of the Happy Hunting Ground. They had lived and died together. They would—perhaps—awake together. But not on the prairies of the West.

CHAPTER XXXIII

THE CAPITULATION

"I'd like to know how it's all going to end."

Mrs. Rickards drew a deep sigh of perplexity and looked helplessly over at Ma, who was placidly knitting at her husband's bedside. The farmwife's bright face had lost nothing of its comeliness in spite of the anxieties through which she had so recently passed. Her twinkling eyes shone cheerily through her glasses, and the ruddy freshness of her complexion was still fair to see. A line or two, perhaps, had deepened about her mouth, and the grayness of her hair may have become a shade whiter. But these things were hardly noticeable.

The change in Rosebud's aunt was far more pronounced. She had taken to herself something of the atmosphere of the plains-folk in the few weeks of her stay at the farm. And the subtle change had improved her.

Rube was mending fast, and the two older women now spent all their spare time in his company.

Ma looked up from her work.

"Rube an' me have been discussin' it," she said. "Guess we've settled to leave the farm, an' buy a new place around some big city. I don't rightly know how the boy 'll take it. Y' see, Seth's mighty hard to change, an' he's kind o' fixed on this place. Y' see, he's young, an' Rube an' me's had a longish spell. We'd be pleased to take it easy now. Eh, old man?"

Ma glanced affectionately at the mighty figure filling up the bed. The man nodded.

"Y' see, things don't seem hard till you see your old man's blood runnin'," she went on. "Then—well, I guess I ain't no more stummick fer fight. I'd be thankful to God A'mighty to end my days peaceful."

Mrs. Rickards nodded sympathetically.

"You're quite wise," she said. "It seems to me you've earned a rest. The courage and devotion of all you dear people out here have been a wonderful education to me. Do you know, Mrs. Sampson, I never knew what life really meant until I came amongst you all. The hope, and love, and sympathy on this prairie are something to marvel at. I can understand a young girl's desire to return to it after once having tasted it. Even for me it has its fascinations. The claims of civilization fall from one out here in a manner that makes me wonder. I don't know yet but that I shall remain for a while and see more of it."

Ma smiled and shook her head at the other's enthusiasm.

"There's a heap worth living for out here, I guess. But— —"

"Yes. I know what you would say. A time comes when you want rest for mind and body. I wonder," Mrs. Rickards went on thoughtfully, "if Seth ever wants rest and peace? I don't think it. What a man!"

She relapsed into silent admiration of the man of whom she was speaking. Ma noted her look. She understood the different place Seth now occupied in this woman's thoughts.

"But I was not thinking about the affairs of this farm and the Indians so much as something else," Mrs. Rickards went on presently, smiling from Ma to Rube and back again at Ma.

The farmwife laid her knitting aside. She understood the other's meaning, and this was the first mention of it between them. Even Rube had turned his head and his deep-set eyes were upon the "fine lady."

"Yes, I was thinking of Seth and Rosebud," she went on earnestly. "You know that Rosebud— —"

Ma nodded.

"Seth's ter'ble slow," she said slyly.

"Do you think he's— —"

"Sure." The two women looked straight into each other's eyes, which smiled as only old women's eyes can smile when they are speaking of that which is the greatest matter of their lives.

"I know how she regards him," Mrs. Rickards went on. "And I tell you frankly, Mrs. Sampson, I was cordially opposed to it—when I came here. Even now I am not altogether sure it's right by the girl's dead father—but——"

"But——?" Ma's face was serious while she waited for the other to go on.

"But—but—well, if I was a girl, and could get such a man as Seth for a husband, I should be the proudest woman in the land."

"An' you'd be honored," put in Rube, speaking for the first time.

Mrs. Rickards laughingly nodded.

Ma sighed.

"Guess Seth has queer notions. Mighty queer. I 'low, knowin' him as I do, I could say right here that that boy 'ud ask her right off, only fer her friends an' her dollars. He's a foolhead, some."

Mrs. Rickards laughed again.

"In England these things are usually an inducement," she said significantly.

"Seth's a man," said Ma with some pride. "Seth's real honest, an'—an', far be it for me to say it, he's consequent a foolhead. What's dollars when folks love? Pshaw! me an' Rube didn't think o' no dollars."

"Guess we hadn't no dollars to think of, Ma," murmured Rube in a ponderous aside.

"Wal? An' if we had?" Ma smiled defiantly at her "old man."

"Wal, mebbe we'd 'a' tho't of 'em."

The farmwife turned away in pretended disgust.

"And you don't think anything will come of it?" suggested Mrs. Rickards, taking the opportunity of returning to the matter under discussion.

Ma's eyes twinkled.

"Ther' ain't no sayin'," she said. "Mebbe it's best left to Rosie." She glanced again at her sick husband. "Y' see, men mostly has notions, an' some are ter'ble slow. But they're all li'ble to act jest so, ef the woman's the right sort. Guess it ain't no use in old folks figgerin' out fer young folks. The only figgerin' that counts is what they do fer themselves."

"I believe you're right," responded Mrs. Rickards, wondering where the farmwife had acquired her fund of worldly wisdom. Ma's gentle shrewdness overshadowed any knowledge she had acquired living the ordinary social life that had been hers in England.

Ma's worldly wisdom, however, was all on the surface. She knew Seth, and she knew Rosebud. She had watched their lives with loving eyes, prompted by a great depth of sympathy. And all she had seen had taught her that both were capable of managing their own affairs, and, for the rest, her optimism induced the belief that all would come right in the end. And it was out of this belief she reassured her new-made friend.

Meanwhile the little blind god was carrying on his campaign with all the cunning and crushing strategy for which he is justly renowned. There is no power such as his in all the world. What he sets out to do he accomplishes with a blissful disregard for circumstances. Where obstacles refuse to melt at his advance, he adopts the less comfortable, but none the less effective, manner of breaking through them. And perhaps he saw the necessity of some such course in the case of Seth and Rosebud. Anyway, he was not beaten yet.

The last of the refugees had left the farm. Seth had been assisting in the departure of the various families. It was a sad day's work, and no one realized the pathos of it more than the silent plainsman. He had given his little all to the general welfare, but he had been incapable of saving the homes that had been built up with so much self-denial, so much thrift. All he could do was to wish the departing folk Godspeed with an accompaniment of cheery words, which, perhaps, may have helped to lighten the burden of some of them. The burden he knew was a heavy one in all cases, but heavier in some than others, for Death had claimed his toll, and at such a time the tax fell doubly heavy.

It was over. He had just seen the last wagon drop below the horizon. Now he turned away with a sigh and surveyed the ruin around him. He walked from place to place, inspecting each outbuilding with a measuring eye. There were weeks of labor before him, and all labor that would return no profit. It was a fitting conclusion to a sad day's work.

But he was not given to morbid sentiment, and as he inspected each result of the siege he settled in his mind the order of the work as it must be done. A setback like this had only a stimulating effect on his spirit. The summer lay before him, and he knew that by winter he could have everything restored to order.

At the barn he made the horses snug for the night, and then, taking up his favorite position on the oat-bin at the open doorway, lit his pipe for a quiet think. He was wholly responsible while Rube was ill.

Sitting there in the golden light of the setting sun, he was presently disturbed by the approach of light footsteps. It was an unusually gay voice that greeted him when he looked up, and eyes that were brighter, and more deeply violet than ever.

Had he given thought to these things he might have realized that there was something artificial in Rosebud's manner, something that told of unusual excitement going on in her bosom. But then Seth, with all his keenness in other things, was not the cleverest of men where women were concerned. Ma's opinion of him was wonderfully accurate.

"Oh, Seth, I just came to tell you! Fancy, no sooner is one excitement over than another begins. I've just learned that Pa and Ma are going to give up this farm. We are going further west, out of the Indian territory, and Rube's going to buy a new farm near some city. Just fancy. What do you think of it?"

For once Seth seemed taken aback. His usual imperturbable manner forsook him, and he stared at the girl in unfeigned astonishment. This was the last thing he had expected.

"We're quittin' the farm?" he cried incredulously.

"That's precisely it," Rosebud nodded, thoroughly enjoying the other's blank manner.

"Gee! I hadn't tho't of it."

The girl broke into a laugh, and Seth, after smiling faintly in response, relapsed into serious thought. Rosebud eyed him doubtfully for some moments.

"You're not glad," she said presently, with a wise little nod. "You're not glad. You don't want to go. You love this place and what you've helped to make it. I know. So do I."

The man nodded, and his dark face grew graver.

"This is our home, isn't it?" the girl continued, after a pause. "Just look round. There's the new barn. I remember when you and Pa built it. I used to hold the wood while you sawed, and made you angry because I always tried to make you cut it crooked—and never succeeded. I was very small then. There's the old barn. We use it for cows now. And do you remember when you pulled down the old granary, and built the new one in the shape of an elevator? And do you remember, Ma wouldn't speak to us for a whole day because we pulled the old hen-roost to pieces and established the hogs there? She said it was flying in the face of Providence having the smelly old things so near the house. And now we're going to leave it all. We're farmers, aren't we, Seth? But Pa is going in for cattle."

"Cattle?" exclaimed Seth.

"Yes. But I'd rather that than another grain farm after this one. I don't think I could ever like another grain farm so well as this."

Rosebud had seated herself at Seth's feet, with her back to him so that he could not see her face. She was dressed in a simple dark gown that made her look very frail. Her golden hair was arranged in a great loose knot at the nape of her neck from which several unruly strands had escaped. Seth noted these things even though his eyes wandered from point to point as she indicated the various objects to which she was drawing his attention.

"Yes, it is home, sure, Rosie," he said at last, as she waited for his answer. "Yes, it's home, sure. Yours an' mine."

There was a long pause. Rosebud leant against Seth's knees; and presently she raised one arm till her elbow rested upon them. Then she supported her head upon her hand.

"But I think it's right to go; Ma and Rube are getting old. They want rest. Rube's got a goodish bit of capital, too," she went on, with an almost childish assumption of business knowledge. "And so have you. Now how much will buy a nice ranch?"

The girl had faced round and was gazing up into Seth's face with all the bland innocence of childhood in her wide open eyes. The gravity she beheld there was profound.

"Wal, I'd say around twenty thousand dollars. Y' see, stockin' it's heavy. But Rube wouldn't think o' that much. Mebbe he'd buy a goodish place an' raise the stock himself. I 'lows it's a money-makin' game—is stock. It's a good business."

Seth had gained some enthusiasm while he spoke, and the girl was quick to notice the change.

"I believe you're beginning to fancy the notion," she said, with a bright flash of her eyes.

"Mebbe."

Seth's reply was half shamefaced. Rosebud removed her arm from his knees and turned away, idly drawing vague outlines upon the dusty ground with her forefinger. She was smiling too. It was partly a mischievous smile, and yet there was something very nervous about it. She was thinking, thinking, and found it very hard to say what she wanted to.

"I wonder if you'd help me to do something I want to do very much?" she asked at last. "Something very, very particular?"

"Why, sure," was the ready answer. "That's how it's allus bin."

"Yes, I know. It's always been like that. But this is something much harder." Rosebud smiled a little wistfully into the strong face above her.

"You ken gamble on me."

"Of course I can. I know that."

Another silence fell. The girl continued to draw outrageous parallelograms in the dust. Seth smoked on, waiting for her. The last rays of the setting sun were shining athwart the golden head which his dark eyes were contemplating.

"You see, I want to buy Pa and Ma the finest ranch in Montana," she said at last. "You see, I've got lots of money," she went on, laughing nervously. "At least I shall have. I'm rather selfish, too, because I'm going to live with them, always, you know. And I'd like to live on a ranch. Pa could own it, and you could be foreman and partner. And—and I could be partner too. Quite a business arrangement. Pa and you would work. That's your share of the capital. I should only find the money, and do nothing. You see? I talked it over with—er—some one, and they said that was quite a business arrangement, and thought I was rather clever."

Seth removed his pipe and cleared his throat. Rosebud had not dared to look at him while putting forward her scheme. Her heart was beating so loudly, that it seemed to her he must hear it.

"Wal," he said slowly, "it's not a bad notion in some ways, Rosie. Ther's jest the matter o' myself wrong. I 'lows you'd make a han'some return to Rube an' Ma. Guess you needn't to figger on me though. I'll stand by this old farm. I ken work it single-handed. An' I kind o' notion the Injuns around here someways."

"But we couldn't do without you."

Seth shook his head. As she beheld the movement, Rosebud's lips quivered, and a little impatient frown drew her brows together. She felt like shaking him for his stupidity.

"Well, I'm just going to do it, Seth. And—and I'm sorry I said anything to you about it. I shall buy it for Rube without telling him. And you'll help me?"

"Sure."

"Quite sure?"

"Nothin' more certain."

The girl's impatience had passed. A demure smile had replaced the frown, as she stared out at the flaming western sky. Presently she went on with a great assumption of calmness.

"I'm in a bit of a difficulty, though. You see, I want to do the thing at once, and I can't because I haven't got the money yet. I want to know if there isn't some means of arranging it. You see I only have a certain income at present. Later on, I shall get the whole fortune. It's that silly business about getting it when I'm married. And, of course, I'm not married yet, am I?"

"No."

Rosebud felt a desperate desire to run away. But she had never realized how difficult Seth was before. His uncompromising directness was enough to upset any one, she told herself.

"Well, I must raise the money now. You see, now."

"Can't be done. You see, the dollars ain't yours till you marry. Mebbe they'll never be yours. Mebbe you won't never marry. I guess every female don't allus marry. No, can't be done, I guess."

"No—o. I never looked at it like that before. No. The money isn't mine, is it? So, of course, I can't do it. Oh, Seth, I am disappointed!"

The girl's face had dropped, and there was something almost tragic in her tone. Seth heard the tone and it smote his heart, and made him long to take her in his arms and comfort her. He hated himself for what he had said.

"Why, little Rosie," he said gently, "I was only jest lookin' straight at it. Guess them dollars is yours. It's jest a question o' gettin' married."

The girl had turned away again. The sky was fast darkening, and a deep grayness was spreading from the east. And now, without turning, she said quietly—

"Yes, I must get married. But there's no one wants to marry me."

Seth drew a deep breath and stirred uneasily.

There was another long pause while Rosebud sat silently and unconsciously listening to the thumping of her own heart, and Seth tried hopelessly to relight a pipe in which all the tobacco had burnt out.

Suddenly Rosebud faced round. The growing darkness concealed the deep flush which had now taken possession of her cheeks, and spread even to brow and throat.

"But I do want that money, Seth," she said in a low tone. "And — and — you said — you promised you would help me."

There was a sharp sound of an empty pipe falling to the ground. Two strong rough hands were suddenly thrust out and rested in a steady grasp upon the girl's rounded shoulders. They slid their way upward until her soft cheeks were resting in their palms.

Rosebud felt her face lifted until she found herself gazing into the man's dark eyes which, in the darkness, were shining with a great love light. Her lids drooped before such passionate intensity. And her heart thrilled with rapture as she listened to his rough, honest words.

"Little Rosie, gal, you don't jest know what you're sayin'. I hadn't meant to, sure, but now I can't jest help it. My wits seem somehow gone, an' I don't guess as you'll ever forgive me. Ther's only one way I ken help you, little gal. 'Tain't right. 'Tain't honest, I know, but I guess I'm weak-kneed 'bout things now. I love you that bad I jest want to marry you. Guess I've loved you right along. I loved you when I picked you up in these arms nigh seven years ago. I loved you when I bandaged up that golden head o' yours. An' I've loved you — ever since. Rosie, gal, I jest don't know what I'm sayin'. How ken I? I'm daft — jest daft wi' love of you. I've tried to be honest by you. I've tried to do my duty by you — but I jest can't no longer, 'cos I love you — —"

But he abruptly released her, and blindly groped on the ground for his pipe. He had suddenly realized that his actions, his words were past all forgiveness.

He did not find his pipe. Rosebud was kneeling now, and, as he stooped, his head came into contact with hers. In an instant his arms were about her slight figure, and he was crushing her to his breast in a passionate embrace.

"Oh, God! I love you, Rosie!" he cried, with all the pent-up passion of years finding vent in the exclamation.

Her face was raised to his; his lips sought hers, soft and warm. He kissed her again and again. He had no words. His whole soul was crying out for her. She was his, and he was holding her in his arms. Cost what it might afterward she was his for this one delirious moment.

But the moment passed all too swiftly. Reason returned to him, and his arms dropped from about her as he realized the enormity of his offence.

"Child—little Rosie," he cried brokenly, "I'm crazy! What—what have I done?"

But Rosebud did not go from him as he had expected she would. She did not stir. Her face was hidden from him, and he could not see the anger he expected to read there. She answered him. And her answer was meek—very, very humble.

"You've let go of me," she said in a low voice. "And—and I was so comfortable—so—so—happy!"

"Happy?" reëchoed Seth.

She was in his arms again. Night had fallen and all was still. No words were spoken between them for many minutes. Those rapturous moments were theirs alone, none could see, none could know. At length it was Rosebud who looked up from the pillow of his breast. Her lovely eyes were shining even in the darkness.

"Seth—dear—you will help me? You will be my—partner in the ranch?"

And the man's answer came with a ring of deep happiness in his voice.

"Yes, Rosie, gal—if you'll make it partners for—life."

Somehow when he came to look back on these moments Seth never quite realized how it all came about—this wondrous happiness that was his. But then—yes, perhaps, he was "ter'ble slow," as Ma Sampson had said.

Popular Books
AT MODERATE PRICES
Ask your dealer for a complete list of

A. L. Burt Company's Popular Copyright Fiction.

Abner Daniel. By Will N. Harben.

Adventures of A Modest Man. By Robert W. Chambers.
Adventures of Gerard. By A. Conan Doyle.
Adventures of Sherlock Holmes. By A. Conan Doyle.
Ailsa Page. By Robert W. Chambers.
Alternative, The. By George Barr McCutcheon.
Ancient Law, The. By Ellen Glasgow.
Angel of Forgiveness, The. By Rosa N. Carey.
Angel of Pain, The. By E. F. Benson.
Annals of Ann, The. By Kate Trumble Sharber.
Anna the Adventuress. By E. Phillips Oppenheim.
Ann Boyd. By Will N. Harben.
As the Sparks Fly Upward. By Cyrus Townsend Brady.
At the Age of Eve. By Kate Trumble Sharber.
At the Mercy of Tiberius. By Augusta Evans Wilson.
At the Moorings. By Rosa N. Carey.
Awakening of Helen Richie, The. By Margaret Deland.
Barrier, The. By Rex Beach.
Bar 20. By Clarence E. Mulford.
Bar-20 Days. By Clarence E. Mulford.
Battle Ground, The. By Ellen Glasgow.
Beau Brocade. By Baroness Orczy.
Beechy. By Bettina von Hutten.
Bella Donna. By Robert Hichens.
Beloved Vagabond, The. By William J. Locke.
Ben Blair. By Will Lillibridge.
Best Man, The. By Harold MacGrath.
Beth Norvell. By Randall Parrish.

Betrayal, The. By E. Phillips Oppenheim.
Better Man, The. By Cyrus Townsend Brady.
Beulah. (Illustrated Edition.) By Augusta J. Evans.
Bill Toppers, The. By Andre Castaigne.
Blaze Derringer. By Eugene P. Lyle, Jr.
Bob Hampton of Placer. By Randall Parrish.
Bob, Son of Battle. By Alfred Ollivant.
Brass Bowl, The. By Louis Joseph Vance.
Bronze Bell, The. By Louis Joseph Vance.
Butterfly Man, The. By George Barr McCutcheon.
By Right of Purchase. By Harold Bindloss.
Cab No. 44. By R. F. Foster.
Calling of Dan Matthews, The. By Harold Bell Wright.
Call of the Blood, The. By Robert Hichens.
Cape Cod Stories. By Joseph C. Lincoln.
Cap'n Eri. By Joseph C. Lincoln.
Captain Warren's Wards. By Joseph C. Lincoln.
Caravaners, The. By the author of "Elizabeth and Her German Garden."
Cardigan. By Robert W. Chambers.
Carlton Case, The. By Ellery H. Clark.
Car of Destiny, The. By C. N. and A. M. Williamson.
Carpet From Bagdad, The. By Harold MacGrath.
Cash Intrigue, The. By George Randolph Chester.
Casting Away of Mrs. Lecks and Mrs. Aleshine. Frank S. Stockton.
Castle by the Sea, The. By H. B. Marriot Watson.
Challoners, The. By E. F. Benson.
Chaperon, The. By C. N. and A. M. Williamson.
City of Six, The. By C. L. Canfield.

Popular Books

AT MODERATE PRICES

Ask your dealer for a complete list of

A. L. Burt Company's Popular Copyright Fiction.

———————————

Circle, The. By Katherine Cecil Thurston (author of "The Masquerader," "The Gambler.")

Colonial Free Lance, A. By Chauncey C. Hotchkiss.
Conquest of Canaan, The. By Booth Tarkington.
Conspirators, The. By Robert W. Chambers.
Cynthia of the Minute. By Louis Joseph Vance.
Dan Merrithew. By Lawrence Perry.
Day of the Dog, The. By George Barr McCutcheon.
Depot Master, The. By Joseph C. Lincoln.
Derelicts. By William J. Locke.
Diamond Master, The. By Jacques Futrelle.
Diamonds Cut Paste. By Agnes and Egerton Castle.
Divine Fire, The. By May Sinclair.
Dixie Hart. By Will N. Harben.
Dr. David. By Marjorie Benton Cooke.
Early Bird, The. By George Randolph Chester.
Eleventh Hour, The. By David Potter.
Elizabeth in Rugen. (By the author of "Elizabeth and Her German Garden.")
Elusive Isabel. By Jacques Futrelle.
Elusive Pimpernel, The. By Baroness Orczy.
Enchanted Hat, The. By Harold MacGrath.
Excuse Me. By Rupert Hughes.
54-40 or Fight. By Emerson Hough.
Fighting Chance, The. By Robert W. Chambers.
Flamsted Quarries. By Mary E. Waller.
Flying Mercury, The. By Eleanor M. Ingram.
For a Maiden Brave. By Chauncey C. Hotchkiss.
Four Million, The. By O. Henry.

Four Pool's Mystery, The. By Jean Webster.
Fruitful Vine, The. By Robert Hichens.
Ganton & Co. By Arthur J. Eddy.
Gentleman of France, A. By Stanley Weyman.
Gentleman, The. By Alfred Ollivant.
Get-Rick-Quick-Wallingford. By George Randolph Chester.
Gilbert Neal. By Will N. Harben.
Girl and the Bill, The. By Bannister Merwin.
Girl from His Town, The. By Marie Van Vorst.
Girl Who Won, The. By Beth Ellis.
Glory of Clementina, The. By William J. Locke.
Glory of the Conquered, The. By Susan Glaspell.
God's Good Man. By Marie Corelli.
Going Some. By Rex Beach.
Golden Web, The. By Anthony Partridge.
Green Patch, The. By Bettina von Hutten.
Happy Island (sequel to "Uncle William.") By Jennette Lee.
Hearts and the Highway. By Cyrus Townsend Brady.
Held for Orders. By Frank H. Spearman.
Hidden Water. By Dane Coolidge.
Highway of Fate, The. By Rosa N. Carey.
Homesteaders, The. By Kate and Virgil D. Boyles.
Honor of the Big Snows, The. By James Oliver Curwood.
Hopalong Cassidy. By Clarence E. Mulford.
Household of Peter, The. By Rosa N. Carey.
House of Mystery, The. By Will Irwin.
House of the Lost Court, The. By C. N. Williamson.
House of the Whispering Pines, The. By Anna Katherine Green.

Popular Books

AT MODERATE PRICES

Ask your dealer for a complete list of

A. L. Burt Company's Popular Copyright Fiction.

House on Cherry Street, The. By Amelia E. Barr.

How Leslie Loved. By Anne Warner.
Husbands of Edith, The. By George Barr McCutcheon.
Idols. By William J. Locke.
Illustrious Prince, The. By E. Phillips Oppenheim.
Imprudence of Prue, The. By Sophie Fisher.
Inez. (Illustrated Edition.) By Augusta J. Evans.
Infelice. By Augusta Evans Wilson.
Initials Only. By Anna Katharine Green.
In Defiance of the King. By Chauncey C. Hotchkiss.
Indifference of Juliet, The. By Grace S. Richmond.
In the Service of the Princess. By Henry C. Rowland.
Iron Woman, The. By Margaret Deland.
Ishmael. (Illustrated.) By Mrs. Southworth.
Island of Regeneration, The. By Cyrus Townsend Brady.
Jack Spurlock, Prodigal. By Horace Lorimer.
Jane Cable. By George Barr McCutcheon.
Jeanne of the Marshes. By E. Phillips Oppenheim.
Jude the Obscure. By Thomas Hardy.
Keith of the Border. By Randall Parrish.
Key to the Unknown, The. By Rosa N. Carey.
Kingdom of Earth, The. By Anthony Partridge.
King Spruce. By Holman Day.
Ladder of Swords, A. By Gilbert Parker.
Lady Betty Across the Water. By C. N. and A. M. Williamson.
Lady Merton, Colonist. By Mrs. Humphrey Ward.
Lady of Big Shanty, The. By Berkeley F. Smith.
Langford of the Three Bars. By Kate and Virgil D. Boyles.
Land of Long Ago, The. By Eliza Calvert Hall.

Partners of the Tide. By Joseph C. Lincoln.
Passage Perilous, The. By Rosa N. Carey.
Passers By. By Anthony Partridge.
Paternoster Ruby, The. By Charles Edmonds Walk.
Patience of John Moreland, The. By Mary Dillon.
Paul Anthony, Christian. By Hiram W. Hays.
Phillip Steele. By James Oliver Curwood.
Phra the Phoenician. By Edwin Lester Arnold.
Plunderer, The. By Roy Norton.
Pole Baker. By Will N. Harben.
Politician, The. By Edith Huntington Mason.
Polly of the Circus. By Margaret Mayo.
Pool of Flame, The. By Louis Joseph Vance.
Poppy. By Cynthia Stockley.
Power and the Glory, The. By Grace McGowan Cooke.
Price of the Prairie, The. By Margaret Hill McCarter.
Prince of Sinners, A. By E. Phillis Oppenheim.
Prince or Chauffeur. By Lawrence Perry.
Princess Dehra, The. By John Reed Scott.
Princess Passes, The. By C. N. and A. M. Williamson.
Princess Virginia, The. By C. N. and A. M. Williamson.
Prisoners of Chance. By Randall Parrish.
Prodigal Son, The. By Hall Caine.
Purple Parasol, The. By George Barr McCutcheon.

Popular Books

AT MODERATE PRICES

Ask your dealer for a complete list of

A. L. Burt Company's Popular Copyright Fiction.

Reconstructed Marriage, A. By Amelia Barr.

Redemption of Kenneth Galt, The. By Will N. Harben.

Red House on Rowan Street. By Roman Doubleday.
Red Mouse, The. By William Hamilton Osborne.
Red Pepper Burns. By Grace S. Richmond.
Refugees, The. By A. Conan Doyle.
Rejuvenation of Aunt Mary, The. By Anne Warner.
Road to Providence, The. By Maria Thompson Daviess.
Romance of a Plain Man, The. By Ellen Glasgow.
Rose in the Ring, The. By George Barr McCutcheon.
Rose of Old Harpeth, The. By Maria Thompson Daviess.
Rose of the World. By Agnes and Egerton Castle.
Round the Corner in Gay Street. By Grace S. Richmond.
Routledge Rides Alone. By Will Livingston Comfort.
Running Fight, The. By Wm. Hamilton Osborne.
Seats of the Mighty, The. By Gilbert Parker.
Septimus. By William J. Locke.
Set in Silver. By C. N. and A. M. Williamson.
Self-Raised. (Illustrated.) By Mrs. Southworth.
Shepherd of the Hills, The. By Harold Bell Wright.
Sheriff of Dyke Hole, The. By Ridgwell Cullum.
Sidney Carteret, Rancher. By Harold Bindloss.
Simon the Jester. By William J. Locke.
Silver Blade, The. By Charles E. Walk.
Silver Horde, The. By Rex Beach.
Sir Nigel. By A. Conan Doyle.
Sir Richard Calmady. By Lucas Malet.
Skyman, The. By Henry Ketchell Webster.
Slim Princess, The. By George Ade.
Speckled Bird, A. By Augusta Evans Wilson.
Spirit in Prison, A. By Robert Hichens.
Spirit of the Border, The. By Zane Grey.
Spirit Trail, The. By Kate and Virgil D. Boyles.
Spoilers, The. By Rex Beach.
Stanton Wins. By Eleanor M. Ingram.
St. Elmo. (Illustrated Edition.) By Augusta J. Evans.
Stolen Singer, The. By Martha Bellinger.
Stooping Lady, The. By Maurice Hewlett.
Story of the Outlaw, The. By Emerson Hough.
Strawberry Acres. By Grace S. Richmond.

Strawberry Handkerchief, The. By Amelia E. Barr.
Sunnyside of the Hill, The. By Rosa N. Carey.
Sunset Trail, The. By Alfred Henry Lewis.

Popular Books

AT MODERATE PRICES

Ask your dealer for a complete list of

A. L. Burt Company's Popular Copyright Fiction.

Susan Clegg and Her Friend Mrs. Lathrop. By Anne Warner.

Sword of the Old Frontier, A. By Randall Parrish.
Tales of Sherlock Holmes. By A. Conan Doyle.
Tennessee Shad, The. By Owen Johnson.
Tess of the D'Urbervilles. By Thomas Hardy.
Texican, The. By Dane Coolidge.
That Printer of Udell's. By Harold Bell Wright.
Three Brothers, The. By Eden Phillpotts.
Throwback, The. By Alfred Henry Lewis.
Thurston of Orchard Valley. By Harold Bindloss.
Title Market, The. By Emily Post.
Tom Sails. A Tale of a Welsh Village. By Allen Raine.
Trail of the Axe, The. By Ridgwell Cullum.
Treasure of Heaven, The. By Marie Corelli.
Two-Gun Man, The. By Charles Alden Seltzer.
Two Vanrevels, The. By Booth Tarkington.
Uncle William. By Jennette Lee.
Up from Slavery. By Booker T. Washington.
Vanity Box, The. By C. N. Williamson.
Vashti. By Augusta Evans Wilson.
Varmint, The. By Owen Johnson.
Vigilante Girl, A. By Jerome Hart.
Village of Vagabonds, A. By F. Berkeley Smith.

Visioning, The. By Susan Glaspell.
Voice of the People, The. By Ellen Glasgow.
Wanted—A Chaperon. By Paul Leicester Ford.
Wanted: A Matchmaker. By Paul Leicester Ford.
Watchers of the Plains, The. Ridgwell Cullum.
Wayfarers, The. By Mary Stewart Cutting.
Way of a Man, The. By Emerson Hough.
Weavers, The. By Gilbert Parker.
When Wilderness Was King. By Randall Parrish.
Where the Trail Divides. By Will Lillibridge.
White Sister, The. By Marion Crawford.
Window at the White Cat, The. By Mary Roberts Rhinehart.
Winning of Barbara Worth, The. By Harold Bell Wright.
With Juliet in England. By Grace S. Richmond.
Woman Haters, The. By Joseph C. Lincoln.
Woman In Question, The. By John Reed Scott.
Woman in the Alcove, The. By Anna Katharine Green.
Yellow Circle, The. By Charles E. Walk.
Yellow Letter, The. By William Johnston.
Younger Set, The. By Robert W. Chambers.

Good Fiction Worth Reading.

A series of romances containing several of the old favorites in the field of historical fiction, replete with powerful romances of love and diplomacy that excel in thrilling and absorbing interest.

DARNLEY. A Romance of the times of Henry VIII. and Cardinal Wolsey. By G. P. R. James. Cloth, 12mo. with four illustrations by J. Watson Davis. Price, $1.00.

In point of publication, "Darnley" is that work by Mr. James which follows "Richelieu," and, if rumor can be credited, it was owing to the advice and insistence of our own Washington Irving that we are indebted primarily for the story, the young author questioning whether he could properly paint the difference in the characters of the two great cardinals. And it is not surprising that James should have hesitated; he had been eminently successful in giving to the world the portrait of Richelieu as a man, and by attempting a similar task with Wolsey as the theme, was much like tempting fortune. Irving insisted that "Darnley" came naturally in sequence, and this opinion being supported by Sir Walter Scott, the author set about the work.

As a historical romance "Darnley" is a book that can be taken up pleasurably again and again, for there is about it that subtle charm which those who are strangers to the works of G. P. R. James have claimed was only to be imparted by Dumas.

If there was nothing more about the work to attract especial attention, the account of the meeting of the kings on the historic "field of the cloth of gold" would entitle the story to the most favorable consideration of every reader.

There is really but little pure romance in this story, for the author has taken care to imagine love passages only between those whom history has credited with having entertained the tender passion one for another, and he succeeds in making such lovers as all the world must love.

CAPTAIN BRAND, OF THE SCHOONER CENTIPEDE. By Lieut. Henry A. Wise, U.S.N. (Harry Gringo). Cloth, 12mo. with four illustrations by J. Watson Davis. Price, $1.00.

The re-publication of this story will please those lovers of sea yarns who delight in so much of the salty flavor of the ocean as can come through the medium of a printed page, for never has a story of the sea and those "who go down in ships" been written by one more familiar with the scenes depicted.

The one book of this gifted author which is best remembered, and which will be read with pleasure for many years to come, is "Captain Brand," who, as the author states on his title page, was a "pirate of eminence in the West Indies." As a sea story pure and simple, "Captain Brand" has never been excelled and as a story of piratical life, told without the usual embellishments of blood and thunder, it has no equal.

NICK OF THE WOODS. A story of the Early Settlers of Kentucky. By Robert Montgomery Bird. Cloth, 12mo. with four illustrations by J. Watson Davis. Price, $1.00.

This most popular novel and thrilling story of early frontier life in Kentucky was originally published in the year 1837. The novel, long out of print, had in its day a phenomenal sale, for its realistic presentation of Indian and frontier life in the early days of settlement in the South, narrated in the tale with all the art of a practiced writer. A very charming love romance runs through the story. This new and tasteful edition of "Nick of the Woods" will be certain to make many new admirers for this enchanting story from Dr. Bird's clever and versatile pen.

For sale by all booksellers, or sent postpaid on receipt of price by the publishers

A. L. BURT COMPANY, 52-58 Duane St., New York.

Good Fiction Worth Reading.

A series of romances containing several of the old favorites in the field of historical fiction, replete with powerful romances of love and diplomacy that excel in thrilling and absorbing interest.

WINDSOR CASTLE. A Historical Romance of the Reign of Henry VIII, Catharine of Aragon and Anne Boleyn. By Wm. Harrison Ainsworth. Cloth 12mo. with four illustrations by George Cruikshank. Price, $1.00.

"Windsor Castle" is the story of Henry VIII., Catharine, and Anne Boleyn. "Bluff King Hal," although a well-loved monarch, was none too good a one in many ways. Of all his selfishness and unwarrantable acts, none was more discreditable than his divorce from Catharine, and his marriage to the beautiful Anne Boleyn. The King's love was as brief as it was vehement. Jane Seymour, waiting maid on the Queen, attracted him, and Anne Boleyn was forced to the block to make room for her successor. This romance is one of extreme interest to all readers.

HORSESHOE ROBINSON. A tale of the Tory Ascendency in South Carolina in 1780. By John P. Kennedy. Cloth, 12mo. with four illustrations by J. Watson Davis. Price, $1.00.

Among the old favorites in the field of what is known as historical fiction, there are none which appeal to a larger number of Americans than Horseshoe Robinson, and this because it is the only story which depicts with fidelity to the facts the heroic efforts of the colonists in South Carolina to defend their homes against the brutal oppression of the British under such leaders as Cornwallis and Tarleton.

The reader is charmed with the story of love which forms the thread of the tale, and then impressed with the wealth of detail concerning those times. The picture of the manifold sufferings of the people, is never overdrawn, but painted faithfully and honestly by one who spared neither time nor labor in his efforts to present in this charming love story all that price in blood and tears which the Carolinians paid as their share in the winning of the republic.

Take it all in all, "Horseshoe Robinson" is a work which should be found on every book-shelf, not only because it is a most entertaining story, but because of the wealth of valuable information concerning the colonists which it contains. That it has been brought out once more, well illustrated, is something which will give pleasure to thousands who have long desired an opportunity to read the story again, and to the many who have tried vainly in these latter days to procure a copy that they might read it for the first time.

THE PEARL OF ORR'S ISLAND. A story of the Coast of Maine. By Harriet Beecher Stowe. Cloth, 12mo. Illustrated. Price, $1.00.

Written prior to 1862, the "Pearl of Orr's Island" is ever new; a book filled with delicate fancies, such as seemingly array themselves anew each time one reads them. One sees the "sea like an unbroken mirror all around the pine-girt, lonely shores of Orr's Island," and straightway comes "the heavy, hollow moan of the surf on the beach, like the wild angry howl of some savage animal."

Who can read of the beginning of that sweet life, named Mara, which came into this world under the very shadow of the Death angel's wings, without having an intense desire to know how the premature bud blossomed? Again and again one lingers over the descriptions of the character of that baby boy Moses, who came through the tempest, amid the angry billows, pillowed on his dead mother's breast.

There is no more faithful portrayal of New England life than that which Mrs. Stowe gives in "The Pearl of Orr's Island."

For sale by all booksellers, or sent postpaid on receipt of price by the publishers

A. L. BURT COMPANY, 52-58 Duane St., New York.

Good Fiction Worth Reading.

A series of romances containing several of the old favorites in the field of historical fiction, replete with powerful romances of love and diplomacy that excel in thrilling and absorbing interest.

GUY FAWKES. A Romance of the Gunpowder Treason. By Wm. Harrison Ainsworth. Cloth, 12mo. with four illustrations by George Cruikshank. Price, $1.00.

The "Gunpowder Plot" was a modest attempt to blow up Parliament, the King and his Counsellors. James of Scotland, then King of England, was weak-minded and extravagant. He hit upon the efficient scheme of extorting money from the people by imposing taxes on the Catholics. In their natural resentment to this extortion, a handful of bold spirits concluded to overthrow the government. Finally the plotters were arrested, and the King put to torture Guy Fawkes and the other prisoners with royal vigor. A very intense love story runs through the entire romance.

THE SPIRIT OF THE BORDER. A Romance of the Early Settlers in the Ohio Valley. By Zane Grey. Cloth. 12mo. with four illustrations by J. Watson Davis. Price, $1.00.

A book rather out of the ordinary is this "Spirit of the Border." The main thread of the story has to do with the work of the Moravian missionaries in the Ohio Valley. Incidentally the reader is given details of the frontier life of those hardy pioneers who broke the wilderness for the planting of this great nation. Chief among these, as a matter of course, is Lewis Wetzel, one of the most peculiar, and at the same time the most admirable of all the brave men who spent their lives battling with the savage foe, that others might dwell in comparative security.

Details of the establishment and destruction of the Moravian "Village of Peace" are given at some length, and with minute description. The efforts to Christianize the Indians are described as they never have been before, and the author has depicted the characters of the leaders of the several Indian tribes with great care, which of itself will be of interest to the student.

By no means least among the charms of the story are the vivid word-pictures of the thrilling adventures, and the intense paintings of the beauties of nature, as seen in the almost unbroken forests.

It is the spirit of the frontier which is described, and one can by it, perhaps, the better understand why men, and women, too, willingly braved every privation and danger that the westward progress of the star of empire might be the more certain and rapid. A love story, simple and tender, runs through the book.

RICHELIEU. A tale of France in the reign of King Louis XIII. By G. P. R. James. Cloth, 12mo. with four illustrations by J. Watson Davis. Price, $1.00.

In 1829 Mr. James published his first romance, "Richelieu," and was recognized at once as one of the masters of the craft.

In this book he laid the story during those later days of the great cardinal's life, when his power was beginning to wane, but while it was yet sufficiently strong to permit now and then of volcanic outbursts which overwhelmed foes and carried friends to the topmost wave of prosperity. One of the most striking portions of the story is that of Cinq Mar's conspiracy; the method of conducting criminal cases, and the political trickery resorted to by royal favorites, affording a better insight into the statecraft of that day than can be had even by an exhaustive study of history. It is a powerful romance of love and diplomacy, and in point of thrilling and absorbing interest has never been excelled.

For sale by all booksellers, or sent postpaid on receipt of price by the publishers

A. L. BURT COMPANY, 52-58 Duane St., New York.

Good Fiction Worth Reading.

A series of romances containing several of the old favorites in the field of historical fiction, replete with powerful romances of love and diplomacy that excel in thrilling and absorbing interest.

A COLONIAL FREE-LANCE. A story of American Colonial Times. By Chauncey C. Hotchkiss. Cloth, 12mo. with four illustrations by J. Watson Davis. Price, $1.00.

A book that appeals to Americans as a vivid picture of Revolutionary scenes. The story is a strong one, a thrilling one. It causes the true American to flush with excitement, to devour chapter after chapter, until the eyes smart, and it fairly smokes with patriotism. The love story is a singularly charming idyl.

THE TOWER OF LONDON. A Historical Romance of the Times of Lady Jane Grey and Mary Tudor. By Wm. Harrison Ainsworth. Cloth, 12mo. with four illustrations by George Cruikshank. Price, $1.00.

This romance of the "Tower of London" depicts the Tower as palace, prison and fortress, with many historical associations. The era is the middle of the sixteenth century.

The story is divided into two parts, one dealing with Lady Jane Grey, and the other with Mary Tudor as Queen, introducing other notable characters of the era. Throughout the story holds the interest of the reader in the midst of intrigue and conspiracy, extending considerably over a half a century.

IN DEFIANCE OF THE KING. A Romance of the American Revolution. By Chauncey C. Hotchkiss. Cloth, 12mo. with four illustrations by J. Watson Davis. Price, $1.00.

Mr. Hotchkiss has etched in burning words a story of Yankee bravery, and true love that thrills from beginning to end, with the spirit of the Revolution. The heart beats quickly, and we feel ourselves taking a part in the exciting scenes described. His whole story is so absorbing that you will sit up far into the night to finish it. As a love romance it is charming.

GARTHOWEN. A story of a Welsh Homestead. By Allen Raine. Cloth, 12mo. with four illustrations by J. Watson Davis. Price, $1.00.

"This is a little idyl of humble life and enduring love, laid bare before us, very real and pure, which in its telling shows us some strong points of Welsh character—the pride, the hasty temper, the quick dying out of wrath.... We call this a well-written story, interesting alike through its romance and its glimpses into another life than ours. A delightful and clever picture of Welsh village life. The result is excellent." —Detroit Free Press.

MIFANWY. The story of a Welsh Singer. By Allan Raine. Cloth, 12mo. with four illustrations by J. Watson Davis. Price, $1.00.

"This is a love story, simple, tender and pretty as one would care to read. The action throughout is brisk and pleasing; the characters, it is apparent at once, are as true to life as though the author had known them all personally. Simple in all its situations, the story is worked up in that touching and quaint strain which never grows wearisome, no matter how often the lights and shadows of love are introduced. It rings true, and does not tax the imagination." —Boston Herald.

Lightning Source UK Ltd.
Milton Keynes UK
UKHW010751070121
376598UK00001B/96